MAELSTROM

OTHER BOOKS FROM

JORDAN L. HAWK:

Hainted

<u>Whyborne & Griffin:</u>
Widdershins
Threshold
Stormhaven
Necropolis
Bloodline
Hoarfrost
Maelstrom

<u>Spirits:</u>
Restless Spirits
Dangerous Spirits

<u>SPECTR</u>
Hunter of Demons
Master of Ghouls
Reaper of Souls
Eater of Lives
Destroyer of Worlds
Summoner of Storms
Mocker of Ravens

<u>Short stories:</u>
Heart of the Dragon
After the Fall (in the *Allegories of the Tarot* anthology)
Eidolon (A Whyborne & Griffin short story)
Remnant, written with KJ Charles (A Whyborne & Griffin / Secret Casebook of Simon Feximal story)
Carousel (A Whyborne & Griffin short story)

MAELSTROM

(Whyborne & Griffin No. 7)

JORDAN L. HAWK

Edited by Annetta Ribken

\

CHAPTER 1

Whyborne

I STOOD AMIDST the press of bodies at the Nathaniel R. Ladysmith museum, desperately wishing I were elsewhere. Preferably back in Alaska; although I'd despised the cold climate, at the moment the memory seemed heavenly compared to the stuffy heat of the crowded grand foyer. Sweat crept down my back beneath my layers of clothing, and I longed to slip outside and remove my gloves. In previous years, I might have at least escaped to one of the open windows in hopes of catching a bit of a breeze.

Unfortunately, the days of my anonymity were over. Almost as soon as I arrived this evening, Dr. Hart and the museum's president Mr. Mathison cornered me. We'd soon been joined by the head librarian, Mr. Quinn, whom I couldn't remember ever seeing outside of the Ladysmith's library before, let alone in formal wear.

The gathering tonight celebrated a rather large donation of rare books to the museum's library. Although my philological expertise tended to the deciphering of more ancient languages, the source of the donation made it of more than usual interest to me.

Two years ago, my husband Griffin and I had traveled to Egypt to assist our dear friend Dr. Christine Putnam. Christine's sister, Grafin Daphne de Wisborg, had joined us, ostensibly in mourning for her dead husband.

In reality, Daphne had used the books in the late graf's library to find a way to communicate with the spirit of Nitocris, Queen of the Ghūls, lurking Outside our ordinary world and awaiting her chance to come back. Daphne, possessed by Nitocris, then murdered her husband and came to Egypt with the intent of turning the world into a wasteland of the dead for her ghūls to rule over. My left shoulder still bore the scar of the bite she'd inflicted with her jackal teeth, as we fought for our lives in the Egyptian desert. As for Christine, losing her only sister in such a terrible fashion...well, she didn't speak of the incident, but it couldn't have been easy.

The letter from the current Graf de Wisborg had taken Christine by surprise; that much I did know. The young graf had found himself in possession of a crumbling castle he had little interest in maintaining, and an extensive library he cared for even less. Daphne's connection with Christine, and thus the museum, had inspired him— and if his generous donation came with the chance to travel and meet rich American heiresses, so much the better.

I'd come tonight not only to please the museum director, but to offer my support to Christine. Her nerves were already stretched thin from the stress of planning her upcoming wedding; this had certainly done them no good. Unfortunately, I could think of no way to politely extricate myself from the director and president.

"This is quite the triumph, don't you think, Mr. Quinn?" asked Dr. Hart. His balding head shone with sweat, and his face flushed red with the heat.

"Indeed." White tie and tails somehow failed to make Mr. Quinn look any less like an undertaker. His silvery eyes went to Dr. Hart, then to me. He then proceeded to stare at me without blinking. "I suspect we'll find many tomes of great value within. Perhaps Dr. Whyborne would care to assist when we open the crates."

His suggestion caught me off guard; cataloging new arrivals wasn't remotely one of my duties. Still, it would give me an excuse to look for the truly dangerous tomes and suggest they be kept under lock and key, before they had a chance to find their way onto the general shelves. "Of course, Mr. Quinn. I'd be glad to assist."

Dr. Hart rubbed his hands together with glee. "The Wisborg Collection will finally wipe the smirk off the faces of those fellows from Miskatonic. Their paltry library will be nothing compared to ours!"

"Now, now," Mr. Mathison said with a good-natured smile. "Let's not forget Miskatonic University is Dr. Whyborne's alma mater."

"Dr. Whyborne belongs to Widdershins," Mr. Quinn said, giving Mathison a rather poisonous glare. "His allegiance, I should say. To the museum."

"Er, yes." I cast about for some means of escape. Once again the elite of Widdershins crowded the Ladysmith's grand foyer, nibbling on canapés beneath the looming hadrosaur skeleton, exclaiming over the carefully curated displays from Nephren-ka's tomb, and silently judging one another's clothing, demeanor, and heritage. "I say, has anyone seen Dr. Putnam recently?"

"Last I saw, she was speaking with the graf," Mathison said, taking a flute of chilled champagne from a passing waiter. I snagged a flute of my own.

"No, no, the graf is being set upon by every heiress in the place," Dr. Hart replied. "The ones with enough money to desire a title to accompany their fortune, that is."

"He looks like Orpheus stalked by the maenads," Mr. Quinn observed wistfully.

I edged away from him—but I also took a quick look about to make certain the graf wasn't actually being torn apart. I assumed as much from the lack of screams, but...well, the former Graf de Wisborg had been killed and eaten by his own wife.

I didn't see the new graf, but I finally spotted Christine near the Nephren-ka relics. Iskander stood beside her, in earnest conversation with my father.

My heart sank. God only knew what Father might be saying to them. To suggest I'd been shocked when Father offered Whyborne House as the venue for Christine's wedding would be an understatement. Obviously he must have some sort of ulterior motive, but what he had in mind hadn't yet become clear. Most likely he thought doing favors for my friends would convince me to abandon my career, return to the fold, and take up my position as the heir of Whyborne Railroad and Industries. It was, I suspected, the same reason Father settled a large amount of stock on Griffin for his birthday last month.

"Excuse me—I need to speak to Dr. Putnam." I hurried away without waiting for an answer. As I wove through the crowd, I caught sight of my friend Dr. Gerritson and his wife. Unfortunately, they appeared to have been cornered by Mr. Durfree and Mr. Farr, a pair of art curators known for their passionate disagreements on anything and everything. I hurriedly ducked behind a gaggle of heiresses to avoid being drawn in.

My champagne had grown warm in the stifling heat. A whisper of magic chilled the glass, frost forming briefly on the outside of the flute before melting. I lifted it to my lips and was promptly jostled from behind. Champagne splashed across my chin and down the front of my shirt.

"Oh, sorry Percy, didn't see you there," drawled Bradley Osborne. He didn't sound sorry at all.

I took out my handkerchief and began to dab ineffectively at my now-wet clothing. "Quite all right, Bradley," I gritted out between clenched teeth. "Accidents do happen." Not that I imagined for an instant this had been an accident.

Bradley observed my efforts at drying myself with a smug smile. "You really ought to watch where you're going. Been drinking a bit more champagne than good for you, eh?"

The old familiar anger ached in my chest. I straightened my spine, which forced Bradley to look up at me. "Actually, I've been speaking with Mr. Mathison and Dr. Hart."

His jovial mask slipped—just for an instant, but enough to let me know I'd struck home. Bradley had spent his years in Widdershins trying to claw his way higher into society. When we'd first met, he'd held me in contempt, for...well, for all sorts of reasons, but not taking advantage of the class I'd been born into was certainly one of them.

Bradley's right hand tightened around his champagne flute; his left he tucked at the small of his back, perhaps to conceal a fist. Then he relaxed and put on a false smile. "I'm sure they found your father's money and name—I mean, your conversation—*most* fascinating."

I forced my expression to remain neutral, even as I seethed within. It wasn't just Father's money that had brought me to the attention of the museum's board and president. Most of the blame lay with my wretched brother Stanford, who'd held Widdershins's upper crust hostage in this very foyer, forcing me to save them.

"Among other things," I replied coolly.

"Ah, yes, other things." He continued to smile, but his eyes were cold and dead as knives. "By the way, how is Mr. Flaherty?"

"I'm quite well," Griffin said from just behind Bradley. "Thank you for your concern, Dr. Osborne."

I felt a thrill of savage satisfaction when Bradley started in surprise. Griffin stepped to my side, his green eyes fixed on Bradley and a smile no more genuine than Bradley's on his lips. The man I called husband always cut a handsome figure, but the tailcoat and white tie suited him very well indeed. His chestnut hair, worn longer than strictly fashionable, curled around his collar.

Unfortunately, Bradley recovered quickly enough. "I'm glad to hear it, Mr. Flaherty," he said even as his lip drew into a sneer. "After all, if I recall correctly, you were shot right over there. I take it the wound no longer troubles you?"

Goosebumps prickled on my arms despite the heat, and I felt as though the marble floor had shifted beneath me. The night Stanford had taken the museum staff and donors hostage, he'd also tried to kill me.

But first he'd shot Griffin, with the clear intention of hurting me. After first calling me a sodomite.

The implication had been obvious enough. But Stanford was a madman who had tried to murder the most powerful people in Widdershins. Polite society put his insults and actions down to lunatic ravings.

Whether anyone really believed that or no...well, Griffin had quietly received an invitation to various museum functions, including this one, with no real explanation as to why. If pressed, no doubt it would be pointed out he'd tried to save everyone at the Hallowe'en tour and been gallantly wounded in their defense. Surely that was worth a few invitations to exclusive events?

And perhaps it was the real explanation. I honestly didn't know and certainly would never ask. But I had no doubts as to Bradley's opinion.

Would he try to use it against us? He hadn't so far, but that didn't mean the day wouldn't come when we'd find police knocking on our door. Or my name in some headline from a tawdry New York paper, as no reporter in Massachusetts would dare risk Father's wrath.

My hand tightened on the champagne flute, the scars beneath my white glove pulling tight. The great arcane maelstrom that underlay Widdershins turned beneath my feet. A breeze ruffled through the gathering, bearing on it the scent of the nearby ocean.

"As I said, I'm quite fine," Griffin replied. "Come, Whyborne—you need to dry your shirt."

He touched my elbow. The breeze died away, and my sense of the maelstrom receded to the back of my mind, in the same place that kept track of my heart beating and my lungs breathing.

"Yes," I said, and let him steer me away.

CHAPTER 2

Whyborne

GRIFFIN LED ME to the discreet staff door in the back of the foyer. The air on the other side was far cooler, and I took a deep breath. "Damn Bradley," I said. "Thank you for your rescue."

"Any time, my dear." Griffin looked up at me, but the dim light made it difficult to read his expression. He moved closer, thighs almost touching mine. "Let's go to your office."

"My office?" I blinked down at him. "I thought we were going to the washroom to dry my shirt?"

"No," Griffin murmured. His voice had taken on a husky edge. "We were getting you away from Bradley before the little breeze I noticed became a gale. Or you lost patience and blasted the man with a lightning strike." Heat laced the smile he offered me. "He didn't have the slightest idea what he was playing with. But I did."

"L-lightning isn't easy to call down," I stuttered, my heart beating faster in response to his nearness, his smile.

"We'll discuss it in your office." His hand brushed across the front of my trousers. "Now."

I hurried to comply. My hands trembled as I unlocked the door. Moonlight streamed through the high windows, illuminating the desk and chair. I tried to keep the place more neatly than my old office in the basement, but my attempts had been only half-hearted, and there were piles of papers stacked in the visitor's chair, on the floor, and over most of the desk.

"If not lightning, then setting him on fire," Griffin said. He closed the door behind us. The lock clicked loudly.

I turned to see him stalking toward me. "Or slamming him into the wall by manipulating the air," he went on. "Or bending the marble around his feet and ankles so he couldn't move."

"Er." I backed up until my hip met the edge of my desk. "I hope I wouldn't do such a thing just because Bradley said something wretched to me."

"Of course not." Griffin stopped inches from me, staring up but not touching. "And I know you wouldn't. But I could see the fire in you. So bright. Trembling. Begging for release."

A soft whimper escaped me.

"I've been watching you the whole evening, you know." He crowded in closer now, trapping me between his body and the desk. His thigh slipped between mine, pressing and rocking just right.

The room seemed suddenly as breathless as the foyer had been. "O-oh?"

He rocked against me harder, sending jolts of pleasure through my rapidly stiffening member. "Mmm hmm. I watched you standing there with Mathison and the rest. Dr. Percival Endicott Whyborne—so aloof. So untouchable."

My heart beat faster, my skin more heated than it had been before. "I'm not."

"You look it, when you feel you're on display. Withdrawn and remote as a statue. None of them see what's underneath that marble shell. The fire just waiting for the right moment to erupt into a blaze. Watching you keep it so tamped down in public, so in control, knowing none of them guess I'd have you on your knees, begging me to fuck your mouth."

Lust tightened my throat—and my trousers. But... "I have to go back out. We do, I mean. They'd see."

The hard line of his erection pressed against my own. "Oh yes. You're right," he purred in such a way I knew he hadn't forgotten for an instant. "We must keep your lips clean, your hair unmussed. I suppose I'll just have to fuck your ass instead."

I took a deep gulping breath against the constriction in my throat. "I have oil in my desk. Used to keep leather scrolls supple."

He leaned in closer, almost but not quite kissing me. His breath smelled faintly of champagne. "Then get it."

Griffin pulled back, just far enough to let me turn around and bend over the desk to grapple with one of the drawers. He took advantage, pressing against my backside in a most distracting fashion, until I fumbled out the small bottle.

Griffin stripped off his gloves before taking it. "Don't move," he ordered. "Stay bent over."

I had just enough presence of mind to remove my own gloves and take out a handkerchief. He shoved me against the desk, kissed the back of my neck, then reached around to unbutton my trousers. In short order, he had my suspenders unfastened, and shoved trousers and drawers alike down. I spared a thought for the cloth wrinkling, but his hands gripping my hips drove everything out of my mind but him.

"You look so handsome," he whispered. The shadows of the museum seemed to swallow his words, as if taking our secret into themselves, even as I took him into me. I gasped, the scars on my right hand pulling as I gripped the desk.

The difference in our height made things awkward, but did nothing to dissuade him. He groaned, leaning in to me and lifting his heels off the floor to push further in. In a few moments, he'd found his rhythm, his breath rough, his fingers digging into my hips.

I bit my lip to keep from crying out, then remembered I couldn't leave a mark anyone would question once I returned to the gathering. So instead I arched my head back, trying to keep my moans quiet.

I'd waited to put a hand to myself, afraid it would be over too soon, but the ache in my cock became too insistent to ignore. "Yes," Griffin gasped hoarsely. Our flesh slapped together, sticky with oil and sweat. "Touch yourself. I can't wait to go back out there. Can't wait to see them all look at you, so cool and collected, the fire contained once again, and never guess I've just come inside you."

His words trailed off into a groan, body stiffening, pushing in as far as he could while he spent himself. A wave of pleasure shocked through me: his cry, his hands on my hips, his rough speech, all excited my blood past enduring. My orgasm rushed through me, and I barely remembered the handkerchief in time to keep my spend from spilling onto the desk.

I blinked sluggishly, senses reeling. "God," I mumbled.

"Not quite, but the confusion is understandable," Griffin teased as he pulled free.

I snorted. "That's the devil you're thinking of."

"I'm wounded." He smacked me lightly on the bottom. "Clean up and let's return to the gathering before anyone wonders what's taking so long."

I unlocked the door with a far steadier hand. To hell with Bradley. He might snipe and bark, but in the end, his character was that of a schoolyard bully, easily cowed when someone of authority chanced by. If nothing else, Dr. Hart wouldn't tolerate a scandal. If Bradley attempted to bring one upon the museum by moving against me, he'd find himself short of a job.

And, for all his bluster, Bradley wasn't a fool. He knew better than to antagonize the museum.

"Oh, hello there, Whyborne," Christine said as I stepped out into the hall. "I'd wondered where you'd gotten off to."

I jumped, heart pounding. "Oh! Christine. We were just, um, drying off my shirt." Which of course I'd not yet had the chance to do, curse it.

She arched a brow. It was always strange to see her in an elegant dress; she preferred far more practical skirts, and wore trousers in the field. "I'm sure you were," she said in a tone meant to indicate she knew I was lying to her face.

"And what are you doing back here?" Griffin asked. He of course seemed perfectly at ease. "I rather thought you'd be missed if you left the gathering."

"Bah!" Christine scowled. "I've a bottle of whiskey in my desk. After listening to everyone stand around, going on and on about how grateful I should be to the graf for donating the Daphne de Wisborg Memorial Collection, I needed a real drink." She pulled a flask from somewhere in the folds of her gown. "Care to join me?"

Griffin took it from her and helped himself. "I'm sorry, Christine. I know this can't be easy for you."

Her scowl only deepened. "Daphne tried to murder us all. I don't particularly care to memorialize her with anything."

"Nitocris had taken her over by then."

"Don't coddle me, Griffin, we both know that isn't true," she said. Griffin passed the flask to her, and she took a long pull before putting it away again. "We should return to the lion's den, before we're missed. And Whyborne, I know it isn't your job, but if you could find a way to look at the books, I'd appreciate it."

"Mr. Quinn has already suggested it," I said.

"Well." She looked mildly surprised. "The man has far more sense than I imagined. Still, I'd take it as a favor if you'd make it something of a priority. We don't want someone summoning Nitocris in the middle of Widdershins."

"Dear heavens, no," I agreed as we followed her back out. "We've far too many home grown abominations as it is."

CHAPTER 3

Whyborne

"**JUST LOOK AT** it," Griffin beamed. "Isn't it wonderful."

"No," I muttered under my breath.

"What was that, my dear?"

"I said it's quite wonderful," I replied. "Yes."

The object in question was a new Oldsmobile Curved Dash motor car. The thing was painted a mixture of black and shocking crimson, accented with the gleaming steel of the tiller and axles.

Two very cheerful men had delivered it at the crack of dawn, having brought it from the rail station. Griffin sold off some of the stock Father gave him for his birthday to purchase it, and had anticipated its arrival for weeks now. My own quiet hopes, that the thing would be lost somewhere in transit, had apparently been dashed.

"Where are we to keep it?" I asked. At the moment, it was parked in front of our gate, but surely Griffin didn't mean to leave it there, exposed to the elements. I didn't think anyone would molest it, if only out of fear I might curse them, but it was rather blocking the street.

Griffin gave me a slight frown. "We're renting Mr. Zanetti's carriageway and carriage house, since he has no use for it." At my blank look, he added, "Mr. Zanetti? Our next-door neighbor?"

"Oh." Griffin was the gregarious one, not I.

He let out a familiar sigh, the one that meant I'd disappointed him in some respect. "Whyborne, you've lived here almost as long as I have. Four years."

"Three and a half."

"And you still don't know our neighbor's name?"

"I know Mrs. Yates," I said, naming the elderly lady across the street.

"Because she looks after Saul when we're gone." He folded his arms over his chest. "Besides, don't you remember me mentioning this? I specifically said our budget could afford the monthly fee he's asking, and you agreed."

"Erm..." It wasn't that I didn't listen to Griffin. I did. But he'd always been quite happy to handle the finances of our shared home, and I'd been equally happy to let him. "The red color is very modern. I think all the other motor cars in Widdershins are black."

Thankfully he let himself be distracted. "It is, isn't it?" A pleased smile crossed his face, lightening his green eyes. "Well, then. Get in."

I blinked. "Get in?"

"Of course!" He handed me a pair of dust goggles, before donning his own. "I'm going to drive you to the museum."

I stared suspiciously at the conveyance. I'd ridden in Father's motor car a few times, but it was three years older and rather slower and more sedate, at least judging by what I'd seen through the curtains when this one was delivered earlier. "Do you even know how to manage it?" I asked.

"One of the fellows who delivered it showed me, while you hid inside with breakfast," Griffin replied. "We took it up and down the neighborhood. Now climb up."

Having no other choice, I picked up my Gladstone bag and clambered in beside him. He cranked the engine, and within moments it chugged loudly to life.

I'd barely settled the goggles on my face before we were off. Griffin gleefully steered the contraption down the street at a speed I found to be far in excess of safety, honking the brass and rubber horn, and letting go of the tiller to wave enthusiastically to gaping pedestrians.

Oh God. He was going to kill us both.

Water Street grew more crowded as we moved out of the residential neighborhood and into one lined with shops and businesses. Griffin dodged a trolley, shouted an apology at the cab driver whose horse he spooked, and hastily swerved yet again to avoid an elderly man making his way across the street. I clutched my Gladstone in one hand, my hat in the other, and closed my eyes so as not to see whatever object inevitably spelled our doom.

The motorcar's abrupt halt jolted them open once again. Somehow, we'd survived long enough to reach the marble steps leading up to the museum's grand front entrance.

"There now, that was much better than taking the trolley, wasn't it?" Griffin asked. His face was flushed, his hair tousled by the wind where it stuck out past his flat cap. "I'm sorry I won't be able to come by for you this evening, but I have a client and I'm not certain of my schedule."

"That's quite all right," I assured him, as I scrambled out.

"Oh look—there's Christine and Iskander." Griffin honked the annoying horn yet again. "Christine! Iskander!"

Everyone on the sidewalk and steps had stopped to stare. I felt the tips of my ears going hot, and wondered if anyone would believe I'd simply happened by and had no connection whatsoever to the madman in the motor car. Probably not.

Christine and Iskander hurried back down the steps. Iskander generally walked to the museum with Christine in the mornings, even if he had no particular business there that day. His modest income from his lands back in England kept any money woes at bay, so long as he watched his budget. Still, I knew he yet hoped for a permanent position at the Ladysmith.

"I say, what a fine machine," Iskander said of the automobile.

"Thank you." Griffin looked as pleased as if he'd built the thing himself. "It has a two-speed transmission, chain drive, and side crank."

"How modern." Christine also seemed unduly impressed. "How fast does it go?"

"According to the salesmen, it can reach up to twenty miles per hour. I haven't tried to go that fast yet, of course, but I hope to put it to the test soon."

I cringed, and Iskander look alarmed. Christine, however, brightened. "Oh, excellent. I don't suppose you'd mind taking us for a turn some time?"

Griffin beamed. "I'd be happy to. I know the wedding has you occupied at the moment, but once it's over, we'll take a drive up the coast. Will that suit?"

"Quite well." Christine stepped back onto the curb.

"I'll see you tonight, Whyborne." Griffin waved at us cheerfully, then sent the motor car back out into traffic, barely missing the director's carriage as he did so.

"Dear lord," I said, turning my back on whatever mayhem he caused next. "I'll be a widower by sundown."

CHAPTER 4

Griffin

I SPENT THE remainder of my morning at home, first attending to the bookkeeping, then sorting through newspaper reports and generally tidying up my office. I'd obtained a cabinet a few months ago, where I locked away anything I didn't wish to simply leave about, including the more confidential information entrusted to me by various clients. As I added some of my notes to one of the files I kept within, I paused to let my hand rest on the oddly cut gem, which sat on a small brass stand.

Last December, I'd agreed to let the Mother of Shadows alter me so we might escape the ancient city buried deep beneath an Alaskan glacier. She'd given me what I'd come to think of as shadowsight—the ability to perceive magic. And she'd sent with me an Occultum Lapidem—a gemstone originally created to allow the umbrae to communicate over distance.

The gems could be perverted to other sorcerous uses as well, even turned against the umbrae. But she'd seen the deepest part of my mind and given me a trust that still humbled me.

I heard a distant whispering when I touched the stone. A soft murmur of voices, as though someone spoke in another room. If I chose to concentrate, the words would gradually become clear. I'd done so a few times, worried about how the umbrae might fare now they were free from their ancient prison. So far, they had both thrived and remained hidden from humanity.

I withdrew my hand, and the whispers ceased. But even as I relocked the cabinet, I felt oddly comforted by the gem's presence.

The bell rang at precisely the time I'd scheduled my new client. I opened the door to find a smallish man with auburn hair and mustache, dressed in a conservative suit. He seemed utterly unremarkable.

I allowed my focus to shift slightly. Thankfully our house wasn't on one of the lines of arcane energy, and I was able to use my shadowsight without being blinded by magical glare. The man looked just as ordinary as he had through my normal vision. He was neither a sorcerer, nor one of Widdershins's inhabitants who could claim an inhuman lineage.

"Mr. Dewey Lambert?" I asked, holding out my hand. "Griffin Flaherty. Please, come inside. Can I offer you coffee?"

He followed me into my office and took the seat I indicated. "No, thank you. I've given it up. Bad for the nerves. I follow the Graham Diet."

"Of course," I said. "Quite sensible." I forewent coffee of my own and took my seat across from him. "Why don't you tell me why you're here."

He perched on the very edge of his chair, looking as if he might flee at any moment. "Mr. Flaherty, I came to you because...I heard you sometimes handle...odd cases?"

The last words were practically whispered. Mr. Lambert struck me as the sort of fellow who would go to any length to avoid being considered "odd." Or even interesting. "Some of my cases have had unusual aspects," I agreed carefully. "You know I've done work for the old families."

Lambert made a face of distaste. "I'm from Boston," he said. "If I'd known what this town was like, I'd never have taken a job here. Sin and depravity everywhere, and nowhere as common as amidst its leading citizens."

I managed to keep my expression neutral, although it took some effort. Having been accused of perversion and depravity myself, my sympathy for Mr. Lambert rapidly slipped away. "Your story," I prompted.

Perhaps he heard the coolness of my tone. "Er, yes. It happened two days ago. I had left work to take my lunch time walk."

"And your work is...?"

"I'm employed at Dryden and Sons, Tailors, on River Street. I fit men's suits. Many of my clients ask for me by name," he added with an air of pride.

"Very respectable," I agreed. I was familiar with the business, although I'd never used their services myself. Most of their clientele were well-to-do—not rich, certainly not members of the old families, but men of means nonetheless. "What happened on your walk?"

"I set off for the park, as I do every day the weather permits," he said. "I take my lunch and eat it in the fresh air."

I made a note on the paper on my desk. "You bring your lunch from home?" I guessed.

He sniffed. "It's the only way to be sure. The last time I ate at a restaurant, the waiter forgot to mention there was pepper in a dish. Pepper!" His eyes bulged in outrage. "I refuse to run the risk of nervous excitement and all the ills which come from it."

I began to regret my decision to hear Mr. Lambert's case. "Naturally. Please, go on—you left the shop, you say?"

"Yes. I hadn't gotten far—perhaps halfway to the park—when I began to feel distinctly odd." He shifted in his chair uncomfortably. "I wondered if I'd taken ill, and cast about for somewhere to sit down, and then..."

He chewed uncertainly on the ends of his mustache. "And then?" I asked.

"Your discretion is assured?"

"Of course," I replied. "You and I might not hail from Widdershins, but I'm certain you appreciate a private detective couldn't remain in business here without a policy of absolute discretion."

He seemed only slightly reassured. "When I told the police, they thought I was drunk. Drunk! If word got back to the store, I'd surely lose my position."

"They won't hear it from me," I said. Dear God, would the man ever get to the point? "Just tell me what happened."

Lambert took a deep breath, as if steeling himself. "I was somewhere else," he said. Fear crept around the edges of his voice. "I'd been whisked in an instant from the sunlit street, to darkness. I couldn't move, couldn't see, couldn't do anything."

I frowned. "You'd been abducted?"

"Yes!" Lambert leaned forward. "I don't know how they did it. They must have hit me over the head or—or I don't know! I tried to move, to cry for help, but I couldn't. I couldn't even see my surroundings."

At a guess, the man had been heavily drugged. "Did you hear anything?"

His eyes widened. "You believe me?"

"Of course." This was far from the strangest thing I'd encountered in my time in Widdershins. "Did you hear anything? Smell anything? Notice any detail that might shed some light on what happened?"

"No." He shook his head, slumping back in his chair. "Nothing. Only darkness. It was...terrifying, not even being able to scream. I don't know how long I lay—stood?—there, wondering what was happening. Then, all of a sudden, I was on the steps of city hall with a clerk yelling at me, accusing me of theft!"

This wasn't the turn I'd expected his story to take. "Let me make certain I understand you aright. You said you were kidnapped, secured somehow in a dark place unable to move or cry out—and then with no transition found yourself outside of city hall?"

"Yes!" His eyes bulged. "I had no idea what was going on, or why some clerk would be shouting at me. I asked him if he'd seen who had left me there, and he looked at me as though I were mad. Then the police came. They heard out the clerk first."

"And what did he say?"

"He claimed I came into the hall of records and asked to see a map of the area from the 1600s." Lambert's expression became incredulous. "As though I'd do such a thing! Why would I care about an old map from before there was even a town here? He said he brought out the map and I examined it. Then I left, and when he turned to put the map away, it was gone."

"Was it found on your person?"

"Of course not!" Lambert scowled at me for daring to make the suggestion. "When the police found nothing, the clerk accused me of passing it out the open window to an accomplice. The police asked for my version of events."

My heart sank. Lambert would have been far better off lying, but I doubted it would have occurred to him to do so. "And you told the truth."

"Of course I did." His mustache bristled with righteous indignation. "I wanted them to investigate my abduction and bring my kidnappers to justice. But the police said I was either mad or drunk, and the clerk was as well. I tried to tell them he must be in league with the kidnappers, but they dismissed me."

It was a bit of a stretch, but I didn't say that out loud. "Do you have any idea why someone would kidnap you? Or why they'd return you to the steps of city hall?"

"No." He shook his head. "I have no enemies, but I suppose one of them might be a dissatisfied customer seeking to discredit me."

"I see." I made another note. "Do you recall the clerk's name?"

"Patrick Tubbs."

The case was indeed odd, as Mr. Lambert had put it. I didn't doubt he told the truth, or at least what he believed to be the truth. I tore off a corner of the paper and wrote a sum on it. "Your case sounds of interest, Mr. Lambert. This is my daily fee. Should I require additional expenses, I'll speak to you about them beforehand."

Lambert frowned at the paper. "This seems a bit high, Mr. Flaherty."

Of course he was the sort to haggle with me. "Then by all means, you may hire another detective to clear your good name."

The suggestion made him look no happier. "I assume the fee is only to be paid should you in fact succeed?"

"That would make it a reward, not a fee." I pasted on a false smile. "I operate under much the same rules as the Pinkertons who trained me, Mr. Lambert. I understand not all do so, but it is how I conduct my business."

In other words, he was free to depart, assuming he could find anyone else who would believe him.

No doubt he had the same thought. He didn't stop frowning, but he did nod reluctantly. Even so, I made certain to have a check for the first day of investigation in my hand before seeing him out.

CHAPTER 5

Griffin

I STILL HAD a few hours before city hall closed for the day, so I made my way to the department of records. I entered to find the clerk seated behind a desk; he rose rather hastily to his feet when I came in. No doubt he felt the sting of the map's loss from under his nose.

"Mr. Tubbs?" I asked, extending my hand. "Permit me to introduce myself. I'm Griffin Flaherty."

I'd come to the hall of records in the course of my work before, but the deputy clerks changed at the whim of the City Clerk, and I'd not met this one yet. Mr. Tubbs was rather handsome, his young face not yet sculpted by lines, his blond hair thick. As we shook hands, his eyes swept over me in a not unappreciative fashion.

"What can I do for you, Mr. Flaherty?" he asked.

I gave him my most charming smile. "I hoped you might answer some questions about the map that disappeared the other day."

His smile wilted. "I already told the police everything."

"I'm not with the police. I'm a private detective, representing a client whose identity is confidential." I looked him straight in the eye. "And I don't think the loss of the map was your fault." Not that I had a clear notion of what was going on, but it seemed doubtful the explanation would be so prosaic as carelessness on Mr. Tubbs's part.

His expression perked up at my assurance. "You don't? You must not be working for Mr. Lambert, then."

No reason to correct his flawed assumption. "As I said, my client requires confidentiality. May I ask you a few questions?"

"Yes, of course. Can I offer you some coffee?"

Not an admirer of the Graham Diet, then. "Thank you; that would be most kind." While he fetched the coffee, I wandered about the room, studying numerous bookshelves stuffed with bound records and a large number of cabinets built for the storage of maps. I knew from experience that most of the maps were surveys of property boundaries. An electric fan turned slowly overhead, and the open windows let in a refreshing breeze. I peered out; certainly it would have been possible for Lambert to have passed the map to an accomplice, but only if Tubbs hadn't noticed him walk over to the window with it. There was also a disturbingly large rat hole in one corner of the room, but it seemed rather unlikely that anyone had trained rats to steal maps.

Tubbs returned with the coffee and saw me looking at the hole. "Awful, isn't it? I put out poison and asked for a carpenter to come seal it. At least there hasn't been any damage to the records."

We sat and sipped our coffee. I had the feeling Mr. Tubbs didn't get many visitors in the ordinary course of a day. We chatted a bit about the ghastly heat, before I drew the conversation around to my investigation. "Do you recall what map Mr. Lambert asked to see?"

"Oh yes." Tubbs nodded. "I should have known something was strange, because the map he asked for dated from 1685, almost a decade prior to Widdershins's founding. It was a large survey of the entire Cranch Valley area."

"And how valuable would such a map be?" Money was never a bad guess when it came to motive, after all.

"I couldn't say, really," he confessed. "I'm sure the right collector would pay well for it, but an early map of the town would be far more valuable. Most of its worth was as a historical document."

An odd choice for a thief, then. "Why wasn't it in the museum?"

"The Ladysmith? Hmph." Tubbs scowled. "To paraphrase the City Clerk, the museum would take every object of note in Widdershins and hoard them away from the rest of us. The Ladysmith already has enough old maps, including some very valuable ones drawn up by Theron Blackbyrne himself. And yet their American History department or their librarians come by every so often and attempt to convince us to give them all of ours. I turned down such a request myself just last week. Pure greed on their part, wouldn't you agree, Mr. Flaherty?"

"Absolutely." A shame Whyborne wasn't here. He would have

gleefully joined in with Mr. Tubbs and heaped abuse upon the American History department in general, and Bradley Osborne in particular. "Was there anything of special interest on this map?"

"I don't believe so." Tubbs shrugged. "Various geographical features, the locations of old Indian villages, that sort of thing."

"I see." I didn't see, actually, but an appearance of confidence never went amiss. "Thank you, Mr. Tubbs. You've been most helpful."

"I'm grateful to have been of assistance." He rose and showed me to the door. We paused there, and he cleared his throat nervously. "If you have any more questions, don't hesitate to send for me. Perhaps I could meet you somewhere more genial than this office to answer them."

The poor fellow wasn't exactly practiced, which made his suggestion even more flattering, as it implied he didn't often arrange such meetings. "I appreciate the offer," I said with as much kindness as I could, "but I feel any questions would best be answered here, in a professional environment."

A blush stained his cheeks. "O-of course. Good-day, Mr. Flaherty."

CHAPTER 6

Whyborne

"I HAVE SOMETHING for you to inspect," said one of the librarians. "A codex. Fifteenth century, if I'm not mistaken."

I resisted the desire to check the clock. I'd spent the day in the library, laboring over the Wisborg Collection. As Christine had said, it wasn't my job, but it would hardly be the first time I'd spent my hours at the museum researching the occult rather than comparing ancient languages. Although to be fair, in this case there was some overlap.

The librarians carefully opened the crates and removed the volumes one at a time. Mr. Quinn had his best men inspect each book and identify the language, if known to them, as well as the name of the volume, if indicated. Any of interest he brought to me.

Most of the hundreds of books were ordinary fare: a number of Bibles, one dating from the medieval period and adorned with the fanciful artistry of the monks who had copied it; the *Histories* of Herodotus; the works of Homer and Shakespeare.

But other, darker, tomes lay mixed in, like adders lurking amidst a pile of sticks. A Latin translation of the *Al Azif, De Vermis Mysteriis*, fragments of the Pnakotic Manuscripts, and of course *Cultes des Goules*. Several others had no name inscribed on them, but a cursory glance showed them to be grimoires of the blackest sort. There was even a book similar to the *Liber Arcanorum*, but oddly altered, as if copied by someone making deliberate changes. That one I told Mr. Quinn to keep under lock and key, and to show to no one but myself. An outrageous demand, but he'd merely bowed and looked unaccountably pleased.

A heavy iron latch held the codex closed. I hoped the stains on the leather cover were from rust. I opened the tome cautiously; although I couldn't have said why, I felt almost as if I touched something alive, an animal that might turn on me at any moment.

There appeared to be no title, and the writing, while in a neat hand, was in no system of letters I'd ever seen before. Was it a code, perhaps? Some alchemists used them to conceal their knowledge from rivals, as did sorcerers. The *Liber Arcanorum* was one such example. But the letters within it had still been Latin, not...whatever this system of writing was.

"Pardon me, Dr. Whyborne," Mr. Quinn said from my elbow.

I started, having not heard his approach. "Oh! I, er, yes?"

One spidery hand fluttered in the direction of the clock. "It is after five."

"Oh, of course." No doubt the librarians wished to end their day and return home. I occasionally worked long hours, although for the sake of matrimonial harmony, I tried to leave as close to five as possible. Was it my turn to cook tonight? Blast, I couldn't remember.

Still, I hesitated over the codex. I'd handled far too many books of dangerous lore over the last few years, and as a consequence had developed something of an instinct. The writing within the codex might be incomprehensible at the moment, but something about it set my nerves on edge.

Another half hour wouldn't hurt. Griffin had said he might be late, given his own work. "I think I'll take this one back to my office," I said, rising to my feet. "I'd like to give it a closer look."

The librarian who'd brought me the codex had drifted up during our conversation. Now he offered me a bow. "Widdershins," he said, in the same tone I imagined an Englishman might say "my lord."

Mr. Quinn gave him a poisonous glare, as if the poor fellow had overstepped his bounds. Why, I hadn't the slightest idea, since I'd been subjected to the librarians addressing me thusly since that awful Hallowe'en of two years ago. The librarian hastily bowed again and departed.

"As you wish, Dr. Whyborne," Mr. Quinn said. "Do let me know if you find the codex to be of interest."

"Of course," I said, scooping it up before he changed his mind. I didn't think he would, given he ordinarily seemed to have no qualms about handing me the darkest of tomes, but one never knew.

I passed a few of my colleagues on the way to my office, all of them making for the exit. "Don't work too late, Percy," Bradley called jovially as I passed. "You wouldn't want to keep your *landlord* waiting for dinner."

Ass.

A visit to the men's washroom was in order, so I left the codex on my desk and made my way through the labyrinthine corridors. A few minutes later, as I returned back the way I'd come, I spotted a familiar form. "Iskander," I called.

He stopped, a relieved smile on his face. "Whyborne! I was just coming to find you, actually. I'm glad to see you haven't left for the day."

I couldn't recall him ever seeking me out on his own. "Is everything all right?"

"Oh! Yes, fine." He hesitated. "I think. There is something that's been weighing a bit on my mind."

I fell into step beside him. "By all means, please tell me. You know I'll do whatever I can to assist."

A rueful smile curved his handsome lips. "I know. Thank you for the offer of hosting the wedding in Whyborne House."

"It wasn't my idea," I said. "That was entirely my father's."

"Oh." The smile faded. "I thought...well."

I'd said something wrong, although I wasn't entirely certain what. "You thought...?"

Iskander sighed. "Massachusetts may not have anti-mis-cegenation laws, but Christine will do her career no favors by marrying me. It's a heavy truth, but wishing things were otherwise won't make them so."

Oh. It hadn't even occurred to me. But of course he was perfectly correct.

"The loss of the firman in Egypt, returning from Alaska virtually empty-handed, marrying a half Egyptian...her career is in jeopardy." Iskander went on. "If Christine were a man, of course, things would be different. But as it is, having the wedding with the stamp of your family's approval—of *your* approval—will help. People respect you."

I snorted. "They respect Father, perhaps. Although I fear Stanford destroyed a good deal of that respect with his antics."

Iskander stopped. "No, Whyborne. They respect *you*. And your father as well, of course, but he wasn't the one who fought your brother or saved the town from the tidal wave the Endicotts raised. Christine told me all about it. *One for the land, and one for the sea.*"

The damned prophecy was going to haunt me for the rest of my life. "Whatever the case, I'm glad Father saw fit to help," I said. "So what is it you need from me?"

Iskander began to walk again. "Holding the wedding in Whyborne House will do us no good if we fail to make the right sort of impression. My father was a diplomat, and my family well enough off to move in certain social circles back in England. I know how these things go. Every eye will be critical, just waiting for some breach of etiquette or taste."

I'd grown up with such critical eyes trained on me, although many had belonged to my own family. "I understand."

"Then you'll appreciate I'm a bit...concerned...that Christine seems to be leaving things to the last minute," he said. "We agreed to divvy up the responsibilities, but when I enquire as to the flowers and other decorations, she says she's been busy and not to worry."

"Oh dear." I'd never had to plan any sort of event myself, but I recalled how much rushing about Miss Emily and the other servants had done well ahead of any large gathering.

"Exactly." He sounded relieved I understood. "I thought if she won't listen to me, she might listen to you. Just...prompt her a bit."

"Of course." How I'd do so without provoking Christine's well-known tendency to stubbornness, I couldn't imagine. But at least if she grew annoyed, it would be with me and not her husband-to-be. "I'll do my best."

"Thank you," he said. "You're a good chap, and—I say, did that fellow just come out of your office?"

A man wearing an unremarkable brown suit and bowler hat strode swiftly away from the now-open door to my office. In one hand, he carried a valise; the other was tucked into his coat pocket.

The devil? "Excuse me?" I called, lengthening my own strides. "Sir?"

He cast a single glance over his shoulder; his left eye was covered by a patch. Then he broke into a run.

CHAPTER 7

Whyborne

"AFTER HIM!" SHOUTED Iskander.

We both took off after the fleeing man, bellowing for security at the top of our lungs. Whoever he was, he seemed to know the layout of the museum far too well for a casual thief. He darted down corridors, cut through the taxidermy room, and knocked aside one of the curators who'd been working late.

Still, I'd walked these corridors for eight years and knew every secret. "Keep after him," I told Iskander, and dashed up the next stairwell.

I suspected the thief made for the service door at the rear of the building, so as to easier lose any pursuit in the back alleys. If I was wrong...well, hopefully Iskander might still catch him. I was out of breath by the time I reached the roof, my lungs burning and my legs aching. Still, I pounded across the flat roof to another access, then down the stairway to the ground floor.

I emerged just as the thief came into sight. "Stop!" I shouted, and summoned wind.

The magic leapt to obey, fueled by the great arcane vortex beneath us. I felt it turning, sensed the flow of energy, the scars on my arm aching as I bent my will to reshape the world. A breeze ruffled my hair, turned into a gale—

The man halted and drew an antique-looking dagger from his pocket. Although nowhere near me, he slashed violently at the air.

The magic fell apart, the warp and weft of the spell severed by the blade. While I stood gaping, he turned and dashed down a side corridor, making for the front of the building.

"Bugger!" Iskander exclaimed. "What happened?"

I forced my aching legs into motion once again. "The dagger—it was like the cursed sword Stanford used—the witch hunter's blade," I gasped. "Spells are useless so long as he has it."

The one-eyed thief exited through a staff door into the public portion of the museum. We followed and found ourselves in the Classical wing. Pale marble statues watched us through blank eyes from the perimeter of the room. The thief slowed just long enough to shove a large pithos into our path. The ancient container crashed to the floor, shattering into ceramic fragments.

"Damn you!" I shouted as I dodged the remnants, trying to keep from accidentally stepping on any pieces and making the damage worse. Bad enough the fellow was a thief, but this destruction went beyond the pale.

We exited the wing, into the grand foyer with its displays of ancient animals and humans alike. Apparently encouraged by his success at slowing us, the man overturned a small display of neolithic weaponry.

It proved his undoing. Iskander scooped up one of the obsidian blades, paused to take aim, and threw it.

The sharp edge of the volcanic glass sliced through the man's coat, shirt, and arm with ease. He let out a cry of agony, the valise tumbling from his hand.

"Stop right there!" shouted one of the guards from the other end of the hall.

The thief ignored the command and the brandished weapon, instead darting through the small door to the side of the main entrance. It was yet unlocked, and in an instant he was gone. The guard ran after him, but I doubted his chances of catching the fellow amidst the evening crowds.

"At least he didn't get away with whatever is in the valise," I said as I knelt to open it. "Your aim was excellent as always."

Iskander picked up the obsidian blade and inspected it carefully. "It doesn't look damaged, just bloody," he said with relief. "What did the fellow take from your office?"

I reached into the valise and pulled out the Wisborg Codex. Apparently my instincts about the volume had been right.

Iskander frowned. "What did he want with that?"

"No idea." I tucked the volume under my arm and rose to my feet. "But I think it best to keep it locked safely away until we find out."

CHAPTER 8

Griffin

THE NEXT MORNING, I interrogated Whyborne over breakfast. He'd arrived home rather late, having spent several hours reiterating his story for the police investigating the attempted theft, and we'd gone to bed shortly after.

"The detective seemed to find it odd that I'm always in the middle of anything that goes wrong at the museum," he said glumly as we settled into breakfast. "As though it were my fault! I'm not the one who brings dangerous items into the Ladysmith. I tried explaining that I merely work long hours and have terrible luck, but I don't think he believed me."

"I take it you're going to examine the codex more closely today?" I poured milk over my cold cereal, then passed the bottle to him.

"Of course. And yes, I'll be careful," he added. "What bothers me is that the thief came prepared to face me."

"The dagger." I frowned. "Might he have taken it from the museum's collection? Did it have the same provenance as the sword?"

"Devil if I know." Whyborne poked unenthusiastically at his cereal with his spoon. "If I recall correctly, Dr. Norris said there was only the sword and the diary, but he might have been mistaken. I wouldn't trust him to know every item the American History Department has squirreled away in its storerooms."

His remark put me in mind of Mr. Tubbs's comments about the acquisitiveness of the Ladysmith's staff. "That reminds me—my case has some aspects to it which would benefit from your expertise. Your sorcerous expertise," I added when he momentarily brightened.

"Oh." He deflated. "Go ahead then."

I told him the details of my case as we ate. "I don't think either Mr. Lambert or Mr. Tubbs were lying," I concluded. "Is it possible Mr. Lambert was under a spell of some sort? Something to cloud his mind?"

"It is possible," he mused, sucking on his spoon thoughtfully. "There are spells for mind control, and the victims are usually disoriented. Sometimes they remember fragments, such as having the sensation of being unable to control their own bodies."

"How ghastly." A shiver ran up my spine at the thought. "As I recall, when the dweller in the deeps influenced your mind, you believed yourself to be somewhere else."

"True," he agreed. "But the dweller didn't cause me to act in such a...coherent, I suppose, fashion as Mr. Lambert. I thought I was in the depths of the ocean, but my body wasn't off having conversations and looking at maps in the meantime."

"No." It wasn't one of my fonder memories. "You didn't behave rationally, whereas Mr. Lambert did. Still, it might be worth investigating." I added more sugar to my coffee. "Assuming Mr. Lambert wasn't simply the victim of some sort of strange fit or mental disorder, someone chose him in particular to steal the map."

"Assuming it was stolen in the first place," Whyborne pointed out. "Remember the evening we came home to find Saul had dragged out your case notes and shredded them?"

I eyed our cat, currently enjoying his breakfast as well. "I couldn't forget. So you think a cat, in some fit of kittenish excitement, came in through the open window and made off with the map?"

"Well, it doesn't sound quite so likely when you put it that way." Whyborne muttered. "But the window was open, and if the electric fan was on, the map may have simply blown away."

"And the fact Mr. Lambert's strange attack took place in the same span of time?" I arched a brow at him. "That seems a bit of a stretch, don't you think?"

"Yes, well. You can hardly blame me for hoping for an explanation that doesn't involved sorcery, can you?"

"That seems a bit hypocritical coming from a sorcerer," I said, but I winked to show I was joking.

Whyborne shook his head. "Jest all you like, but you know as well as I that cases involving sorcery tend to end with a great deal of screaming and blood. Often ours."

"The screams or the blood?"

"Both." He sipped his coffee. "Has the morning paper come yet?"

"Let me check." I rose to my feet. "Don't look so glum, my dear. Perhaps we'll have some luck, and someone was merely playing a cruel prank on Mr. Lambert. No blood or death involved."

"I hope you're right."

I retrieved the newspaper from the porch. My heart sank as soon as I read the headline.

My face must have betrayed me as I walked back to the kitchen, because Whyborne set aside his spoon. "Griffin? Is something wrong?"

"I fear your hopes have been dashed," I said, and laid the paper on the table.

HORRIBLE MURDER OF A CITY CLERK! blared the headline. And beneath, in smaller type: *Mr. Dewey Lambert arrested for bloody crime.*

CHAPTER 9

Griffin

AN HOUR LATER, a policeman led me to Mr. Lambert's cell.

The jail was as dreary as I remembered it, having been held here briefly myself on murder charges. That day had been one of utter misery. First Whyborne had broken off our nascent relationship thanks to my own foolishness. Then I'd been arrested for the murder of Madam Rosa, one of my informants who had died horribly. At the time, I'd made no true friends in Widdershins save for Whyborne, and all of my old friends from my Pinkerton days had abandoned me when I went to the madhouse.

I'd sat here alone and afraid, every remembered terror from my confinement in the asylum playing itself out over and over again in my mind. Until Whyborne's godfather, Addison Somerby, came to pay my bail and take me away from here. I'd felt a moment of hope.

And then things had gotten exponentially worse.

My heart raced with remembered fear, and I took a deep breath to calm it. I wasn't a prisoner. I was no longer the stranger in town, friendless save for the cat that had shown up starving in my back yard. I was here as a free man and would leave the same way.

Unlike poor Mr. Lambert.

"Mr. Flaherty!" He rose to his feet as I stopped outside his cell. His face was drawn and pale, his mustache chewed to tatters. His drab appearance looked even more out of place amidst the iron bars and moisture-stained brick walls. The smell of mildew and piss filled the air, and I recalled how it had infiltrated my clothing and hair when I'd been held here.

I glanced at the policeman. "May I have a word with my client?"

"Sorry, sir." And the fellow did look sorry. "You ain't his lawyer, so Detective Tilton says I'm not to leave you alone with him."

I kept my expression neutral. I ordinarily did my best to avoid the police, for the sake of both my profession and my private life. But it was unavoidable to come into contact with them at times, and Detective Tilton and I had crossed paths before. He'd made it clear he considered me as much a brute as any Pinkerton strike breaker. As I thought him too eager to jump to conclusions, not to mention too willing to be bribed by the old families, the dislike was mutual.

"Of course," I said. Turning my back to the officer, I asked, "How are you holding up, Mr. Lambert?"

"How do you think?" He wrung his hands unhappily. "Do you have any idea what they've accused me of doing?"

"I read the account in the newspaper."

He groaned and sank back down onto the edge of his iron cot. "The newspapers...I'll lose my position for certain. The scandal..."

"Don't lose hope." I stepped up to the bars and wrapped my hand around one of them. "Just tell me what happened, from your perspective."

"I was asleep in my rooms last evening—I live in a boarding house with other bachelors—when my landlady woke me. She said the police wanted to see me." His face twisted. "I'll be lucky if she hasn't already thrown all my possessions into the street!"

"I'm certain she'll be understanding," I said, more to calm him than because I thought it the truth. "Please continue."

Lambert swallowed convulsively. "I-I thought the police had come about the map. That they'd found it, perhaps, or-or something, although why they'd visit in the middle of the night I couldn't imagine. Instead, they arrested me. They said I...they said I killed him."

"Mr. Tubbs." I tried not to think of the man as I'd last seen him: his tentative smile, his disappointment when I'd refused his offer to meet away from his job.

"Yes." Lambert swayed back and forth. "Detective Tilton showed me photographs. It was...horrible. Unspeakable."

If Tubbs had died half as hard as the *Widdershins Enquirer Journal* claimed, no wonder Lambert looked so shaken. "What evidence did Detective Tilton present against you?"

"He said I must have done it. That I was angry after the

accusation of theft, and it drove me into a murderous rage." Lambert blinked rapidly, but the tears broke loose and slid down his face anyway. "When I protested my innocence, he suggested I was either a liar or a madman."

"But there was nothing else?" I prompted. "Nothing of yours at the scene?"

"Of course not! How could there have been? I'm an innocent man, Mr. Flaherty. You must believe me!"

The desperation on Lambert's face would have moved a far harder heart than mine. "I do," I reassured him. "I have one last question for you. Have you experienced any more incidents like the one which first led to your encounter with Mr. Tubbs?"

He shook his head vehemently. "No."

"No loss of memories? Moments of disorientation? Strange visions?"

"No."

I hoped he was being honest, for his sake. Certainly he seemed sincere...but at the same time, he might deny it out of fear such an episode would be used against him.

Could the map have been a misdirection all along? Did someone harbor a grudge against Mr. Tubbs and wish to discredit and kill him? It was hard to believe, given what I'd seen of the man, but I couldn't simply dismiss the possibility.

"Thank you for your time, Mr. Lambert," I said. "I suggest you hire a lawyer, if you haven't already. In the meantime, I'll see what I can discover."

"Thank you, Mr. Flaherty." Lambert blinked back tears. "And please, hurry. My life rests in your hands."

CHAPTER 10

Whyborne

As soon as I reached my office, I removed the Wisborg Codex from the safe where I'd locked it away the night before. The cryptic letters of the first few pages seemed to mock me. Still, the very fact someone else was interested in the tome suggested the writing could be deciphered, if one only had the correct key.

Would someone from the Cabal know anything about the book? My only contact with them had been through Revered Scarrow in Alaska, who claimed them a loose confederacy of sorcerers opposed to the Endicotts. Which didn't necessarily make their intentions good ones, but Scarrow had saved Griffin and Iskander's lives. I was willing to give his organization the benefit of the doubt.

I skipped forward a few pages in my inspection, only to be stopped by a brilliant splash of color. A drawing of a plant filled most of a page—some sort of cycad, perhaps, although I was no botanist. I paged through slowly and found more illustrations, plants and animals alike, all of them beautifully rendered and most of them rather fantastical. I paused at the hideous illustration of a monstrous hybrid that looked like a rat with a human face. The artist had certainly possessed a horrible imagination.

The door to my office burst open unceremoniously. "What the devil, Whyborne!" Christine exclaimed as she stormed in. Miss

Parkhurst hovered behind her, looking apologetic. "Kander told me what happened last night, after I'd left to go home. Why on earth didn't you call on me?"

Miss Parkhurst cast me an uncertain look. "Would you care for some coffee, doctors?"

"No, I think Dr. Putnam has already had a bit too much," I replied. Miss Parkhurst retreated hurriedly, closing the door behind her. "We hardly knew someone was going to try to steal the codex, Christine."

Christine dropped into the chair across from me. "Is that the codex? Why did someone want to steal it?"

"I've no idea." I eyed the rattish horror so carefully inscribed on the page. "Given the craftsmanship and age, it has a certain value. In other circumstances I might have thought a collector wanted to make off with it before we had a chance to have it properly cataloged. But the witch hunter's dagger suggests otherwise."

"Not if the collector belongs to one of the old families," she countered. "Or someone else who knows you're a sorcerer."

"Then why not wait until I left for the day?"

"I imagine they thought you had. Kander said you'd walked away from your office for a moment," she pointed out. "Speaking of which, how did the fellow know it was in your office instead of the library?"

"Yet another question I don't have an answer for." I rubbed my eyes tiredly. "I assume he was watching the library...watching me... somehow."

"How unsettling." She reached out and turned the codex around to examine the picture. "Almost as unsettling as that thing."

"Quite." I hesitated, but there was nothing gained by delaying. "How are the wedding arrangements coming?"

She frowned slightly. I had to admit, it wasn't the sort of question I would normally ask. I tried to look innocently curious. "Fine," she said.

"Oh good." I nodded. "So you've made arrangements with the florist?"

"Not yet," she said. "Why?"

I bit back a sigh. Christine's family might not have ranked with the Vanderbilts or the Whybornes, but they'd had enough money to move in society. She really ought to know better.

"The ballroom and dining room at Whyborne House are quite large," I said. "A considerable quantity of flowers will be required. It isn't fair to the florist to wait until the last minute and then expect miracles."

Christine scowled. "I don't expect miracles, Whyborne. I...oh."

Her expression cleared. "Of course. I'm sorry, old fellow."

"Er..." Should I question whatever misapprehension had led to her agreement, or take advantage of it? "It's quite all right."

"I'll make an appointment for us to visit the florist tomorrow," she said. "Or, even better, we'll ask Miss Parkhurst to do so, as you'll be coming with me."

I'd assumed by "us" she'd met herself and Iskander. "I am?"

"Of course!"

"But...oh, very well." If it moved things forward, I'd resign myself. "Will you give me the codex back now?"

"Yes, yes," she said, turning the page. "It's very...oh."

She turned the volume so I could see as well. Unlike the fantastical illustrations that had come before, this creature was all too real. All too familiar.

A ketoi.

"Blast," I said softly.

"A family portrait?" Christine asked.

I shot her a dark look. "This isn't funny." The ketoi was beautifully rendered, from its lithe body to its mouth full of shark teeth, to the stinging tentacles of its hair.

Filled with a sense of new urgency, I turned a few more pages, revealing a progression of what looked like star charts. An umbrae.

A longer page folded into the codex, which when extended showed a Mother of Shadows on one side and the dweller in the deeps on the other.

"What did Daphne say?" I asked. "She knew I wasn't human. She said she smelled the ocean in my blood." I flipped back to the ketoi.

"There are other sources," Christine pointed out uneasily. "The *Unaussprechlichen Kulten* for one. Or the knowledge may have belonged to Nitocris. It doesn't mean this is the book that taught Daphne how to...do whatever she did."

"She called to the Outside, and Nitocris answered." I shook my head. "I don't like this, Christine. I don't like this at all."

Miss Parkhurst tapped lightly on the door. "Dr. Whyborne? Mr. Flaherty is here to see you."

"Send him in." I gave Christine a pointed look. "Do you see? *Some* people know to ask Miss Parkhurst before they come barging in here."

"Why the devil should Griffin, of all people, have to ask to see you?" she countered.

Griffin stepped inside. My greeting died in my throat, and the sober expression on his face brought me to my feet. "Griffin? What happened?" A hopeful thought occurred to me. "Did the motor car suffer some mechanical failure?"

"What? No, of course not." He'd removed his hat, but kept it in hand, absently tapping it against his thigh. "It's the case I'm working on. There's been a murder, and I think...well. Is Iskander somewhere about?"

"Indeed," Christine said, rising to her feet. "I'll fetch him. He's busy photographing some of the older artifacts."

Griffin's mouth pressed into a grim line. "Tell him to bring his camera. And his knives."

CHAPTER 11

Griffin

As THE MOTOR car would only seat two, we paid a brief visit to Whyborne House at my request. A bit over two hours later, a coachman drove us up the coast road north of Widdershins in a spring wagon. Even though Niles had been out, Fenton assured us that "Mr. Whyborne left instructions to treat any request from you as if it came directly from him, Master Percival." As a result, Whyborne sulked most of the way out of Widdershins.

Once away from the town, the coast became a lonely, bleak place. Stunted trees clung to the sea cliffs, their branches bent by the constant winds. A line of poles bearing telegraph and electrical wires marched alongside the road. Many seemed to be in disrepair, and I wondered if the electrical company abandoned their upkeep after Stormhaven Lunatic Asylum had been destroyed. Crows and seagulls perched on the leaning poles, watching with curiosity as we passed by.

"You probably saw the newspaper accounts," I said to Christine and Iskander, who sat side-by-side across from Whyborne and me. "But here are the facts."

I related the details of my case. "Last night, Mr. Tubbs's body was found at a farm up the coast," I said. "The farmer, one Mr. Robinson, thought he glimpsed lights in a distant pasture as he prepared for bed. Taking up his shotgun, he went to investigate. Fortunately for him, the perpetrators had already left by the time he arrived to find the body."

"And Lambert didn't have another...episode?" Whyborne asked.

"He claims not. He might be saying so to make himself less suspicious in front of the police, of course, but I find myself believing him." I reached into my coat. "After I spoke with him, I stopped by Detective Tilton's desk. Tilton wasn't in, but he'd carelessly left some photographs of the murder behind."

Whyborne's eyes widened. "You stole one?" he asked in a scandalized whisper.

"Good man," Christine said, reaching for the photo.

"The details aren't distinct," I explained as I handed it over. "It looks to have been taken at night, with only the police lanterns to illuminate the scene. Still, one can see the brutality of the crime all too well."

"I'd say," she said with a frown.

Iskander peered over her shoulder. "Good lord."

The picture showed poor Mr. Tubbs, his lifeless body sprawled across a low, blocky stone. His clothing had been torn aside, and sigils painted on his skin in some dark substance. His throat had been cut, and his chest pried open.

Whyborne accepted the photo from Christine and studied it. "His heart?"

"Missing," I confirmed.

"He wasn't just murdered," Iskander said. "His death seems to have been part of some ritual."

"Those stones in the background are hard to make out," Christine said, "but they don't look natural."

"According to the newspaper, Mr. Robinson found the body amidst some old Indian standing stones." I tucked the photograph away again. "Which is why I requested you all to accompany me. I want to look over the site, but I'm neither sorcerer nor archaeologist. Nor am I as adept at camera work, should we wish to document the area."

"Not to mention going alone would be foolhardy," Iskander added.

"That, too," I agreed.

The carriage rocked slightly as we turned onto a narrow lane leading off to the west. The coast fell behind, and the landscape became slightly less inhospitable. Shrubs and real trees soon hemmed in the lane, and fields lined with rock walls lay beyond.

Eventually the coach drew up in front of a small farmhouse, its sides weathered but still sturdy. An elderly woman tottered out onto the porch to greet us, her face creased into a frown.

"We don't want to talk to no more reporters," she snapped as I climbed out.

I beckoned Whyborne to follow me, then approached her with my hat in my hand. "I assure you, ma'am, we aren't reporters," I said. "Permit me to introduce myself. I'm Griffin Flaherty, a private detective. This is my friend Dr. Percival Endicott Whyborne, and—"

"Whyborne," she said. She peered at him through narrowed eyes.

I focused on my shadowsight. No mark of sorcery lay on her, but there was...something not quite human. The blood ran thin in her, but I was certain she was a ketoi hybrid.

"Good afternoon," Whyborne said, a bit stiffly.

"Hmph," she said. I couldn't tell if the sound was meant to indicate approval or its opposite. "My husband found the body in the far field, over that way." She indicated the direction with a jerk of her head. "Just follow the lane there, past the barn and the hayfield, 'til you come to the high hill with the big oak. He was laying right on the altar stone."

Whyborne looked aghast. "Altar stone?"

"I'm not saying we used it as such," she said defensively.

"Of course," I said quickly. "Thank you, Mrs. Robinson. Your cooperation may set an innocent man free."

She shook her head. "I don't want to hear nothing more about it. There's things decent folk know to leave alone, and this is one of them."

She shuffled back into her house and shut the door decisively. "I suppose that makes us indecent folk," Iskander remarked when we climbed back into the carriage.

"I've always said as much," I replied, signaling the driver to continue on. "She was one of your distant cousins, Whyborne."

He looked at me in surprise. "A ketoi hybrid?"

"Yes." I glanced at him. I'd grown used to the sight over the months, the odd feeling that the untameable spikes of his hair would suddenly become tentacles, or I'd tug his collar down and discover gills beneath. "More human, though."

"Do you think they're involved?" Christine asked, twisting around to peer back at the farmhouse.

"The Robinsons or the ketoi?" Iskander asked.

"Either."

"No," Whyborne said firmly. "That is, I can't speak for the Robinsons, but Persephone would never sanction murder."

"I would never cast aspersions on Persephone," I said carefully, "but Lambert's odd episodes..."

"Were nothing like those the dweller caused in me!" he exclaimed.

"You said so yourself! And do I have to remind you that Persephone is my sister?"

"I know." I held up a hand for peace. "And Persephone risked her life to stop war with the land. I haven't forgotten. But not all of the ketoi wanted that peace. It's too early to discount any possibilities."

Whyborne folded his arms over his chest, back to sulking again. I resisted the temptation to roll my eyes.

Cows watched us pass from behind a fence, their dark eyes mildly curious. Their animal scent perfumed the air, mingled with sweet hay and sun-kissed grass. It brought back unexpected memories of my youth in Kansas: muscles aching from a long day of hard work, the feel of warm hide beneath my hands, the clang of the bell summoning us to dinner.

"It seems a well run farm," I remarked. My voice came out slightly thicker than I'd intended. Whyborne caught it, of course, and cast me a concerned look.

"If you say so," Christine said. Like Whyborne, she'd lived her life in cities. Or in tents in the wastes of Egypt. But Iskander looked nostalgic; perhaps he thought of the rural estate in England where he'd grown to manhood.

The lane grew more rutted the farther we went. We left the cows behind, and soon I spotted the hill Mrs. Robinson had mentioned. An enormous oak sprouted just short of the crown, spreading its hoary arms wide.

Whyborne shaded his eyes against the westering sun. "Look, at the hill crest. Are those the stones we saw in the background of the photograph?"

Something about their shape seemed horribly familiar...but no. Surely I was simply being paranoid.

"This is as close as I can get, sir," the driver said as the carriage creaked to a halt at the foot of the hill.

"Thank you," Whyborne replied as he climbed out.

"Should I bring my camera?" Iskander asked, gesturing to his bag at his feet.

I scanned the area carefully, but there looked to be nowhere for any attackers to conceal themselves. Likely whoever had done this was long gone. "Yes," I said. "But bring your knives as well. Just in case."

We started slowly up the steep hill. "There's a line of arcane power here, isn't there?" Whyborne asked when we were halfway to the crest.

I nodded. It burned in my shadowsight, a wide swath of blue fire, feeding into the great vortex that lay beneath Widdershins. "Yes."

The stones cast long shadows across the grass, and the late sun stained them orange, save where blood had lent them a darker hue. Some of the stones had fallen long ago, but the rest of the menhirs stood higher than a man. At the eastern end of the circle lurked a rough stone block—the altar Mrs. Robinson had referred to, no doubt.

Centuries of weathering had blurred the figures carved thereon, but I made out hybrid abominations reminiscent of the terrible Guardians that Blackbyrne and his ilk had raised. On another face, what could only be ketoi swam alongside a tentacled titan.

All boiled and pulsed with the same blue fire as the maelstrom, as if its power had been drawn up into the stones somehow.

"I wish you could see this, Whyborne," I said. I reached for one of the stones, but at the last minute thought better of the gesture and let my hand drop.

His look sharpened. "What is it?"

I described the scene as best I could. "So is the magic from the ritual?" he wondered aloud. "Or did the stones always look like that, and that's why the murderer chose to conduct it here?"

"I won't pretend to be an expert on either sorcery or North American archaeology," Christine said, "but doesn't this site remind you of anything?"

Iskander frowned. "Not particularly."

But it wasn't Iskander to whom she spoke. "It looks like the stone circle on the island in the lake," I said, half amazed my voice didn't tremble. "Where Blackbyrne and the Brotherhood meant to open a gateway to the Outside."

Whyborne let out a long sigh. "Well, then. It seems a visit to my father is in order."

CHAPTER 12

Griffin

I AWOKE TO a sharp rapping on our door.

The bedroom was dark, without even the light of the moon to seep in through the window. A soft breeze stirred the curtains, bringing with it Widdershins's distinctly fishy scent. We'd thrown back the coverlets, and I felt Whyborne stiffen beside me, his naked skin lightly filmed with sweat where our bodies touched.

"That isn't Christine's knock," he whispered.

My mind sorted through possibilities as I sat up. A potential client in dire need? A neighbor in some sort of distress?

The knock came again, this time much more heavily. "Mr. Flaherty!" a voice called from the front yard. "It's Detective Tilton. Open the door."

Whyborne let out a soft gasp, and my heart started into my ribs in fear. Wild images chased themselves through my mind—the police bursting in, finding Whyborne and I in bed together. Hauling us off to jail. Standing beside him in a docket, both of us facing ruin at best, hard time in jail at worst.

"Go," I said, switching on the light and reaching for my nightshirt.

He didn't have to ask, sliding out of the room and into the darkened corridor. A moment later, the light in what was ostensibly his bedroom came on. He'd remember to muss the bed sheets, I told myself, even as I snatched up the pillow his head had rested on and arranged it behind mine, as if I'd used it as a prop. Damn, I should have given it to him, to exchange for the one in his bedroom, the dampness of sweat a guarantee he'd indeed slept on it.

It was too late now. I tied my dressing gown about my waist as I left my room and paused in the study. A photo taken by Iskander showed Whyborne and I on the couch together, and I tossed it hastily into a drawer for concealment, before making my way down the stairs.

Had my theft of the crime scene photograph provoked Tilton too far? Or, as with the investigation that had ended with me in his jail years ago, had my prying angered the wrong people?

"I've got the door, Whyborne!" I called once I reached the hallway, loud enough for Tilton to hear. Just a landlord assuring his friend and lodger that the situation was under control, and there was no reason to bestir himself from his entirely separate bed.

Tilton stood on the stoop, dark rings around his eyes. From the stubble on his face, I guessed he'd been roused from bed himself not long ago, and in too much haste to shave. I gave him a look of concern. "Detective Tilton, is everything all right? You don't seem well."

He shook his head, and for a moment seemed to be at a loss for words. "I'd say everything is far from all right, Mr. Flaherty. I've come about your client. Dewey Lambert."

The tight knot of fear loosened in my gut. He hadn't come for Whyborne and me after all.

Then his words registered, and a new kind of fear touched me. "Mr. Lambert? Is he all right?"

It was a stupid question; Tilton wouldn't have been on my doorstep at this hour if nothing was wrong. "I'm afraid Mr. Lambert died tonight in his cell," Tilton said, a tremor in his voice. "The circumstances surrounding his death were...odd."

Odd. The same word Lambert had used when he came to me in the first place. And now the poor bastard was dead.

"Odd how?" I asked cautiously.

"You need to see for yourself." Tilton glanced past me. "And I'd appreciate it if you'd bring Dr. Whyborne with you."

My spine stiffened. "Dr. Whyborne?"

Tilton met my gaze, but there was no challenge or anger in his eyes. Just fear. "Word gets around in this town, Mr. Flaherty. There's an official version of what happened at the museum that Hallowe'en. Of the freak wave that almost wiped Widdershins off the map, only to die away just in time. And then there's...another version, let's say." He looked away. "I don't mean to imply Dr. Whyborne has any... expertise...in these sorts of things. I'm just suggesting that if you happen to bring a curious friend to the morgue with you, I'd be indebted."

Technically, there was no reason even for me to go. With Lambert dead, there was no one paying me to look into the case. I had no business investigating his death; rather, I should leave the matter to the police and be done.

Tubbs had died horribly on a stone altar very like the one on which the Brotherhood would have sacrificed me. And now Lambert was dead as well, in a manner that disturbed the Widdershins police, who ought to be fairly inured to the bizarre by now.

"Of course," I said. "Allow me to wake Dr. Whyborne and apprise him of the situation."

CHAPTER 13

Whyborne

THE EASTERN SKY was still black when we arrived at the city morgue. Tilton led the way into the large front room, where the unidentified dead lay on display, in hopes some desperate spouse or child or mother might recognize them. I'd only set foot here once before, when coming to view the body of Miss Emily, the maid who'd helped raise me after Mother fell ill. I still couldn't think of her without a mix of grief and anger, for all the secrets she'd kept from us.

The smell of death was heavy in the summer heat, so thick I almost tasted it. I glanced at Griffin, but he betrayed no disgust, his face carefully neutral in the presence of so many police. The officer just behind him looked distinctly green, however.

An unjust flicker of pleasure went through me at that. Of course the police would—I desperately hoped—think nothing of knocking on our door in the middle of the night. Never realize we'd suffered those moments of heart-pounding fear, when I contemplated the lawyers Father could muster, the judges he might bribe.

But I hated that I had to be afraid at all.

Tilton spoke with an attendant, who beckoned us after. We passed through a small door into the inner workings of the morgue. The thick walls held in a coolness absent in the viewing room, though the reek of death didn't lessen, as if it had seeped into the very floor over time.

The officer remained outside the room, while Griffin and I accompanied Tilton and the attendant within. Two bodies lay on the steel tables tonight. Tilton didn't bother to ask which belonged to Lambert, but made straight for the sheet soaked through with blood.

Not a good sign.

The attendant reached for the sheet, but Tilton held up his hand. "Before you see the body, allow me to explain what happened. Or what little we know of what happened." His skin had taken on a pasty hue. "According to the officer on duty, everything was normal when he checked on the prisoners. There was Lambert in his cell, and one of the Waites in another, worse off for drink and passed out cold in his cot. The officer on night watch put out the light and went back to his post just outside. Everything was quiet for an hour or two. Then, just before midnight, the screaming began."

Tilton took a deep breath, his eyes fixed on the bloody sheet. "The officer rushed back to see what was going on, but by the time he arrived, Lambert was dead. He was no new recruit, but he said the screams..." Tilton passed a hand over his face. "I'll have to keep a close eye, make sure he doesn't turn to drink to silence them in his dreams."

At his signal, the attendant pulled back the sheet. The face of the dead man was frozen in an expression of horror and agony. His chest gaped open, ribs and sternum a splintered ruin, fragments of bone pushed outward, as if something had shoved its way through his body. I was glad not to have anything in my stomach.

Griffin leaned closer, a frown drawing down his brows. "What the devil happened to him?"

"Some kind of animal attacked him," the attendant said unexpectedly. "Dr. Greene took a look at him at Detective Tilton's request. Some monster chewed its way through his body. Teeth marks are clear, and you can see some of the hairs still stuck in the wound."

Bile burned my throat, and I swallowed hard. "Dear lord." I rather wished I could sit down. But Tilton had brought me here for a reason. "What sort of creature would do...this?"

"Nothing natural," Griffin murmured. He continued to inspect the wound far more closely than I would have been comfortable with. "I take it your officer saw nothing when he entered the jail, Detective Tilton?"

"Just Lambert and a great deal of blood."

A chill went through me. What could have savaged the man in such a way, then simply vanished? And from a locked cell, no less?

"You don't have to make any guesses as to what caused this in my hearing," Tilton said, his gaze focused on me now. "I don't want to know. Cause of death on the certificate will be heart failure. Ordinarily I wouldn't trouble you, Dr. Whyborne, but given Mr. Flaherty's involvement, I thought you might want to know."

The attendant didn't look surprised by any of this. How many disturbing corpses were quietly whisked away under the convenient label of heart failure?

"Did the other prisoner see anything?" Griffin took a step back from the table. "Hear anything?"

"Just the screams." Tilton shrugged. "They woke him from his stupor. He said it was too dark to make out anything, and I'm inclined to believe him."

"I see." Griffin watched as the attendant tugged the sheet back up over Lambert. "Thank you, Detective Tilton."

Tilton's mouth thinned. "We haven't seen eye to eye over the years, Flaherty," he said. "To be honest, I would have preferred you set up shop in Boston or Arkham."

Griffin's mouth quirked slightly. "'Widdershins always knows its own,'" he quoted.

That damned prophecy. But Tilton glanced uncomfortably at me, then away. "So it would seem. And I'm not fool enough to challenge it. As of now, my part of the investigation is closed, and I'd like it to stay that way. These are no doings for an honest policeman."

We parted ways in front of the morgue, Tilton heading back to the police department. Griffin and I stood together on the walk. The eastern sky had begun to turn gray, and the first birds chirped from the trees shading the road. "Honest my eye," Griffin said as the clop of hooves faded. "Still, it's good to have him out of the way. It gives me a bit of a freer hand, without having to wonder if I'm to be hauled in for impeding an investigation."

"Quite." My eyes ached from lack of sleep. "What do you think happened?"

"I was going to ask you the same question." Griffin looked up at me. The street lamp found the occasional lighter strand amidst his chestnut hair, gleaming like gold. "Clearly sorcery was involved. The only question is: what form did it take?"

I shook my head slowly. "Blast if I know. There are tales of spectral hounds savaging or carrying people off, but I would have to research to discover if they're real or just folklore."

"Talk to your father first," Griffin advised. "He may be able to set us on the right track."

"Unless he's involved himself," I muttered. "What if he's trying to revive the Brotherhood?"

"If that were so, he would have encouraged you to join in his efforts." At my skeptical look, Griffin sighed. "I know you don't want to hear it, but your father cares for you. Perhaps even more importantly, he's come to respect you."

"Ha, ha," I said. "Very amusing." Father, *respect* me? He'd sooner throw all of his money into the river.

Griffin frowned. "At the very least, he couldn't imagine he'd get away with any sorcerous dealings behind your back. And given we helped destroy the Brotherhood the first time around, that would be rather foolhardy on his part."

"I suppose." I stretched, my back popping audibly. "It must all be related, though. The standing stones and Tubbs's murder, Lambert's fit and the map, and now Lambert's death."

"Agreed." Griffin looked pensive. "Perhaps there is some clue to be found in the background of one of them. I'll pursue that possibility. You speak to your father. If he has nothing useful—or perhaps even if he does—we should consider summoning Persephone tonight to make sure there's no ketoi connection."

I'd not felt the dweller's press against my mind, but Griffin was right. We had to be certain. "Very well," I said, peering blearily in the direction of the rising sun. "But first things first. Do you imagine there's anywhere we can find a cup of coffee?"

CHAPTER 14

Whyborne

BEFORE SETTLING INTO my desk at work, I sent word to Father, requesting we meet. His reply was prompt, suggesting we share lunch at Whyborne House. With nothing else pressing to occupy my time until then, I turned my attention back to the Wisborg Codex.

Translating the cryptic letters seemed imperative, given one attempt at stealing the manuscript had already been made. If only I had some idea what language it might be written in. Latin, Greek, or Aklo seemed likeliest, but likelihood was hardly certainty.

I stared at the illustration of the ketoi. What if the symbols belonged to whatever system of writing they used? Did they have a system of writing? I felt a fool for never having asked Persephone or Mother. But we'd always had other things to speak of in our infrequent meetings: Mother wanted to hear of my life, and Persephone wished to learn sorcery. I had been a poor brother and son indeed, not to have asked more about their lives beneath the sea.

I worked on the cipher, to no avail, for several hours. Shortly before lunch, Christine came in. She held a large envelope in one hand, which she tossed onto my desk. "Iskander developed the photographs from yesterday," she said, taking her usual seat.

I'd fortified myself with cup after cup of coffee, but my interrupted sleep was making itself known nonetheless. Perhaps I'd grown immune to the stuff after so many years of consumption. "Thank you, Christine."

"You look awful," she said bluntly.

"How kind of you to say." I signaled to Miss Parkhurst. "Could you bring more coffee, please?"

"Of course, Dr. Whyborne, Dr. Putnam." Once she'd bustled off, I said, "Detective Tilton came knocking at our door in the wee hours of the morning."

Christine's dark eyes widened in alarm. "Are you all right? I swear, if the police think they can just—"

"I appreciate your concern, but his visit concerned Griffin's case," I said, before she started threatening Tilton with bodily harm. I gave her a quick summary of the details.

"I'm going to have lunch with Father," I finished, as Miss Parkhurst brought in our coffee. "Perhaps he'll be able to enlighten us on some details."

Christine frowned at me. "Miss Parkhurst made our appointment with the florist this afternoon."

Blast. Had she told me? I couldn't recall. "I don't really know much about flowers..."

"Whyborne," Christine said threateningly.

Miss Parkhurst looked up from stirring just the right amount of sugar into my coffee. "I don't mean to be too bold, but perhaps I might be of help?" she suggested uncertainly. "That is, I know I'm only a secretary, but I follow all of the society columns, especially the weddings. Just...just in case."

For some reason, she turned absolutely scarlet. Why she seemed so embarrassed I couldn't guess; the very fact the newspapers ran such columns, lavish with detail, proved many people shared her interest.

"And I have a good eye," she hurried on. "For colors and the like."

Recalling the puce scarf she'd knitted me, I had severe reservations. The gift had probably saved our lives, but it wasn't the most flattering of shades, to put it mildly.

Christine, however, looked relieved. "If you're willing, then please, join us. I've no head for this sort of thing, and Whyborne is even more hopeless."

Miss Parkhurst pinked again. "I suppose I could take the afternoon off, then, if Dr. Whyborne agrees it's all right."

"Don't be absurd!" Christine exclaimed. "You're his secretary. This might not be within your job description, but if anyone asks, we'll just pretend he had you cataloging something in a distant storeroom or some such. There's no reason for you not to get paid, especially as you're doing a favor to us."

"Agreed. Thank you, Miss Parkhurst," I said, taking the coffee she passed to me. "I appreciate all the kindnesses you've done me over the years, this latest one not the least."

"Oh." She turned even pinker and all but fled the room. I watched her go, a bit mystified.

Christine shook her head. "Poor girl."

"What? Why? Is something wrong?"

"Never mind." Christine sipped her coffee, then prodded the envelope with the photographs. "Are you going to take those to show your father?"

"I ought to, I suppose." I picked up the envelope and pulled out the photos, shuffling through them. Iskander had captured several angles of the standing stones as a whole, before taking a number of photographs of each side of the altar stone. As I inspected the worn carvings, one image caught my eye.

I opened the codex, flipping hurriedly through the pages. "Christine, look. This image—the swirl symbol on the altar and the one in the book."

Her eyes widened. "They're identical." Then she frowned. "If the symbol is from some European system of the arcane, that must mean the stones date from the colonial period at the earliest."

My heart beat very loudly in my ears. "Perhaps." I turned to the folded page, slowly unfurling the image of the Mother of Shadows. "But the Eltdown Shards from England and the city of umbrae in Alaska were connected."

"Which doesn't mean that's the case here," she replied firmly. Then she wavered. "Although it does raise the possibility. Damn it."

"Yes." I closed the codex again carefully. "I'll take the codex with me when I meet Father. Perhaps we'll be lucky, and he'll have the answers we require."

And, I added silently, not be behind it all himself.

CHAPTER 15

Griffin

DRYDEN & SONS, TAILORS proclaimed the sign above the neat shop on River Street. The electric trolley rolled past behind me. Shoppers, mainly women and servants at this hour, went in and out of the large department store nearby. The omnipresent smell of fish strengthened as the wind blew from the direction of the market, replaced a moment later by the more noisome scents from the cannery.

A small bell rang above the door as I entered the shop. A man in an excellent, though somber, suit immediately came forward to greet me.

"Good morning, sir, welcome to Dryden and Sons," he said with a smile. The electric lights lent a sheen to his receding gray hair, and sparkled from the rims of his silver glasses. "How may we be of service?"

"Mr. Dryden?" I guessed as we shook hands. "My name is Griffin Flaherty. I'm afraid I've come with unfortunate news concerning one of your employees."

Dryden paled and glanced about, although I'd taken care not to speak anything specific in the hearing of any other customers. "I see. Please, join me in my office."

Small and cramped, the office was filled with cloth samples, catalogs, and other tools of the tailor's trade. "This is about Mr.

Lambert, isn't it?" he asked as we sat down. He didn't sound at all pleased, and I noted he didn't bother to offer me any refreshments.

"I'm afraid Mr. Lambert is dead," I said.

Dryden went even paler. "Oh no. How?"

"Heart failure," I said dryly.

"I see." Dryden stared off into nothing, then shook himself. "Forgive me, Mr. Flaherty, but are you with the police?"

"I'm a private detective. Mr. Lambert hired me to clear his good name." A small lie would go farther to explain my investigation than the more fantastical truth. "He paid me before I had chance to render services to him, and as a result, I feel I'm still in his employ. I would prefer he not go to his grave with a stain on his reputation."

Dryden frowned. "You didn't come here to give me the news of his death. What is it you want, Mr. Flaherty?"

Here was where things became tricky. "Were there any customers dissatisfied with Mr. Lambert?"

"Certainly not!" Dryden seemed shocked by the very idea. "We at Dryden and Sons pride ourselves on seeing that every customer leaves this shop happy."

"If I may be blunt, that seems a bit of a tall order, people being as they are," I said. "You could give some men a free suit cut from gold cloth, and they'd complain about the fit."

The corner of his lip twitched in an attempt not to laugh. "True. But there were none who complained particularly about Mr. Lambert. Certainly not to the point where they'd go to such lengths to discredit him."

"Was Mr. Tubbs—the man who originally accused Mr. Lambert, and whose murder Mr. Lambert was arrested for—among your clientele?"

"No." Dryden's lip curled slightly. "We serve a...more refined class of gentlemen."

In other words, poor clerks just starting out in life weren't welcome. "Of course," I said. "It would be a great help to have a list of the customers Mr. Lambert served in the last few months, if you have such a thing about."

Dryden's brows climbed toward his receding hairline. "We would never share the details of our clients without their permission," he said. "I cannot believe you would even suggest such a thing."

I had expected as much, but I'd hoped he would cooperate. Time for a bit of bribery, then. "I understand," I said soothingly. "Your customers are all gentlemen of a certain station in life. Although you'd never simply give out their names, their recommendation of your shop to others is valuable to your reputation."

His eyes narrowed suspiciously. "Naturally."

"And of course, having persons of a certain caliber being seen to patronize this store helps a great deal as well."

"Your point, Mr. Flaherty?"

Whyborne was going to kill me. "What if I said I could ensure that Dr. Whyborne—Niles Whyborne's son, heir to the Whyborne fortune—acquired his next suit from you?"

Greed flashed through Dryden's eyes, although he struggled to conceal it. "That would be a coup," he allowed, "but I can't imagine how you would accomplish such a thing."

At least everyone in Widdershins didn't instantly associate the two of us. "We belong to the same society," I lied, twisting my wedding ring to draw his attention to it. With the protective runes and white pearl, it looked like the sort of thing a secret society might bestow on its members. And in Widdershins, no one would dare question which society, for fear of drawing the wrong sort of attention.

"I see." Dryden looked torn for a moment, then nodded. "Very well, Mr. Flaherty. So long as you're discreet."

"Absolutely," I promised.

"Then allow me to get Mr. Lambert's appointment book for you."

CHAPTER 16

Whyborne

"**GOOD AFTERNOON, MASTER** Percival," Fenton said as I stood on the stoop in front of Whyborne House. "Your father awaits you in the dining room."

"Thank you, Fenton." I stepped inside and handed off my hat to the maid who silently appeared to take it. My Gladstone with the codex and photographs, I kept with me.

Fenton led the way, as though I might get lost in the house I'd grown up in. I watched his straight back as we walked, his bearing perfect, as though not a moment passed when he wasn't conscious of the part he played in upholding the dignity of the family.

I'd never been particularly good at doing my part for the dignity of the family. First as a sickly child, my health embarrassing in a house concerned with raising robust sons to become captains of industry. Later, as a scholar who turned his back on the masculine struggle of business to read dusty tomes locked away in a museum. As a result, Father had always looked at me with a certain amount of disdain, while fawning on Stanford. Fenton followed Father's lead, of course.

And now Stanford was locked away with madmen for the murder of our sister, while I remained.

We entered the dining room, and Fenton bowed. "Master

Percival," he announced me unnecessarily.

Any other family would have chosen a smaller room to eat in, and reserved the dining hall for entertaining. Not us. No, we had to sit at one end of a table long enough to seat twenty, our voices echoing amidst the high rafters.

"Percival," Father greeted me as I took my seat. "It's good to see you."

"Thank you, Father." Despite the summer heat outside, the dining room felt cold. Or perhaps it was I who was cold. With Mother gone, what little warmth that penetrated this mausoleum of a house had faded as well. Nothing about it seemed like a home to me any more—not that it really ever had.

The servants laid out our meal of poached fish in a parsley sauce. "How is Griffin?" Father asked.

"A pair of strange deaths—and more—connected to one of his cases is why I've come," I replied. Hadn't I said as much in my note?

Father gave me an irritated look. "I know that, Percival. I was merely enquiring after his health."

"Oh." It was unspeakably odd, to have my father asking after my lover. The younger version of myself, who'd suffered through endless meals at this table, while Father dissected my every failing, couldn't have imagined it. "He is quite well. He purchased a motor car not long ago."

Father's eyes lit up. "Oh? What model?"

I told him, and he asked a number of questions about the infernal thing that I was wholly unqualified to answer. The subject took us through the meal, at least, and at the end Father rose to his feet. "Let's retire to the study, and you can show me what you've brought."

Once in the study, he seated himself behind the massive desk. I sat across from him, feeling even more uneasy than usual. None of my memories of the room were pleasant, but the last time I'd set foot in it, I'd nearly destroyed it with wild magic. All the while screaming at Father that I hated him.

If he recalled the incident, he gave no sign, merely waiting while I passed him the photographs and explained the circumstances surrounding Griffin's case. "The standing stones are very like those on the Somerby Estate," I finished. "So I must ask: is the Brotherhood regrouping?"

"No," Father said, but he frowned as he studied the photographs. "But you're right about the stones. These are very similar. According to the Brotherhood's lore, the standing stones predated the founding of the town. Blackbyrne took the lake and the land around it for his own precisely because of their presence. But I wasn't aware there were more such ruins in the area."

"I see." I believed him...or thought I did, anyway. He might employ subterfuge when it suited him, but answering a direct question with a lie wasn't in his character. "And the ritual murder?"

"Could have been performed for a number of reasons." He sat back in his chair. "I was never involved in the sorcerous aspect of things, you know that."

"But you were at certain gatherings." I'd not absolve him so easily. "The one on Walpurgisnacht, when Leander drowned in the lake. The one where Blackbyrne meant to bring something in from the Outside and clothe it in Leander's resurrected flesh—and feed Griffin to it, may I remind you. I'm sure many more of which I'm unaware."

Father scowled. "Yes, yes. My point is, there are many reasons someone might be interested in these ruins. And the Brotherhood was far from the only source of knowledge about them. Our lore held that Blackbyrne himself learned such things from the Man in the Woods."

A shudder ran through me. "Nyarlathotep."

"If you prefer." Father shrugged. "I've little interest in religion."

"Perhaps if you did, you would have removed yourself from the Brotherhood," I said. "Nyarlathotep was a god of chaos. I've seen his temple amidst the wastes of Egypt. The faceless statues and blasphemous carvings." He'd been worshipped by the heretical pharaoh Nephren-ka, until the pharaoh's death. After, the priests of the other gods had done their best to expunge both from the record. But traces had remained, and against all odds, Nyarlathotep's name reappeared in the Middle Ages as the Man in the Woods, who tutored witches and sorcerers in the black arts.

"It's only a story," Father said crossly. "Look at you—you wield great power, but you discovered it on your own, through study. Not by selling your soul to the Devil, or whatever foolishness men like Blackbyrne spread about in order to enhance their reputations."

"I have power because I'm an Endicott," I replied, as much as I hated it. "And I'm not at all certain there's no truth behind the legends. Nitocris was all too real."

Father looked skeptical, but then, he hated to imagine anything might be out of his control. Even he would find it hard to bully an immortal creature with vast sorcerous knowledge.

I changed tactics. "This symbol," I said, pointing to the odd swirl on the photograph of the altar. "Do you recognize it?"

"Not particularly."

Curse it. If the man had to be steeped in an evil cult, at least he might have had the decency to learn something useful. I drew out the Wisborg Codex and laid it before him. "What about the script in here?"

He perused it. "No. I don't..."

His voice faded away, as he paused on the image of the ketoi. An odd expression passed over his face. If I hadn't known better, I would have thought it sorrow, or even loneliness. But that was absurd.

"At least the Brotherhood isn't involved directly," I said. "What of the others who survived? Might one of them be behind this?"

He seemed to recall himself, closing the codex gently. "It's certainly possible. I'll make discreet inquiries."

"Thank you. But be careful," I added awkwardly, the memory of Lambert all too fresh in my mind. "Whatever was sent to kill Lambert...well, presumably it might be turned against others."

To my surprise, a small smile creased his lips. "I'll be cautious."

"I don't suppose you have any ideas what might have murdered Lambert in his cell like that?" I asked without much hope.

"A few." He sat back, tapping his chin thoughtfully. "From time to time the Brotherhood needed persons...removed. We tried to keep it as discreet as possible, which Lambert's death most certainly was not. But at times we needed to send a warning."

"Is that what you think this is?" I asked. "Could someone be warning Griffin off the case?"

"Or you." Father didn't look pleased at the thought. "As for what might have killed him, there are many possibilities. Hounds of tindalos, nightgaunts, shamblers..."

It was a depressing litany. "How did you ever think any of that was justifiable?"

His frown deepened, but now it was turned on me. As usual. "Look around you, Percival. Do you think this house just grew up out of the ground? I worked for it, and my father before me, and his father before him. Sacrifices must be made."

"Funny how it was always other people making those sacrifices," I said bitterly. "Or should I say *being* sacrificed on the Brotherhood's altar."

"Don't play the saint with me," he growled. "Our willingness to get our hands dirty ensured you grew up in comfort. Do you imagine you'd have been happier born in the tenements? You would never have survived infancy amidst the disease-ridden rabble there. And if you had, do you imagine you'd be where you are now? Of course not— you'd be laboring in the cannery, or driving a nightsoil cart, or mucking out a livery stable. So I've had quite enough of you looking down your nose at those whose actions you've reaped the benefits of."

I wanted to argue. Griffin's life had begun in the tenements of New York, hadn't it? And look how well he'd done for himself.

But I wasn't Griffin. I slumped back in my chair. "I didn't come here to fight. Thank you for your help. I should return to the museum —Christine has an appointment at the florist's this afternoon."

He gave me a smile that I didn't trust for a moment. "I'm glad your friends accepted my offer," he said. "Before you go, however, I have a request."

"A request?"

"A favor, more like."

I bit back a curse. Of course he hadn't just offered Whyborne House to Iskander and Christine out of the goodness of his heart. Certainly not because he wished to make me happy by helping my friends. I should have guessed there would be a price from the start. "What is it?"

"I want you to bring your sister to dinner."

I blinked, uncertain I'd heard him correctly. "You want me to bring Persephone to...dinner? Here?"

"Of course," Father said. "She's a Whyborne. She ought to know where she comes from."

I stared at him blankly. "You do realize Persephone can't just wish herself human, don't you? Once the change is made, it's permanent. She belongs to the sea."

"Don't patronize me," Father snapped. "I'll send a closed carriage for her. No one else will be here save for you and Griffin."

"You're inviting us?"

"Of course." He frowned. "Although I suppose you might as well bring Dr. Putnam and Mr. Barnett with you, too, as they know Persephone already. I also want you to accompany me to see Stanford."

Silence followed his pronouncement. Eventually I gathered my wits enough to say, "You want me to visit Stanford. At the asylum."

He looked irritated. "I don't believe I stuttered."

"Are you insane?" I exclaimed. "Stanford tried to kill me! He would have killed Griffin if he were a better shot! Why the devil would I want to visit him?"

"Because he asked for you," Father replied.

This was absurd. Father had clearly lost his wits. "Asked for me how? In chains? My head on a platter?"

"Your brother regrets his actions."

"I'm sure he does!" I would have laughed, could I have found the humor in it. "After all, he ended up locked in an asylum, instead of the uncontested ruler of Widdershins with an army of ketoi at his back, ready to spread his reign across the eastern seaboard. I imagine he very much regrets not murdering me the way he murdered

Guinevere."

Father flinched, and I almost regretted my own words. But Stanford had killed our oldest sister to keep her from telling Persephone and me his plans. She died in my arms. "I won't forgive him," I said savagely. "Not for that. Not for Guinevere, or for Miss Emily, or for hurting Griffin. There's nothing he could ever do or say that would change my mind."

"No one is asking you to forgive him," Father said. "Stanford wishes to make amends, for the sake of his own conscience."

"I'm under no obligation to make anything easier for Stanford's conscience."

"Percival. You're being churlish." His glower made me feel as though I were ten years old again.

If I refused, would he rescind his offer to host Christine's wedding at Whyborne House? Had he finally realized that browbeating me would never bring me under his thumb, and so found a new way to force me to comply with his wishes?

Probably. "Very well," I said stiffly. "I will *ask* Persephone if she'll come. I can't order her to do so. And I'll go with you to visit Stanford at the asylum.

He nodded graciously. "I'm glad you decided to be reasonable."

"Since when has reason ever had anything to do with *this* family?" I muttered, rising to my feet. "Don't bother Fenton. I can see myself out."

CHAPTER 17

Whyborne

"**This is so** exciting!" Miss Parkhurst gushed. "I just love weddings, don't you, Dr. Putnam?"

I was still in a foul temper from my visit with father when we climbed out of a cab in front of the florist's shop. The large windows showed an explosion of color within: scarlet roses, blushing lilies, vibrant violets, and golden sunflowers. I felt as though I ought to shield my eyes from the rainbow assault.

"Not at all," Christine replied, her hands on her hips as she surveyed the shop like a general prepared for battle. "Given the current state of our laws and society, they far too often mark a woman surrendering what little independence she has to the whims of a man."

"I...oh." Miss Parkhurst cast me a pained glance.

"I, er," I said. "That is, that can often be true, I am aware." Griffin's tales of murderous husbands from his days in the Pinkertons had opened my eyes to various realities. And if they hadn't, Daphne's sorry history certainly would have. I couldn't say I approved of her solution, but desperation often drives people to do things they wouldn't consider otherwise. "But Iskander is a fine fellow."

"Indeed." Christine nodded her head once, sharply. "You'll note I waited quite a while after meeting him before marriage, Miss Parkhurst. One must be absolutely sure of compatibility on all matters." She nodded again, and a small smile touched her mouth. "All matters."

Miss Parkhurst blushed. "Yes, well, we should go inside."

I shot Christine a dark look behind Miss Parkhurst's back. Christine ignored me, of course, and instead started for the door. "We'd best get this over with. Come along, Whyborne."

The mingled scent of a dozen different species of flower struck us as soon as we stepped within. My nose tingled, and I sneezed.

A plump woman beamed at us from behind the counter. "Can I help you...oh! Mr. Whyborne?"

"Dr. Whyborne," Christine and I chorused.

"Oh, I'm so sorry." She bustled out, her cheerful smile fixed in place. "May I say I'm so pleased the Whyborne family chose to patronize my humble shop?"

I ground my teeth. I'd spent my entire life fleeing Father's legacy, and yet, here I was, "Mr." Whyborne, all the humble progress I'd made on my own superseded by Father's money.

"Yes," I said, as civilly as I could manage. Her expression suggested I'd taken on...how had Griffin described my aspect? Cold? Haughty? Aloof?

I turned to Miss Parkhurst and Christine, and gave them a bow. "Ladies. Do as you will."

Which ultimately amounted to the shopkeeper and Miss Parkhurst doing as they would. I lurked in a corner, mopping at my running nose and trying not to sneeze. They discussed colors with great enthusiasm, while Christine nodded along, her expression that of a hunted animal.

"What will your bridesmaids wear?" the florist asked.

"Er..." Christine's eyes widened in panic. "I don't...that is I forgot..."

I barely managed to restrain myself from clapping my hand across my eyes in despair. Of course she had.

"That is...Miss Parkhurst!" Christine turned to my secretary, a bit frantically. "Will you be my maid of honor?"

Miss Parkhurst's eyes widened. "Are you certain?"

"Why not?"

I cringed, certain I'd spend the next six months trying to make up for Christine's rudeness. But Miss Parkhurst's expression bloomed like one of the flowers. "Oh...yes! Thank you so much, Dr. Putnam! I'd love to!"

She hugged Christine. Christine looked horrified and patted her lightly on the shoulder. "Er, yes, you're quite welcome."

After, there was no curbing Miss Parkhurst's enthusiasm. "That was exhilarating," Miss Parkhurst said as we climbed back into our cab, which Father's money had paid to keep waiting for us. "Oh, it will all be so beautiful!"

As she'd ultimately chosen a combination of violently purple lilacs, paired with scarlet roses, I could only say, "It will certainly be something to see."

CHAPTER 18

Whyborne

"I STILL CAN'T believe Father," I said that evening. "Asking me to visit Stanford, as though our shared blood somehow matters more than all the horrible things he did."

"I'm certain Niles appreciates your cooperation," Griffin said. He'd purchased a bathing costume at the beginning of the summer, for when we went to the coast to visit Persephone and Mother. I perched on the edge of the bed, watching him change into it. I'd tried to coax Saul up for petting, but he was more interested in the corner of the room. He sat on the floor, ears forward, occasionally sniffing and pawing at the baseboard.

"You have met Father, haven't you? The man doesn't appreciate my cooperation, he sees it as his due." I gestured to Saul. "And now mice are trying to chew our house apart."

"Saul will take care of it," Griffin said. "As for your father, why do you think he wants you to go to the asylum with him? Simply because Stanford asked?"

"Oh, who knows," I muttered. "He probably wishes there were some way to combine the two of us. Stanford's personality with my sorcery. He'd have the perfect son."

Griffin bent to brush a kiss over my brow. "Stanford imprisoned and beat him. Hardly the perfect son."

"Still preferable to the one he has left, no doubt." I held up my hands at Griffin's protest. "It hardly matters. I will give Persephone her invitation. If she wishes to satisfy her curiosity, I suppose I'll have no choice but to accompany her."

"As will I." Griffin frowned. "But isn't Niles worried about the servants seeing her? Surely he doesn't mean to cook and serve dinner himself."

I laughed at the thought. "Dear heavens, no. Even when he was in the army, he had personal servants to cook his meals and clean his dishes. I'm certain any servants on hand will be like Fenton, trusted with the darkest secrets of Whyborne House." The way Miss Emily had been. But she'd had secrets of her own.

Griffin shook his head and pulled his coat on over his bathing costume. "It seems very odd to me."

"I suppose." I'd grown up with servants, some of whom had been in Widdershins nearly as long as we had. "But how was your day? Did you get the list of customers from Mr. Lambert's employer?"

"Yes." Griffin chewed at his lower lip thoughtfully. "Most names I didn't recognize, although it seems several of your colleagues get their suits there. Dr. Norris, Dr. Osborne, and Mr. Quinn were all on the list. Oh, and you'll be shopping there as well."

"I will?"

"I needed a bribe to convince Mr. Dryden, and the Whyborne name carries weight," he said.

"Griffin!" I protested.

"I'll make it up to you," he promised with a suggestive leer. "Now come along."

We left Saul to his rodent hunting. Griffin insisted on driving, of course, although at least the streets weren't nearly so crowded this time of day. Griffin pulled the motor car off the road, and we walked down to the isolated beach. Once on the shore, Griffin reached into his pocket. "I'm going to throw the summoning stone," he warned me.

I nodded and made certain I was mentally prepared for its strange call. Just in case, I turned my back as well. There came a soft splash as he threw it out into the waves.

"There," he said. "No effects? You don't feel the need to dash out into the ocean?"

"No," I assured him. "Although perhaps it's a good thing I don't swim."

"Perhaps." He kissed me and began to strip off the coat and trousers he'd put on over his swimming costume. I took it from him, folding it neatly on a rocky outcropping. "Are you certain you don't want to come in?" he asked.

"I don't have anything to wear."

"The ketoi wear nothing but jewelry and skirts of gold netting," he pointed out. "No one will be scandalized by nudity."

"I'm certainly not going to parade around in front of my mother and sister with no clothes on!" I exclaimed.

He shrugged. "As you wish."

I climbed atop the outcropping and lit the small lantern we'd brought with us. I had brought a book on cryptography, hoping for more ideas as to how to decipher the codex, and read while Griffin splashed about in the water. Moonlight sparkled off the waves, and the heat of the day yielded to a more pleasant warmth.

I paused in my reading to watch Griffin. I could make out the white stripes of his bathing costume, and wished suddenly I might see him better. He cut such a fine figure in it. Perhaps one day I would quell my fear of water and try swimming with him. We'd float, buoyed by the waves, and he'd catch me to his strong body. He'd kiss me, his mouth tasting of brine, and we'd wash onto the shore, bodies intertwined...

The sight of a fin cutting the water broke me from my reverie. I straightened sharply. "Griffin!" I called. "Look—"

His bobbing figure vanished from sight, as something powerful jerked him beneath the waves.

CHAPTER 19

Whyborne

GRIFFIN REAPPEARED A moment later, choking and spluttering. The monster that had dragged him under surfaced beside him. Her mouth split into a grin, revealing row upon row of shark's teeth. Stinging tentacles spread out around her shoulders, and she reached for Griffin with a hand tipped with claws.

"Are you all right?" my sister asked, laughing.

"Is trying to drown your brother-in-law a greeting ritual among the ketoi?" But Griffin laughed too, even as he wiped water from his face.

More figures broke the water, although most of them remained back from the beach itself. Persephone rode the next wave in, accompanied by our mother.

I couldn't help but smile to see them. I took up towels, passing one to Mother, another to Persephone, and the last to Griffin. As soon as Mother was dry enough, I hugged her.

My whole life, she'd been ill, her body frail from long sickness. Until she took to the sea, that is. Now she was strong—not just healthy, but honed from a life of swimming beneath the waves. Her skin felt sleek as a dolphin's, bleached white marked with swirls of blue.

"Percival," she said, when I drew back. A frown creased her brow, and she looked up at me with eyes that remained unchanged from her transformation. They were my eyes as well, and Persephone's. "Is something wrong? Why did you summon us?"

"Indeed." Persephone handed the summoning stone back to Griffin, and he quickly wrapped it in silk to quiet its song. "It's several days early for our monthly visit."

Griffin and I tried to come every full moon, to meet them on this beach for a few hours at least. The only other time I'd summoned them early had been to bring the news of the death of Griffin's father.

"Something is wrong," I said carefully. "Although it may have nothing to do with the ketoi."

Mother sank down on the rock and gestured for me to join her. "Then tell us."

Griffin and I did so, to the best of our ability. When we finished, Persephone shook her head. "It isn't the god. He sleeps deep in the abyss, and we hear his dreams on certain nights."

"That's what I said." I leveled a look at Griffin.

"I said it needed to be investigated, not that I believed it true," he replied, unruffled. "No stone unturned."

"Quite so." Mother patted his knee.

"And the system of writing?" I'd copied down some of the opening lines of the Wisborg Codex, and passed the paper to Persephone. "Is it familiar to you?"

"No." She shook her head. "It's nothing I've ever seen beneath the sea."

Mother tapped a claw against her chin thoughtfully. "You said these standing stones looked similar to the ones you encountered on the Somerby estate. Have you gone to inspect those as well?"

Griffin shook his head. "No. Who owns the estate now?"

"Addison died without an heir," Mother replied. "Before I left for the sea, no one had taken up residence there."

"Father might know." I hesitated, but I'd made a promise. "Persephone, I have a request to make."

"Oh?" Her tentacles suddenly unfurled, darting for my head. I ducked, but felt them across my scalp. "Is it to—how do humans say? —style your hair?"

"Stop it!" I batted at the tendrils. Persephone had a fascination with my hair, particularly when it came to vexing me about it. She laughed gleefully. Griffin, the traitor, laughed as well.

"If you're quite finished," I said, "when I went to see Father today, to inquire about the Brotherhood...he asked me to extend an invitation to you."

Her laughter died away. "An invitation?"

"To have dinner with us in Whyborne House. He said you're a Whyborne, and you ought to know where you came from." I shrugged apologetically. "I told him I'd pass it along, nothing more."

To my surprise, she didn't immediately reject the idea. Her tentacles twitched against her shoulders, but whether that indicated agitation or some other emotion, I wasn't entirely certain.

"I am curious," she said at length. She turned to our mother. "Should I go?"

Mother sighed. She took Persephone's hand in one of hers, then reached for mine with the other. "He is your father," she said carefully. "And he did always try to do well by his family. He failed at it utterly, at least when it came to our sons. But he did try."

I didn't know what to say. I couldn't imagine how she must feel, speaking of the man she'd spent the better part of her life with.

She hadn't loved him. But love was often an afterthought, when fortunes became involved. Even at the time, the Whybornes had wealth, though not the empire Father had built with the railroad. Mother and Father had been socially and financially suitable, and that's what had mattered.

"If you're curious, you should go." Mother squeezed Persephone's hand. "It will do no harm to see the place and to meet him. After all, it isn't as if he could try to convince you to marry some wealthy scion of business to consolidate yet another fortune."

Griffin chuckled. "I would love to see her debut. Do you think Maison Worth designs around fins?"

"They say one can find any fashion in Paris," Mother replied with a toothy smile. "But I don't think it will come to that. Bring one of my old gowns, assuming Niles hasn't thrown them out. He'll find it easier to face her with clothing, even if we do have to rip holes to make it fit."

CHAPTER 20

Whyborne

THE NEXT MORNING, I stood in the office of Dr. Norris, the head of the American History Department. A cabinet along one wall displayed dishes that once belonged to Thomas Jefferson, and a gigantic portrait of George Washington loomed behind Norris's desk. The office smelled of leather and expensive cigars. Had the suit Norris wore been fitted by the doomed Lambert?

"Thank you for looking into my request," I said. My skin prickled as he regarded me. The codex—and thus its attempted theft—seemed linked with the standing stones. And Norris both worked at the museum and knew Lambert.

Then again, it was rather difficult to imagine Dr. Norris sneaking into the woods to summon an ancient chaos god. Mr. Quinn, on the other hand...

"Naturally, Dr. Whyborne," he said. At least he remembered my name now. "I met your father not long ago, you know. I'm sure he mentioned it to you."

Oh. Of course he only remembered my name because of Father. Was the man to take over every aspect of my life?

"Oh yes," I lied through gritted teeth. "About my request..."

"Straight to business, eh?" Norris laughed. "Like father like son, as they say."

My nails bit into my palms. I forced my hands to relax. "They do say that, yes. Was the witch hunter's dagger a part of our collection?"

"I was under the impression we had only the sword and diary," he said, "but one of the curators found the original letter of donation. There was a dagger and some other items—shackles, I think. But where the items are stored...we aren't entirely certain."

Damn it. "So it's possible the dagger was taken from the museum?"

He shrugged. "The fellow would have had to hunt through storerooms to find it."

"I see." I wasn't certain which scenario was worse—that the dagger came from the museum, or that there might be more such weapons out in the world, likely to turn up at any inconvenient moment. "Thank you, Dr. Norris."

He waved a negligent hand. "Give my best to your father."

As I stepped out of his office, I found Bradley Osborne arguing with Norris's secretary. Bradley's face flushed red as he said, "But I requested this two weeks ago!"

"And when Dr. Norris finds the time to accommodate you, I'm sure he'll let you know," the secretary replied icily.

"I—" Bradley broke off when he saw me. His flush deepened. "Very well," he snarled.

I tried to slip quietly past, but of course it wasn't to be. Bradley pursued me down the hall, not speaking until we were well out of earshot of the secretary. "Have a nice chat with Dr. Norris?" he asked.

I disliked the brittle quality of his voice. "Quite nice," I replied, as neutrally as I could.

"I suppose you think it means something, that you have his ear," Bradley said. "And the director's. I suppose you imagine it makes you special. Well, you aren't."

I stopped. We were alone in the corridor, and I felt a little flicker of fear at the sight of Bradley's anger, his clenched fists. I might be taller, but his physique suggested he belonged to an athletic club.

The maelstrom turned beneath me, as much a part of my awareness as the rush of my blood through my veins, the rhythm of my breath. If he raised a hand to me, he'd regret it. "Do you have something you wish to say to me?" I asked coldly.

"I'm here because of my own merit," he said. "My own hard work. You? The director only hired you out of hopes your father would contribute generously to the museum."

"Then he was disappointed," I snapped. At least for the first few years, although to be fair, that had changed.

Bradley snorted and shook his head. "Everything you have—your job, your friends, everything—is because of an accident of birth. You don't deserve any of it."

My scars ached, and wind whispered down the corridor. "Go to hell."

He smirked. "A little close to home, eh, Percy?"

I should never have betrayed my anger. Swallowing back the words of power I longed to speak, I turned on my heel and walked away. Bradley's mocking laughter echoed behind me.

CHAPTER 21

Whyborne

WE WENT TO the old Somerby Estate that night. I'd suggested going during the day, like a sensible person, but Griffin in turn pointed out we were technically trespassing, and there was a reason most criminal undertakings took place under the cover of darkness.

It wasn't a trip I was at all eager to make, but Mother's suggestion to investigate the standing stones had been a valid one. A quick note to Father revealed he didn't know if anyone had bought the place, so Griffin ended up at city hall once again. A search through the property deeds revealed only that a company headquartered in Boston had purchased it less than a year ago. A Pinkerton Griffin had worked with in the past was stationed in the Boston office, so he sent a letter requesting the man look into the company on his behalf.

Christine and Iskander accompanied us, both of them wanting a closer look at the site to compare it with the one on the Robinson farm. Although I doubted we'd need their archaeological expertise, I welcomed their presence, if only because of my dark memories of the island. I couldn't help but feel as though the place were cursed in some fashion.

We avoided the estate itself, as the standing stones were on an island, and we needed to approach by boat. I clung to the sides of the craft and tried not to look at the black water. The moon rode low, its beams largely blocked by the dark bulk of the Draakenwood. It was very quiet. No night birds called from the forest. There came the soft slap of water against the boat, the whisper of Griffin and Iskander's oars, and the occasional plop of a fish breaching the surface after an insect, but nothing more. The island loomed against the stars, thick trees concealing the standing stones from casual view.

I hated this lake. Leander, the boy I'd been hopelessly in love with as a youth, had died in its waters. I'd come close to dying myself, and had a terror of drowning ever since. Then Griffin, Christine, and I had nearly perished on the island while trying to stop Blackbyrne from opening a doorway to the Outside. I'd never wanted to come back here again.

Not to say Griffin or Christine likely did either. I twisted around to look at Griffin, who sat directly behind me. I found he'd been watching me already, and a little smile touched his handsome face when our eyes met.

It was all right, I told myself. We were all right. We were alive and together, and this accursed lake would claim none of us if I had anything to say about it.

The little dock had fallen into disrepair, but was still serviceable enough. I scrambled out of the boat as soon as it drew alongside.

"Be careful," Christine snapped. "You're going to send us over!"

Her voice rang across the lake, the unnatural stillness carrying the sound farther than it would have otherwise. Christine looked taken aback and clapped a hand to her mouth. "Sorry," she whispered.

There came a loud rustling from the bushes next to the dock, as though something forced its way through the tangled growth. I jumped at the unexpected sound. "What was that?"

"Just a muskrat or something like," Griffin said soothingly as he tied up the boat. "Perfectly natural."

"Nothing about this island is natural," I muttered.

The path leading from the dock to the standing stones was so overgrown I could barely discern it, even when Griffin directed the beam of his police lantern on it. "This way," he murmured, and started forward.

I wanted to snatch him back. To bundle him into the boat and return to shore, away from this place.

"Hurry it up, Whyborne," Christine said from behind me. "The sooner this is done, the sooner we can leave."

She had a point. I forced my reluctant feet to move, following Griffin toward the heart of the small island. Tree branches snatched at my clothing and tried to knock off my hat. The faint scent of death and rot seemed to hang over the place, although perhaps it was simply my memories coloring my perceptions. The undergrowth continued to rustle not far from us; there must have been an entire clan of muskrats living here.

At last the trees gave way, and we stumbled out into the clearing around the standing stones.

And it was a clearing. The forest had begun to encroach upon it, but someone had removed the saplings, trimmed back the branches, and cut away the brambles. The place might not look as well used as when the Brotherhood conducted their unholy rituals here, but it had obviously been tended to recently.

"Not the best of signs," Iskander remarked.

"No," Griffin agreed. "Neither is this."

He directed the beam of his lantern onto the altar stone. The dark stains on it were too fresh to have been made when the Brotherhood occupied the estate.

"The site is on an arm of the maelstrom, just as the other standing stones were," Griffin said. He stepped further into the clearing, his body tense and his revolver in his hand. "And these stones are infused with power as well."

The undergrowth rustled again, louder this time. A dark shape emerged and scampered up the altar stone. For a moment, I thought it a giant rat. Matted brown fur covered its misshapen body, and the naked tail trailing after it was scabbed and unhealthy. Did the thing have some disease, to show itself to us so boldly?

Then it reached its perch atop the altar and turned to us. In place of a rat's muzzle, it had the twisted, leering face of a man.

CHAPTER 22

Griffin

"Good gad!" Christine exclaimed in revulsion. My own gorge rose at the sight of the abomination on the altar stone. I'd seen enough to think myself inured to horrors, but there was something so profoundly *wrong* about the creature that I could hardly stand to look at it.

But look I had to, because it raised forepaws that more closely resembled human hands. A strange, tittering sound issued from its distorted mouth which sounded like a chant.

A chant to which voices responded from all around us.

We'd been expected, it seemed.

Four men appeared, one at each of the cardinal points. Each held a wand of some sort before him, a twisted skein of magic glowing from the polished wood. Within moments, they were joined by another man —one with an eye patch, who wore an odd, loose-sleeved shirt and held a dagger in his visible hand.

"It's the thief from the museum," Iskander said.

Whyborne didn't waste time with words. He *burned* in my shadowsight, the power of the arcane river beneath his feet flooding into him as he called upon it. Blue fire lit his eyes, and the scars on his right arm showed even through his clothing, lines of power inscribed upon his skin. He thrust out his hand toward the one-eyed man, and the world responded to his will.

His spell twisted through the air in my shadowsight, like a needle piercing the warp and weft of the universe itself, tugging on the very threads of reality. The wind leapt up, howling over the open water, shaking the trees—

Then the edge of the dagger found it. The spell shattered, broke, threads snapping and fading into nothing.

Damn it.

The monstrous rat creature still called from the altar, the cultists responding to it. Light glinted from Iskander's blades, and Christine hoisted her rifle and sighted on the abomination. I raised my revolver, intending to put a bullet through the head of the one-eyed man.

The chant reached a crescendo, and the magic in the wands flared. The web of a spell spread out from each, racing across the ground like a sudden frost, lines intersecting and tangling with one another. I tried to shout a warning, but the magic reached me first.

Dizziness swept over me, and my revolver grew unspeakably heavy. I tried to aim it, but instead my arm fell slowly to my side. Lethargy gripped me, and I swayed on my feet. I thought Christine moaned, but I couldn't turn my head to be sure.

I had to move. Had to break free. We were defenseless otherwise, easy prey for the one-eyed man approaching with his knife.

Weariness lapped over me like a wave. So much easier to just close my eyes. My knees grew weak, and I stumbled. Perhaps I should just lie down. Sleep.

"No," Whyborne said, like a man trapped in a nightmare. "G-get back."

I forced open eyes I hadn't even realized I'd closed. The cultist with his dagger was almost on Whyborne now. There came the clink of metal from somewhere on the thief's person, and I saw some sort of shackles hanging from his belt.

They meant to use those on Whyborne. Do something to him.

Hurt my Ival.

No.

It took every ounce of stubbornness I possessed, but I forced my legs forward: one, then the other. "Get away from him," I snarled, and lifted a revolver that felt heavy as an anvil.

The one-eyed man spat a curse. Keeping his knife raised defensively, he grabbed for me with his other hand.

Only it wasn't a hand that emerged from his odd, loose sleeve.

I had but a glimpse, before a thick, slimy tentacle wrapped itself around my throat.

The spell fell away from me and the world went dark, save for the lantern light. The anti-magic of the witch hunter's blade blinded my shadowsight. I would have cried out if the tentacle around my neck hadn't squeezed tight. I clawed at it madly, trying to breathe. Suckers gripped my flesh, squirming nauseously against my skin.

"How dare you, worm?" the cultist said. "Your blood will feed—"

"No," Whyborne growled, and grabbed at the tentacle arm.

He missed, the spell of lethargy sending him staggering. Instead, his hand closed around my shoulder.

The world exploded. Heat burned through me, and my skin tingled. I felt as if I'd grabbed a live wire, electricity surging through my veins.

Whyborne gasped, and I felt it in my mouth. His heartbeat seemed to thunder in my chest alongside my own. Flashes of emotion and fragments of thought sparkled in my brain, there and gone too fast for me to comprehend.

The one-eyed man shouted and leapt back, tentacle whipping free, as if we'd scorched him. The world around me lit up once again, filled with arcane radiance. Whyborne made a slashing gesture with his hand, and the sticky web of the spell was obliterated in surging magic, burned away by the power of the maelstrom.

All four of the other cultists shrieked and released their wands. Christine let out a blistering string of curses, and her rifle fired at almost the same instant Iskander threw his knives. Two of the men went to the ground, dead or dying, and the other two beat a hasty retreat.

The taste of blood filled my mouth, accompanied by the scent of burning and hot iron. The rat creature fled, and the one-eyed man ran after it, both vanishing into the darkness.

Silence fell, and we were left amidst the stones and the dead. The wands lay scattered about the clearing, their glow soft now, the magic quiescent.

Whyborne released my shoulder. "Griffin?" he asked, but the sound of his voice was faint and far away. The ground was close, though, and drawing rapidly nearer. Even so, I fell into darkness before reaching it.

CHAPTER 23

Griffin

"HOW ARE YOU feeling, darling?" Whyborne asked.

I lay on our couch at home, Saul curled up on my legs. Whyborne perched on the edge of the cushion, holding out the steaming cup of tea he'd made me.

I'd awoken as Whyborne and Iskander hauled me out of the boat. My mouth tasted of blood, and my throat was mottled with bruises and sucker marks. A look in the mirror once we'd returned home showed the whites of my eyes had gone red with burst capillaries.

"The powder has taken care of the worst of my headache," I assured him. I took the tea, inhaling the scent of bergamot. "I'm certain this will do me wonders."

He watched me anxiously as I sipped the tea. Guilt stirred in my gut—I'd frightened him, even though I certainly hadn't meant to do so. I reached out and took his left hand in mine. The light from the lamp burnished the deep gold of our wedding rings.

"What happened?" I asked. "There on the island. You touched me, and..."

Saul stood up to investigate, standing on my stomach and putting his head between us. Whyborne stroked him with his free hand, eyes distant. "I've been thinking about it ever since it happened. I have a theory. I don't know if it's true, though, or just wild conjecture."

"What is it?"

"The umbrae that touched your mind in Chicago and Egypt, the Occultum Lapidem, all created certain pathways, if you will." His mouth flexed into a small frown. "Which the Mother of Shadows used to communicate with you. Not to mention the little queen."

Old pain flared in my chest. So much hurt and grief there beneath the glacier, in the ancient city built by nothing human. But love, too. "It felt a bit like that," I said, turning over the thought in my mind. "When the Lapidem connected us, there at the end. Not as intense, but I had...glimpses, I suppose, of your thoughts and emotions."

"Which lends credence to my theory." Whyborne sighed and redirected his gaze to our joined hands. "Those pathways are still there, still intact, and now stronger than ever."

I arched a brow. "More of a highway than a path, then?"

He snorted. "Only you could joke about such a thing. But yes. With the power of the maelstrom already flowing through me, I saw the magic through your eyes. The lines of the spell. Once I knew what I was up against, I tore it apart at its weak points."

"I'm glad." I took another sip of my tea.

"As am I, but..." he turned his gaze back to me and sighed. "It hurt you. We shouldn't do it again."

"We would have died otherwise!" I protested. "What if—"

"No." He held up a hand to forestall me. "I know what you're going to say, Griffin. But I'm not risking your life."

"Whyborne—"

"I said no!" Pain twisted his features, and he looked away. "Don't you see? People—*humans*—don't tap directly into such power for a reason. Even Theo and Fiona used a wand when they drew on the vortex. The power would have burnt them to ash otherwise. I won't let that happen to you."

Curse it. I reached out and put my hand over his. "You *are* human. In every way that matters."

He made no reply, only shook his head.

I sighed. Better to let the matter drop for the time being. It wasn't as though we didn't have plenty of other concerns. "That...*thing*. On the island. What was it?"

"The Wisborg Codex has an illustration of such a creature," he said. "Which makes me wonder if everything in it is real. It's not a happy thought."

"So you've no idea what it might have been."

"I do, as a matter of fact. You've heard the legend of witches' familiars?" Whyborne took my empty cup from me and set it aside. "In Salem, during the witch trials, some of the accused said they'd been given demons in the shape of rats and dogs to serve them. Ordinarily I wouldn't put stock into such tales, especially given how the confessions were extracted."

"But?" I prompted.

"But Blackbyrne fled Salem to found Widdershins." He met my gaze, worry clear in his dark eyes. "Moreover, the *Liber Arcanorum* mentions the Man in the Woods will give such familiar servants to tutor aspiring sorcerers in magic, if they will agree to serve him."

"The Man in the Woods," I said. "You mean Nyarlathotep?"

"Yes." He sighed. "The one-eyed man tried to steal the codex."

I shuddered. "His arm...it wasn't like that when you saw him before, was it?"

"No." Whyborne shuddered as well. "I don't know what happened to him. He failed to steal the codex...perhaps that was his punishment."

I touched the tender skin of my throat. "This case gets worse with every conjecture."

"I'm afraid so." Whyborne sighed. "We already know the standing stones are connected with the worship of Nyarlathotep, thanks to the association with Blackbyrne. It isn't much of a stretch to imagine the rat creature is a familiar given by him to an aspiring sorcerer."

God, what a tangle this was. "So you think Nyarlathotep is a real being? Something from the Outside, perhaps, like Nitocris?"

Whyborne didn't look happy at the thought. "It's certainly possible."

"Damn it." I tilted my head back and stared at the ceiling. My eyes ached. "All right. So we have a connection to Blackbyrne and his ilk. Two sets of standing stones, both of which seem to have had some sort of bloody ritual conducted on them. But to what end? Are there any other standing stones in the area?"

"Not that I know of," Whyborne said. "Then again, I didn't know of the set on the farm...oh."

The expression on his face said he'd had the same thought as I. "The stolen surveyor's map. The one that showed Indian villages and the like on it. What if it indicated the locations of the standing stones? And what if the two sites we now know about aren't the only ones?"

"If there are more, there are likely to be more sacrifices," I said.

"Yes." Whyborne fell silent for a long moment. "Christine gathered up the wands before we left. I'm going to examine them tomorrow and send a letter to Reverend Scarrow. With any luck, someone in the Cabal will know what to make of all this."

"Good idea. And there is one more question."

"What's that?"

"The cultists, the rat familiar...they were expecting us. Waiting for us on the island. How did they know we would be there, tonight?"

Whyborne cursed softly. "That's a good question."

"Yes." I rubbed gingerly at my painful eyes.

He brushed a lock of hair gently from my forehead. "You're still not well. Let's get you to bed."

"Are you trying to seduce me, Dr. Whyborne?" I asked in a rather feeble attempt at humor.

But instead of rolling his eyes, he only smiled. "If you like."

My headache had receded, and my eyes didn't trouble me enough to become a distraction. "I think I would like, yes."

He took my hand, and I let him pull me to my feet and lead me to his bedroom. Once there, he kissed me softly, his mouth gentle against mine.

We undressed slowly, unhurried, helping one another with buttons. I brushed my hand across his chest, tracing the shape of his ribs, delighting in the feel of his skin beneath my fingers. "Lie down," he said, so I did, stretching out on the bed and waiting to see what he had in mind. Anticipation of his touch woke my cock, bringing it to lazy attention.

He only looked at me, as though memorizing the shape of my body. I took the advantage to do the same. I'd wanted to seduce him from the day we met, to delve beneath the frosty exterior and reveal the passion I sensed boiling within. Years later, and I knew that passion, knew *him,* more intimately than I'd ever known anyone else. And he knew me.

"Are you going to spend all night looking?" I teased.

"No." He climbed on top of me, straddling my hips. The friction of his thigh against my cock drew a pleased moan from me. His lips brushed mine, his hands drifting over my chest. "You frightened me," he whispered against my mouth. "When you collapsed, my heart nearly stopped. You were so still when Iskander and I carried you back to the boat."

"I didn't mean to scare you, my dear."

"I know." He kissed me again, deeper this time. I shaped the planes of his back with my fingers, slid my hands down and cupped his taut buttocks in my palms. He pressed his body against mine, his hips starting to move, rubbing us together. "I love you. I couldn't...if I lost you..."

I wrapped my arms around him and rolled onto my side, taking him with me. His leg tightened around my hip, and his arms slid around me, holding me in turn. We clung to each other, kissing and rubbing, letting desire build. I started to draw back, thinking to look into his face—but the sight of my bloody eyes would probably remind him of his fear. So I slid my hand to the underside of his thigh, pulling him tighter, our cocks trapped between us.

"Feel this," I growled. "I'm not lost, not even close to it. Feel me, Ival; feel how I'm alive, how badly I want you."

"Y-yes," he gasped against my lips. His movements became more urgent, and I grinned with the joy of it. I loved his busy mind, but I also loved when I could make it all stop, take away every thought and replace it with raw sensation. His breath came like the gasps of a drowning man, and his leg pressed into my hip as he rocked and rutted against me.

He stiffened. Heat spread across my belly, even as he bit my shoulder in blind passion. Even before he'd finished, he grasped my cock with his hand, tugging urgently, as if begging me to join him. I shivered and moaned, and spilled against his stomach.

We lay quietly for a while, semen and sweat drying on our skin. "Are you reassured of my health?" I asked at length.

He sighed and snuggled closer. "Somewhat. Enough to sleep, at least."

"Good." I kissed his forehead.

His breathing evened out soon after. As tired as I'd been, I'd hoped to join him. But my sleep proved restless that night. Wild dreams of ketoi and umbrae, of the leering face of the rat-thing, kept me tossing and turning. The dreams mingled with the sound of chewing, accompanied by half-asleep glimpses of Saul patiently stalking mice in our walls.

CHAPTER 24

Whyborne

THE NEXT NIGHT, we rattled up to the rise overlooking the beach in Father's carriage. Griffin sat across from me, dressed in his best suit, paired with a green bow tie and vest. Ordinarily, they would have looked striking on him, bringing out the emerald of his irises. Tonight, however, they seemed to only emphasize the bloody red sclera.

Seeing him collapse last night, with blood leaking from the corner of his mouth...for a horrifying moment I'd thought him dead, burned up by the power of the maelstrom. Because of my touch.

I'd never felt the differences between us so keenly. I could draw on the power of the maelstrom only because I wasn't fully human. What had Bradley said, about accidents of birth? He didn't know the half of it.

"Did you examine the wands today?" Griffin asked.

I'd taken one to the museum with me, and left Griffin with strict orders not to overexert himself while I was gone. Whether he obeyed me or not, I wasn't certain. If not, he'd at least made the pretense, as I'd returned to find him curled up with Saul. My suggestion he remain in for the evening, rather than subject himself to my family, was met with a roll of the eyes, however.

"Yes." I stared out at what little of the scenery was visible in the darkness. "They're inscribed with various arcane sigils, most of them related to the spell they cast. As for the rest, some of them are hinted at in *Unaussprechlichen Kulten,* suggesting they were associated with certain medieval cults. Which, given the involvement of the Man in the Woods, makes sense. I sent a letter detailing them to Reverend Scarrow, to see if he knows any more. In the meantime, I've put them all in your locked cabinet."

The carriage slowed to a halt. "We'll return in a few moments," I told the driver as we exited.

He'd been in service to the Whybornes for most of his life, so he only nodded and said, "Yes, sir." As if there was nothing at all odd about going to a lonely place along the coast to pick up a passenger. Given the doings of my father and brother, this was likely not the strangest request ever made of him.

Griffin followed me, carrying the valise we'd brought with us. The path led past a sharp bend and a tumble of boulders, concealing this secluded cove from the road. Persephone and Mother waited for us on the beach, golden jewelry shining in the moonlight. Two other ketoi waited with them; I recognized Stone Biter, the male, but the female was a stranger to me. Persephone's tentacle hair writhed nervously around her shoulders when she turned to greet us.

"Brother," she said. "Brother's-husband." Her hands twisted together, claws gleaming in the moonlight.

"You don't have to go," Mother reminded her.

"I want to." Persephone stilled her hands and nodded, as if to herself.

Griffin held out the bag. "We brought a dress and a heavy veil," he said. "Were this Boston, I'd say it would rouse rather than allay suspicion, but as this is Widdershins I'm sure no one will look twice."

While Mother played handmaiden to Persephone, Griffin chatted with the ketoi. I was just as bad at making small talk with ketoi as with humans, so kept mainly silent.

"There," Mother said a short time later. "You'll...well. You won't be naked."

It was perhaps the best thing that could be said about Persephone in a dress. I'd brought one without sleeves, but they'd had to rip the seams anyway to fit it over the fins on her arms. The indigo silk looked odd against the pearlescent white and dark swirls of her skin. She took an experimental step, her batrachian feet hidden beneath the long skirts.

"Human women wear this?" she asked skeptically, plucking at the skirts. "Why?"

"It isn't so bad once one becomes accustomed," Mother replied.

Persephone pulled on the veil. With her hands hidden, she almost looked...well, not human, exactly. But a quick glimpse in dim lighting, and someone might assume her one. I glanced at Griffin, and saw he was trying very hard not to laugh.

"We should go," Griffin said, and offered Persephone his arm. She looked at it dubiously.

"Good luck," Mother told me. Then she turned and vanished beneath the waves, taking the other two ketoi with her.

CHAPTER 25

Whyborne

"**I wish I** might have seen out," Persephone said wistfully as our carriage drew up in front of Whyborne House. We'd kept the curtains drawn over the windows once we reached town, and the interior now smelled of a mixture of Griffin's cologne and seawater.

Despite her disappointment over covering the windows, she'd spent the ride enthusiastically bouncing up and down on the seat beside me, apparently entranced by the cushioning. Now that we'd arrived, her nervousness seemed to have returned, and she shrank back just a little when the door swung open to reveal Fenton.

"Good evening," he said, offering her his hand. "Welcome to Whyborne House, Miss Persephone."

"I remember you." Even though the veil hid her face, her tone turned bright. "You drove Brother and I in the motor car to kill the Endicotts."

"I have a motor car now," Griffin said as we climbed out after her. "Perhaps we can go for a ride one night, Persephone."

Bad enough he was trying to kill me with the accursed thing; now he wanted to add my sister to his list of victims?

Father awaited us in the foyer. His expression remained impassive, but I thought I saw a flicker of...what? Pain? Regret?... when Persephone removed her veil to reveal her seething hair and orca skin.

"Persephone," he said, his voice thick. "It's good to finally meet you."

She stepped forward, then stopped. "And you, Father." She looked around at the marble, the priceless vase on its gilded pedestal, the sweeping grand staircase. "This is very different from brother's house."

From her tone, I guessed she preferred my accommodations. Perhaps she sensed the disappointments and distances that had soaked into these walls, the silent resentments and angry quarrels. Or perhaps I merely projected my own experience onto her reactions.

"This is still Percival's home," Father said. "And it is yours as well." He took a step back and gestured toward the dining room. "Dr. Putnam and Mr. Barnett are already here. Fenton will bring them from the parlor to join us for dinner."

We followed him to the dining room. Persephone's silk skirts rustled loudly as if to emphasize her awkward gait. Christine and Iskander joined us, and Iskander's eyes grew round at the sight of her dress. Christine only snorted. "Honestly, Whyborne, why didn't you say something? I could have lent her something more sensible."

As we sat, Persephone seized a fork, holding it in her fist like a barbarian. "I know this! This is a fork," she declared.

To my shock, rather than look horrified, Father smiled indulgently. "Indeed it is. That one is for the fish course."

"Fish?" She cocked her head to the side. "Is it...cooked?"

His smile faded. "You don't care for it?" Then he shook his head. "Of course—I don't suppose you exactly have ovens and fires beneath the sea, do you? I didn't think. Cook will bring some raw for you."

I just managed not to gape at him. After haranguing me for every tiny infringement of what he saw as propriety over the years, he practically fell all over himself for Persephone. If I'd made such a request, he would have refused it without hesitation. Certainly he wouldn't have gone so far as to suggest it himself.

"Yes," she said slowly. "Or...do you have waffles?"

Father blinked. "Waffles?"

"Yes. Or are those for special occasions?" She cast me a questioning look. "Like our birthday?"

"No," Griffin said, grinning. "Waffles are not reserved only for birthdays."

"Then my brother and I will have waffles," she said, smiling broadly. Fenton paled sharply at the sight of her rows of teeth, and even Father looked shaken.

"I'm sure Percival—" Father began.

"Would love waffles," I finished for him with a glare.
He sighed. "Then waffles you both shall have."

CHAPTER 26

Griffin

IF NOTHING ELSE, dinner at Whyborne House was never boring. While the rest of us dined on mock turtle soup, celery salad, and stuffed lobster, Whyborne and Persephone ate their waffles, with Whyborne giving their father a defiant glare at every bite. For his part, Niles inquired as to Persephone's life beneath the sea.

"And...Heliabel?" he asked hesitantly. "Is she well?"

"Her sea name is Speaker of Stories," Persephone told him. She poured more syrup onto her waffles. "She is well. Happy. I think she will be a matriarch soon."

"The matriarchs are the true power among the ketoi, are they not?" Christine asked.

"Yes and no." Persephone licked her fork thoughtfully. Niles looked slightly pained at her manners, but said nothing. "They decide many things—what cities we trade with, when it is time to perform the ceremonies for the god, other things. I say when it is time for war; I stand before the god. Other things."

"Very sensible," Christine said. "Humans could learn a great deal from your kind."

Niles didn't press further, and the conversation moved onto other topics. He missed his wife, though; that much was clear.

But Heliabel didn't miss him. If she had, she would have returned to visit before now, or at the least taken this opportunity to accompany Persephone. Instead, the suggestion had never been raised, not even by her children.

I couldn't help but pity Niles. I tried to imagine how I would have felt, had Whyborne gone to the sea and never returned, never reached out to me again in the smallest way. I would have wondered what I'd done wrong. If he hated me or was simply indifferent, and which possibility was worse.

When dessert was at last cleared away, Niles said, "Persephone, would you care to learn a bit about our family history? Where you came from?"

She nodded. Her tentacles hung loosely around her shoulders, her earlier nerves having vanished with dinner. "Yes."

"We should view the ballroom and discuss wedding plans," Iskander said with a glance at Christine.

"Of course. Ask Fenton if you need anything." Niles rose to his feet. "Griffin, would you care to accompany us?"

"Very much so," I said.

"Are you well?" he inquired, as we walked back to the foyer. "Your eyes..."

"We ran afoul of magic at the old Somerby estate last night," I said with a grimace.

"Ah." He nodded. "I'd worried it was a consequence of your shadowsight."

"Not directly, at least."

"That's good. Before we go upstairs, here's something you might find interesting." He gestured down the hall leading to his study. "I've had a telephone installed, to better keep pace with happenings in New York."

The telephone sat on a small table in a nook once occupied by a Roman bust. "I'll have Fenton demonstrate its manner of operation the next time you visit," Niles offered.

"I don't see why one can't simply rely on the telegram," Whyborne said, eyeing the telephone with an air of distrust. "Why on earth must you *talk* to people when you can simply write a short message?"

Niles and I exchanged exasperated looks. Whyborne noticed and scowled at us both.

We followed Niles up the grand staircase to the third floor. The hall, which ran to the family quarters, was lined with oil paintings. I'd passed by them before, of course. Once on my way to view—among other things—the room Whyborne had slept in as a youth. The other had been to inspect Guinevere's belongings, hoping for some clue as to who had murdered her.

Niles stopped in front of what looked to be a very old portrait, its paint darkened as if it had at one time hung above a smoky fireplace. "This is Fear-God Whyborne," he told Persephone. "He left England to try his luck in the colonies."

"What Father means to say," Whyborne put in, "is he fled England one step in front of the hangman's noose. I can't recall, Father—was he arrested on charges of thievery or whore-mongering?" He snapped his fingers. "Oh no, wait I remember. It was both."

Niles's thick brows drew together in disapproval. "He was a resourceful man, who came to this land penniless and died a respected land owner."

"And by resourceful, you mean 'fell in with a necromancer and practiced black magic against anyone who stood in his way.'"

Niles's frown deepened. "He didn't practice sorcery himself, but yes, he did what he needed to for his family. Who were grateful for his sacrifices."

Persephone peered at the portrait. "He was very ugly, even for a land dweller," she remarked.

"Moving on," Niles grated between clenched teeth. "Here we have his eldest son and daughter, George and Prudence."

"Her body was never found," Whyborne said. "You'll note, sister, that the Whyborne family tree doesn't have many branches on it."

"And the Endicotts a few too many," I said, hoping to lighten the mood. Although perhaps doing so by reminding everyone of murderous sorcerers who wanted Whyborne and Persephone dead wasn't the best way to go about it.

We continued on, Persephone and I admiring the paintings while Whyborne and Niles bickered. Their voices grew louder and louder the further we went, and I noted a vein standing out on Niles's forehead.

"My younger brother, Charles," Niles said.

"I didn't know Percival had any uncles." I examined the portrait curiously. The man depicted looked to be perhaps twenty-two or -three at the time it had been painted, handsome but stern.

"Of course not," Niles growled. "Percival will go on and on about the misdeeds of our distant ancestors, but the bravery of his own uncle is never mentioned."

"He died long before I was born!" Whyborne objected hotly.

"As did Fear-God and the rest, but you have no qualm slandering them!"

I cleared my throat before the quarrel grew any worse. "I'd like to hear the story, and I'm certain Persephone would as well."

"Yes." She touched the gilded frame lightly with her clawed fingers. What would her uncle think to see her? Would he greet her as family, or curse her as an abomination?

Niles gazed up at his brother, hands folded behind his back. "Charles was captured during the war—we served in different units, and it was some time before I learned what had happened to him. He was sent to Camp Sumter."

I'd heard stories of the prison for union soldiers, and of the atrocities that had led to its commander's trial and execution once the war ended. "I'm sorry."

"Oh, he survived that." Bitterness coated Niles's words. "He lived through starvation and plague and God alone knows what other horrors. And when it was over, he made for Ohio, to recuperate with our mother's family before returning to Massachusetts. His transport ship was the *Sultana*."

Persephone's tendrils contracted slightly in distress. "I do not know what that is, Father."

"A steamship." His mouth was a tight line. "Overcrowded and poorly maintained. The boiler exploded and carried nearly two-thousand men to the bottom of the Mississippi River. Charles was one of them."

"How awful," I said quietly.

Niles took a shaky breath. "He survived so much, only to be struck down by capricious fate. It destroyed our parents. Father wasted away from grief and died later that year. Mother found new life in her grandchildren—Stanford was born the next year—but she died when Percival was still quite young."

"I remember," Whyborne said. "Or rather, I recall her funeral more than the woman herself. All the black clothing and weeping, shutting her away in the mausoleum, seemed very confusing at the time."

"I'm certain it did." Niles straightened his shoulders and turned away. "Well. We should return to our guests, before they think we've deserted them."

Whyborne and Persephone went ahead, but Niles lagged behind. I slowed my steps to match his. "Thank you," I said. "I appreciate that you shared such a personal story with me."

He nodded. "It seemed appropriate." A hesitation, then: "I never had anything against you, Griffin. I know that must be difficult to accept, considering how we first met, but it is true. I didn't realize Percival was...fond...of you at the time, not until he nearly died trying to undo the Brotherhood's mistake."

What mistake did he refer to? Trusting Blackbyrne, or killing innocent people for their own ends? I didn't ask; the answer would change nothing at this late date, and likely lead to us quarreling as well. "I see."

"Percival was always stubborn, from the moment he was born." Niles frowned at his son's back. "I dare say Persephone is probably the same, given how she stood up to the old chieftess that Hallowe'en. But I had hoped he would eventually see reason and wed."

"It would never have happened," I said. "Even if I hadn't come along." At Niles's look, I shrugged. "I've known many men with a wife and children, who seek...different...pleasures among other like-minded fellows. I might, had things gone otherwise, have fallen in love with a woman and married. And been perfectly faithful to her. But Percival's nature is not thus, and he couldn't change it for you any more than he could have made himself shorter, or altered his eyes to look like yours instead of Heliabel's."

Niles was silent for a long moment. Then at last he said, "I hadn't realized."

"I know." I wasn't certain how much to say, what sort of confidences this man might want. But for Whyborne's sake, I'd try my best. "But don't underestimate him because of it. I prayed to change, when I was younger. If it were possible, I would have done it in an instant." I tipped my head back and studied the ornate ceiling. "Whyborne—Percival—never would have. Not even to please all of society, no matter what the cost. And God knows the man is pig-headed at times, but don't mistake courage for stubbornness."

We reached the bottom of the stairs. Iskander was speaking warmly of the ballroom's gallery to Whyborne, while Christine had a slightly blank look on her face. "I see," Niles said at last.

I paused, so we remained just out of earshot. "My adoptive father died before we reconciled. I have no wish to see you and Percival suffer the same."

"Thank you." Niles met my eyes, and I shook my head at his calculating look.

"I won't be your advocate. Only you can do that." I fixed my gaze on Whyborne, looking so uncomfortable in the very home in which he'd grown up. "My first duty is to him, always. But he can't see clearly when it comes to you, and I'll try to remind him of that, if it becomes necessary."

Niles let out a long breath. "I understand," he said at last.

We rejoined the others. Whyborne glowered at me, folding his arms across his chest, although I didn't know why he'd be upset with me.

"You're going to be married here?" Persephone asked Iskander and Christine. Her hair curled around her shoulders in delight. "Oh! Have you decided where to place the skulls?"

"Skulls?" Christine asked, seeming intrigued.

"Or teeth. Trophies of your enemies." Persephone regarded the space, then pointed. "There would be a good place."

Christine sighed. "I'm afraid we don't have any skulls, or anything else of the sort."

Persephone looked dubious. "I could lend you Dives Deep's skull. I've kept it for my own wedding."

"Would you?" Christine asked, a slightly fiendish grin on her face.

"No!" Iskander stared at her in horror. "Don't be absurd, Christine."

"Oh, very well." She turned to Persephone. "What else would you suggest?"

Persephone regarded the room. "Shells. Shark's teeth. Pearls. I will bring some to you."

"Excellent!" Christine clapped her hands. "Between you and Miss Parkhurst, this wedding business is all but taking care of itself."

Persephone beamed. Iskander looked speechless. I took pity on him, and said, "For now, we'd best return Persephone to her people."

"Yes, thank you for your hospitality, Mr. Whyborne." Iskander shook Niles's hand. "We can never repay your generosity."

"You've stood by Percival when he needed it most," Niles said gruffly. "It's the least I can do."

Whyborne's hands tightened on his arms, and his mouth went white at the corners. As we made our farewells, Niles said, "Did you receive my note, Percival? We'll visit your brother the day after tomorrow at the asylum."

"I received it," he said, looking even gloomier than before. He spoke little when we made our goodbyes and remained quiet during the ride back to the beach with Persephone. She was quiet as well, hidden once again beneath her veil.

"What did you think of it all?" I asked her.

"It seemed very strange." Her hands brushed against the silk of her skirts, as if musing on their texture. "Even stranger to think I might have lived there. If the Endicotts' spell hadn't nearly killed us, if we had been born in our due time, I would have grown up there as a human." She shook her head. "I can't imagine it."

The carriage slowed to a halt. I climbed out first, helping Persephone down. "Shall we walk you to the beach?"

"If you'd like. You can take back the clothing."

The dress was ruined, but the silk might be sold as scraps. "All right."

When we rounded the rocky outcropping onto the narrow strand, we found a dozen or so ketoi awaiting us. They stood and sat on the rocks, lean bodies alert. Fins cut the waves just off shore.

Persephone straightened and her face grew grave. I suddenly saw not my admittedly odd sister-in-law, who loved waffles and brightly colored shells, but the chieftess who ruled the city beneath the waves. "Calls Dolphins?" she asked, striding toward them. "What's wrong?"

A ketoi who must be Calls Dolphins rose from her perch on a rock. She looked fierce even for one of their kind, a long spear held in one hand. Scars raked one side of her face, the eye socket empty and glaring. Her pattern of dark swirls and spots looked like war paint.

"Sings Above the Waves." She bowed her head slightly to Persephone. "There's been a disturbance I thought you'd wish to know about. Broken Tooth tasted blood near the Reef of Sighs. She went to see what had been injured, and discovered this." Calls Dolphins gestured to a dark shape lying on the sand. "The land dwellers will wish to see it as well."

I approached warily, my heart sinking as I realized it was a body. The dead man hadn't been in the water long enough for the fish to start in on him, at least. Waterlogged clothing hung loosely on his frame, having been torn aside to expose his throat and chest. Much as with poor Mr. Tubbs, his throat had been cut, and his sternum cracked open to remove his heart.

CHAPTER 27

Whyborne

IT WAS QUITE late by the time we finally returned home. Although the water had washed off any sigils painted on the dead man, I had no doubts he had been killed by whoever had made the sacrifices at the standing stones on land. Griffin searched the body carefully, while the carriage driver hastened with me back to town to alert the police. The ketoi vanished into the sea before the police arrived, and we answered a number of tiresome questions as to what we'd been doing driving along the coast road so late at night. I heavily implied I'd been on business for my father, which was somewhat true. Invoking his name had the expected effect, and we were soon on our way with an apology for keeping us so long.

I didn't want to be in trouble with the police. Of course I didn't. But the fact I had to use Father's name to avoid questioning burned almost as badly as the fact I'd been willing to do so.

I jammed my hat onto the stand while Griffin locked the door behind us. It fell off onto the floor, and Griffin scooped it up, hanging it and his own gently. "Will you tell me what's wrong, my dear?"

Was the man blind? "Oh, just some maniac cultists going about murdering people, for God only knows what horrible purpose," I snapped. "And trying to add us to the number, I might add. Nothing at all."

He sighed. "You were unhappy before we even left Whyborne House. And not the usual sort of unhappy you become when we're there."

My hands curled, the scars on the right pulling across my knuckles. "I'm shocked you noticed. I thought you were too busy making friends with Father."

"What?" His eyes widened slightly. "You're angry with me because I talked to your father?"

"Of course not." I turned my back and stalked down the hall.

Griffin came after me. "Then why?"

"Because I see what he's doing!" The words exploded out of me, far louder than I'd meant to speak them.

Griffin caught up with me in the study. "Whyborne. Ival." He seized my elbow, forcing me to stop. Arcane energy crackled between us, responding to my tattered emotions, but he didn't let go. "I don't know what you mean. What is Niles doing?"

"Exactly what he's always done. Tried to bend me to his will." I sought to pull free, but Griffin refused to let go. "When it was just me —when I was alone and friendless—he had no way in. His only choice was to pit his will against mine and try to wear me down. But now he thinks to bribe my friends so they can do his work for him!"

Griffin gaped at me. "Bribe your friends?"

I tore free of his grasp and stalked to the cold fireplace. Several photos of the two of us held place of honor on the mantelpiece, including one Iskander had taken just last month. Griffin and I sat on the couch, his arm around my shoulders as he gazed up at me. I looked back down at him, laughing at some foolish joke he'd made, my hand resting on his knee.

I glared at the photo. "Don't pretend you don't see it, Mr. Private Detective. Offering to let Christine and Iskander wed in Whyborne House, showering you with enough stock to buy the blasted motor car, 'oh here, Persephone, let's get you waffles.'"

"You're being irrational." Griffin put his hand on my shoulder. I shook it off. "Without Christine and Iskander, we would have both died several times over. Why shouldn't he offer to aid them as a way of thanks?"

"Thank them for saving me? If they'd abandoned me to die, he'd have given them a damned medal. At least until Stanford's fall from grace."

"Your father never wanted you dead," Griffin said with an air of patience that irritated me even further.

Bitterness choked me with the taste of bile. "He ignored me until he needed a replacement for Stanford. Now he's determined to make me over in Stanford's image no matter what. He saw I had friends who cared for me, so now he's going to win you all over with money and gifts, until nothing matters about me to anyone except that I'm his son. He'll shower affection on my sister he would never have shown me, to get her on his side. Donate to the museum until Dr. Hart cares more about his money than any skill of mine."

"Ival—"

Tears stung my eyes, blurring the photograph. I blinked them back savagely. "I fought so hard to make my own way, to create a life that belonged only to me. But all my independence was just an illusion. One snap of his fingers, and I'm once again nothing more than Niles Whyborne's son. How long until he begins to drop hints in Christine's ears, in Persephone's, in Dr. Hart's, that I would surely be better off working for him? How long until my own friends want me to stop being so stubborn and repay my kind, generous father for all he's done?"

"Oh, my love." Grief choked Griffin's voice. "I didn't realize you felt this way."

"How else would I feel?" I closed my eyes, unable to look at the photograph any longer. "What did he offer you tonight?"

"Nothing." The floor creaked behind me as he stepped closer. "I gave him some things to consider, I believe. And I told him that my first duty was to you, no matter what." He took a shaky breath. "Ival, please, look at me."

I didn't want to, but I couldn't resist the note of pleading in his voice. His poor eyes had gone even redder, and tears clung to his lashes. Guilt stung me immediately—I'd hurt him with my own pain, even when I'd never meant to. "Griffin, I'm sorry." I reached for him.

He gripped my upper arms, keeping me from drawing him closer. "Can you really believe such things of us?" he asked. "Christine would die for you, without a moment's hesitation. I risked unleashing the umbrae on the world, because you're more important to me than everything else in it. How could you imagine, even for a second, that we'd betray you like that?"

I felt utterly miserable. "I...I don't know. Because I'm afraid..." I trailed off, because I wasn't even entirely sure what I feared. "You don't know what he's like. How far he'd go."

"The man would have opened a portal to the Outside and remade the world," Griffin said. "I'd say I have a good idea of how far he'd go." His fingers tightened on my arms. "I don't wish to upset you, but have you considered, even for a moment, that his actions aren't part of some grand scheme?"

"No." I shook my head. "Because it would mean he cared about me as something more than a tool that might be of use to him, if he can only find how to make it work."

Griffin sighed and pulled me to him. I pressed my face into his hair. The familiar scent of his cologne, of his skin, spread a balm over my soul. His hand stroked my back tenderly. "What can I do?" he asked. "What will make this less painful for you? I can send back the motor car, if you'd like."

My one chance to get rid of the evil machine, and I couldn't take it. "No. You're right. I know you and Christine and Iskander wouldn't trade me for Father's thirty pieces of silver. I just...it seems so clear to me what he's trying to do, and no one else can see it, and I'm afraid of losing everything I've fought for. Of losing myself."

Griffin pulled back just far enough to wipe a tear off my face. "I understand. I wish I could make this easier for you. Promise me you'll say something next time, instead of letting it fester."

"I will." I kissed him gently. "I'm sorry."

"Don't apologize." He offered me a rueful smile. "You've held me all the times I've crumbled." His reddened eyes searched my face. "I would do anything to make you happy. You know that, don't you?"

I nodded, feeling like a fool. Everything that had seemed not just possible, but inevitable, inside my own head sounded like utter nonsense once spoken aloud. Of course the man who faced his greatest fears to come after me beneath the glacier in Alaska wouldn't be seduced by the ability to buy a motor car. And Christine would tell my father to go to the devil if he dared suggest I leave the museum for Whyborne Railroad and Industries.

As for the rest of the world, I couldn't prevent them from seeing me as Father's son first and myself second. But perhaps, so long as I had my friends, it didn't matter so much.

CHAPTER 28

Whyborne

THE NEXT MORNING, I stared at the Wisborg Codex on my desk, as if I could unlock its secrets by sheer will alone. Beside it lay a map of Widdershins and the surrounding countryside.

There was a pattern here, if only I could see it. Clearly the cultists had made a deal with Nyarlathotep and received the twisted rat-like familiar in return. Equally clearly, or at least likely, they had used some sort of mind control to force Lambert to help steal the old map from city hall. While under their enchantment, he'd distracted Tubbs while the familiar made off with the map through the rat hole Griffin had mentioned seeing in the hall of records. Now they conducted sacrifices to reach some unknown goal.

They knew about me, and knew my history well enough to set up an ambush on the island. Had they guessed I'd go to it eventually, after seeing the site of Tubbs's murder, whose stones so closely matched? Had they in fact counted on it?

Even more disturbing: how had they known I'd be there that night?

As for Lambert, they had to be behind his death as well. Some hideous animal had chewed through him, and I had the horrifying feeling his killer had sat chittering at us from the island's altar stone.

I turned the pages of the codex slowly, examining the

illustrations. The rat familiar. The ketoi. The umbrae. The dweller in the deeps and Mother of Shadows. Was there a connection, or had the creator of the codex simply listed every horror he knew of in some sort of bestiary of abominations?

There was a connection between ketoi and umbrae, though. According to the Mother of Shadows, some long-vanished race had created the ketoi and umbrae as slaves. The umbrae rebelled; the ketoi preserved no memory of that time, but presumably they had done so as well.

Unnatural as we of ketoi blood were, we weren't things of the Outside. The umbrae and we were solidly of this world, unlike the yayhos or Nitocris. Or even the rat-thing, if it was indeed something brought from the Outside by Nyarlathotep. Whatever—whoever—Nyarlathotep might even be.

The medieval rantings in the *Arcanorum* and elsewhere cast him as a sort of demon, if not the Devil himself. Nephren-ka had worshipped him millennia before as a god of chaos. Knowing what little I did of the Outside, I suspected he—or perhaps they—were a different order of being altogether. Something alien to our sphere of existence.

And what would such a being, or race of beings, want with human sorcerers? Why aid them with the gift of the rat-thing tutor? What was the point behind the sacrifices our adversaries had made? How had they known of the codex and the witch hunter's dagger?

The door opened and Christine wandered in. Without asking permission, she seated herself across from me. "Kander asked me to pass along our thanks to you and your father again," she said.

"Yes." I twisted my wedding ring absently on my finger. The reminder of last night stung, and I felt a fool all over again. "Just remember Father doesn't do anything that doesn't benefit him in some way."

She gave me a shrewd look. "I won't. And neither will Kander. His father was a diplomat, if you recall. He knows all about treading lightly and watching his words."

I smiled ruefully. "I'm glad."

Christine peered at me. "You look awful," she said bluntly.

"Thank you," I muttered. A frown appeared on her face when I told her of the ketoi waiting for us on the beach, growing deeper and deeper as I spoke of the dead man. When I finished, she said, "Has the poor fellow been identified yet?"

"Not that I'm aware. Griffin was going to visit the morgue and the police station this morning." I pushed the map toward her. "I've marked the locations of the standing stones—the ones we know of, anyway—and of the reef where the body was thrown into the sea."

She inspected it. "Any thoughts as to why the murderer has suddenly turned to sacrificing people at sea?"

"No." *Was* there a connection with the ketoi? "I'd hoped the method of the murders might shed some light, but there's nothing. Maybe if I could read this blasted codex it would help."

"Hmm. Well, good luck." She rose to her feet. "I have to go and have my wedding dress fitted this morning. It seems a lot of expense and nonsense, if you ask me, but I suppose it makes Kander happy. I'll see you this afternoon."

I spent the next hour or so catching up on my actual work—in this case translating a cuneiform tablet, which proved to be a fragment from the Epic of Gilgamesh. Peter Jensen had published a German translation last year, and I located my copy and thumbed through it, until I came to the scene where Gilgamesh dreamed of the coming of his great friend Enkidu.

Or perhaps more than friends. *"I pressed myself upon him like a wife,"* was Jensen's translation of Gilgamesh's dream.

My thoughts wandered for a while, circling between verb forms and meanings, and tales echoing down the ages, until a knock on the door interrupted me. "Dr. Whyborne?" Miss Parkhurst said. "There's a telegram for you."

Puzzled, I took it from her. It proved to be from the Reverend Scarrow.

SUSPECT INVOLVEMENT OF A CULT CALLED THE FIDELES STOP THEY SEEK WHAT THEY CALL THE RESTORATION STOP HAVE CONNECTIONS TO NYARLATHOTEP AND OTHER BEINGS FROM THE OUTSIDE STOP EXCEEDINGLY DANGEROUS STOP HAVE HEARD OF FRAGMENTARY COPIES OF THE CODEX YOU DESCRIBE BUT NEVER A COMPLETE VOLUME STOP LONGER LETTER TO FOLLOW STOP

"Fideles. The faithful." I murmured. "But Faithful to what?"

My voice sounded very quiet in the emptiness of my office. Whatever this Restoration might be, I doubt it would do us any good. Did they seek to spread the worship of Nyarlathotep, as had happened in Egypt and other places throughout history? Or did they have some other goal?

The distant sound of gunfire echoed through the museum.

CHAPTER 29

Whyborne

I BOLTED OUT of my office, chair falling to the floor in my haste. Miss Parkhurst stood at her desk, face pale. Distant screams sounded, accompanied by another shot.

"Dr. Whyborne!" Miss Parkhurst ran toward me. "Something terrible is happening!"

I caught her by the upper arms and pushed her in the direction of my office. "Go inside and lock the door behind you."

"But what about you?"

"I'm going to see what's happening." Perhaps I could be of help. Explode the gun with my fire spell, if nothing else.

Her eyes widened, but she nodded. "B-be careful, please."

"I will," I assured her. "Now hide, and don't come out until I return."

She nodded. I hurried on my way, breaking into a run as I reached the main corridor. The babble of frightened voices sounded all around me, accompanied by the slamming of office doors as various colleagues barricaded themselves inside.

I rounded a corner and nearly collided with Dr. Gerritson. His face was flushed, sweat standing out across his brow. "Durfree's gone mad. Started shooting at Mr. Farr in the colonial art gallery. I'm going to fetch Mr. Rockwell."

The animosity between Mr. Durfree and Mr. Farr was long-standing, and Christine and I had joked more than once that they'd end up dueling in one of the galleries. I'd never thought they would actually go so far, however.

"Good idea," I said. "I'll try to talk sense into them, or...or something."

He clapped me on the arm and hurried on his way.

I let myself in through the staff door onto the gallery floor and immediately froze. Several visitors crouched behind display cases of colonial silverware, clutching at purses and handkerchiefs. Bullet holes showed in the wall, as well as the center of the portrait of Theron Blackbyrne. Mr. Durfree must truly be out of his mind; given his dedication I'd have sooner believed he'd set himself on fire than do injury to anything in his beloved collection.

The man himself stood in the center of the room, gun held loosely by his side. "Come out, Farr!" he called. "You've thwarted me far too many times. Since the day you were hired, you've been nothing but a millstone around my neck, challenging my every word. It ends here!"

I caught sight of Mr. Farr, tears streaming down his face as he hid behind a plinth supporting a magnificent silver punch bowl. My heart pounded in my throat, and I hesitated. Durfree might have lost his senses, but he was a colleague. Anyone else, I would have set fire to the powder in the gun without a second thought. But I knew this man —perhaps not well, but we'd sat in the same all-staff meetings and attended the same excruciating galas.

Where were the blasted guards?

"Stop!" I shouted. "You don't wish to do this, Mr. Durfree. Put the gun down."

He turned, his contemptuous expression transmuting to one of rage. For a moment, I thought he might shoot me instead. "Go away, Dr. Whyborne. This doesn't concern you."

"Of course it does," I said, hoping to waste time until the damned guards appeared. "You're frightening the visitors. If you'd just put away the gun, I'm sure the director would be happy to hear out whatever grievance you have against Mr. Farr."

"Jacob, please!" Farr called, his voice thick with tears. "This isn't you! I don't—I don't understand what's happening."

There came the pounding of boots against the marble, and two guards skidded to a halt at the gallery entrance. "Put down the gun, Mr. Durfree!" one ordered as he leveled his own weapon.

A strange, ugly smile touched Durfree's face. He meant to shoot them, or try. Someone was about to die, either him or the guards, or both.

I reached for the maelstrom, and it reached back, like a lover taking my hand. Fire sizzled on my tongue, but I let the old, familiar spell slip past and reached for something else.

The air around the gun went cold as an Alaskan night. Frost raced across the iron barrel, down onto the grip, adhering to skin. Durfree cried out in pain and dropped the gun in reaction.

And stood blinking, staring down at his hand with a bewildered expression. "What happened? Where—"

He didn't get the chance to finish his thought before one of the guards wrenched his arms behind his back.

"What are you doing?" he shouted, and the very real fear and confusion on his face turned my blood colder than the iron of the pistol. "How did I get here? What's going on? Why are you putting me in handcuffs?"

I started forward, intending to question him. But before I could, Miss Parkhurst ran through the staff door, her face a terrified mask.

"Dr. Whyborne!" she cried, and threw herself into my arms.

Her timing was atrocious. I patted her awkwardly on the back. "There, there," I said. "It's all right. Mr. Durfree is quite contained. I just need to speak to—"

"There was a—a creature in your office!" she sobbed. "It came in through the window and stole the book from your desk!"

CHAPTER 30

Whyborne

"THIS IS UNACCEPTABLE," Dr. Hart thundered. "Unacceptable, do you hear me?"

"Yes, sir," I said in the direction of the blotter on his desk. Miss Parkhurst echoed the sentiment from the chair beside me.

I felt like a schoolboy dragged before the headmaster. Dr. Hart's day had already been ruined by one of his staff going mad and damaging a valuable work of art. Now I'd come to tell him the Wisborg Codex had been stolen from inside my own office.

Impatience warred with embarrassment. I had to get out of here and let Griffin know what had happened. The way Mr. Durfree had behaved, his sudden confusion, seemed far too similar to Lambert's experience.

"It isn't Dr. Whyborne's fault, sir," Miss Parkhurst offered tentatively.

"It is entirely Dr. Whyborne's fault!" I risked a glance up; Dr. Hart's round face had gone red with anger. I lowered my gaze hurriedly again. "Keeping a valuable artifact like the Wisborg Codex just lying about in your office was utterly irresponsible. That is doubly true, given there was already one attempt to steal it!"

"I usually locked it in the safe," I protested. "The only reason it was out was because I was distracted by the gunshots."

"It shouldn't have been in your office at all," he countered. "Mr. Quinn should never have allowed you to remove it from the library. I shall be having words with him next."

I hunched my shoulders. Now I'd not only lost the codex, but managed to get Mr. Quinn in trouble as well. I didn't want to contemplate what sort of revenge he might exact. Hopefully it would restrict itself to journals becoming mysteriously misplaced when I asked for them, rather than anything more...exciting.

"Dr. Whyborne couldn't have known some sort of—of creature would climb in the window!" Miss Parkhurst shuddered at the memory. "I thought at first it was a large rat, but then I saw its face..." she trailed off, all the color draining from her skin.

I could only imagine her horror at confronting the rat familiar. "What's important is that you're safe, Miss Parkhurst." I patted her shoulder uncertainly, and she cast me a grateful look.

Dr. Hart shook his head. "Rats, stealing books? Forgive me if I find your explanation a bit far-fetched."

"It wasn't a rat!" She stared unhappily at her hands, bunched in her skirts. "I don't know what it was."

I did...or had an idea, at least. But even given what the director had seen that night two years ago, I could hardly start raving about sorcery and sacrifices and monsters from the Outside. Not without sounding like a lunatic.

"It was a frightening situation," I said. "First the gunshots, then a large animal coming into the office where Miss Parkhurst was hiding. Whatever the creature might have been, I believe she is telling the truth."

The director gave me a narrow look. He appeared to guess I was leaving a great deal unsaid. "I see. As much as it pains me to remind you, Dr. Whyborne, this museum has a certain reputation to uphold. These sorts of debacles cannot be tolerated."

In other words, keep sorcery away from the Ladysmith. I wanted to protest that I hadn't brought it here—not intentionally, at least. But one look at his face told me he wouldn't appreciate an argument.

"Yes, sir," I told the blotter.

Dismissed, we slunk past the director's secretary. Once we were safely in the hall, I said, "I'm sorry, Miss Parkhurst."

"Don't be—you stood up for me." She offered me a tremulous smile. "And you tried to keep me safe, while rushing off to stop Mr. Durfree, no matter the danger to yourself. You're so brave."

I flushed. I certainly hadn't felt brave at the time. "That's very kind of you, Miss Parkhurst. I—"

"Barking up the wrong tree there, Maggie," Bradley said.

God. I was going to strangle him.

I turned slowly, moving in time with the distant heart of the maelstrom. A breeze ruffled my hair, and my tongue tasted of burnt iron. Bradley stood before me, smirking. "Percy here is nothing special."

"And where were you?" I asked, swallowing back the words of power I longed to speak instead. "Cowering in your office?"

To my surprise, he didn't flinch. "Not at all. I had an important meeting elsewhere, away from the museum." He looked about disdainfully. "I've found these little halls a bit too confining. Though I expect you'll be here until you die."

"Excellent news," I said. "I wish you well somewhere far away from here."

"Oh, don't worry, Percy. I'm sure I'll stay close." He gave Miss Parkhurst a final leer and strode off, humming brightly to himself. I took a deep breath, trying to calm the churn of rage in my blood.

"He's just jealous," Miss Parkhurst said unexpectedly. At my startled look, she said, "Well, you *do* things, don't you? You retrieved the stolen scroll from the Nephren-ka exhibit, and went to Egypt and Alaska with Dr. Putnam, and ran to help today, and saved everyone when, er...well, your brother." She looked at me apologetically. "Dr. Osborne hasn't done any of that. In fact, I bet he *was* hiding in his office today!"

Her fierce defense brought a smile to my face and drained the last of my anger. "I thank you, Miss Parkhurst. Although I hope you're wrong about the latter. Just between the two of us, I'd much prefer Dr. Osborne found employment elsewhere."

CHAPTER 31

Griffin

WHYBORNE AND I followed Detective Tilton through the police station to the jail.

It was my second trip to the police station in one day. I'd come around that morning to find out if anyone had identified the corpse pulled from the ocean last night. No one had, although tattoos on his body suggested he might have been a sailor. If so, we'd be lucky to ever discover his name. Widdershins was a port town, and ships crewed by men from all over the world put in at our docks. Unless the fellow had a particular friend aboard who might remain behind to search for him, his captain would probably assume he'd passed out drunk somewhere, hire a replacement, and sail off again.

On the slim chance someone might have pertinent information, I visited a few of my old contacts in the more questionable parts of town. I'd come away with no answers, although two of them hinted that an unusual number of strangers had come into Widdershins as of late. The disreputable boarding houses and hotels near the docks were crowded with men who seemed intent on staying for longer than the usual few days.

What it meant, I didn't know, but the implications worried me. When I arrived home, I found even more reason to fear: a note from Tilton, asking me to come to the station to interview the suspect involved in the attempted murder at the Ladysmith.

He'd given no more details. If something terrible had happened, why hadn't Ival contacted me himself? Had he been shot? Tilton surely would have said, but…

I didn't clearly recall steering the motor car from our house to the museum, although the lack of dints suggested I'd done so successfully. The work day had ended, and I spotted Ival coming down the stairs almost as soon as I pulled up to the curb. If not for the presence of so many of his colleagues, I'd have flung my arms around him in relief.

"I'm sorry," he said, once we were underway and I had the opportunity to express my displeasure at not hearing from him sooner. "The director cornered me. I'm in a bit of trouble."

He explained Durfree's odd behavior and the theft of the codex as I drove. "I don't think it was a coincidence," he finished as I stopped in front of the police station.

"No," I agreed. "Neither do I."

Mr. Durfree sat in the same cell Lambert had died in. He cradled his head in his hands, body slumped, the very picture of despair. As with Lambert, no trace of anything magical lingered about him.

"Mr. Durfree?" Whyborne asked tentatively.

Durfree's head snapped up. "Dr. Whyborne?" He rose to his feet. "Have you come to tell them I didn't do it?"

"Er." Whyborne looked desperately uncomfortable. "Not precisely."

"Dr. Whyborne witnessed your rampage," Tilton said.

Durfree sagged back. "But I…how? I don't understand." His eyes sought Whyborne's desperately. "You're here to make a statement against me?"

"They're here to interview you," Tilton said. "I suggest you answer all their questions as honestly as possible."

Durfree looked even more confused. "Interview me? But I've already told you everything I know, detective."

I stepped forward, extending my hand between the bars. "Permit me to introduce myself, Mr. Durfree. I'm Griffin Flaherty."

He roused enough to shake my hand. "Yes, I've seen you about the museum, haven't I? Dr. Whyborne's brother shot you."

Well, it had been my most dramatic moment, at least so far as the museum staff were concerned. "Indeed. Detective Tilton contacted me because I recently had a client whose circumstances were similar to your own."

Durfree glanced again at Whyborne, as if seeking comfort in the familiar. "Similar? How?"

"I don't wish to prejudice your account by planting any

suggestions," I said. "Just tell Dr. Whyborne and I what you remember of events."

Durfree hesitated. I nudged Whyborne. "Er, yes," he said. "Tell us what you remember. Any detail might be important."

"Very well." Durfree took a deep breath. "I spent the morning overseeing the restoration work on one of our newer acquisitions." He held up a bandaged finger. "I assisted with a frame and sliced myself. Afterward Anthony—Mr. Farr—and I lunched together, as we often do."

"Did you quarrel?" I asked.

"Well, yes." Durfree wrung his hands desperately. "He disagreed with my selection of paintings to be lent to the Metropolitan Museum of Art for their exhibition on Colonial portraiture. But it was nothing serious! We often disagree."

Tilton pounced. "In fact, you have a reputation for it."

"No, we..." Durfree blanched. "We do, but...I hold Mr. Farr in the highest regard. I'd never threaten his life."

I had the distinct feeling their relationship was far more complicated than most might assume. Of course I couldn't ask questions of an intimate nature with Tilton listening in, so instead I said, "Please, continue with your account."

"I returned to my office." Durfree bit his lip. "And then...suddenly I was in a dark place. I couldn't move. I struggled and tried to cry out, but I couldn't." He shook his head. "I've never been so frightened. I didn't know what had happened, how I had gone from my office to wherever I was. Then I was standing in the gallery, and my hand hurt. And someone had shot the portrait of Theron Blackbyrne!" Durfree buried his face in his hands, and his shoulders heaved. "They're telling me I was going to kill Anthony, but I never would! I'd never..."

God. I let out a long sigh. "I believe you."

"As do I," Whyborne said quickly. "Set your mind at ease, Mr. Durfree."

"Gentlemen, if we may speak privately a moment," Tilton said, indicating the way we'd come.

We left Durfree behind, retreating just far enough that he wouldn't hear our words. "What do you think happened to the fellow?" Tilton asked in a low voice. "Some sort of—of hypnosis, perhaps?"

Clearly he was grasping for any explanation he might safely put into a report. "Something like that," I said neutrally. "Whoever compelled Mr. Lambert surely did the same with Mr. Durfree."

"And Lambert died in custody." Tilton scowled. "I don't want another body in my jail. Is he in danger?"

Whyborne glanced back at the cells. His expression probably

seemed calm to Tilton, but I noted the tiny muscle tightening in his jaw, the way his eyes narrowed a fraction. "I suspect he is. The, ah, *hypnotist* doesn't seem eager to leave alive anyone who might lead police in his direction."

It wasn't the precise truth, but close enough for Tilton. The detective considered, then nodded. "I'm sure the judge will be amenable if you wish to stand for the bail, Dr. Whyborne."

Just as Addison Somerby had stood for me, once. At least we wanted to keep Durfree alive. "I think that for the best."

"Of course," Whyborne said. "Do I need to speak with the judge, or...?"

"I think we can suspend procedure in this case." Tilton must want Durfree out of his jail. For a moment, I almost felt sorry for the detective. Policing Widdershins must be something of a hopeless job even under ordinary circumstances. "I'll see he's released."

We returned to the main office. A rather distraught looking gentleman sat near the front desk, springing to his feet upon spying us. "Dr. Whyborne! What are you doing here?"

"Mr. Farr?" Whyborne seemed equally surprised. "That is, I came to speak with Mr. Durfree."

"They won't let me see him." Farr wrung his hands together miserably. "But I have to know why! Why would he do such a thing?"

Tilton had already left us, no doubt to set the wheels in motion for Durfree's release. Lowering my voice, I said, "Mr. Farr, did you notice anything odd about Mr. Durfree? Besides him trying to kill you, that is."

Farr started to shake his head, then stopped. "There was nothing earlier. We had lunch together. But then...when I saw him with the gun...he seemed so strange. Not himself. The way he spoke to me about our little debates, as though they were far more serious than they actually are. As if we'd never..." He caught himself.

Poor fellow. "We have reason to believe Mr. Durfree wasn't acting under his own volition," I said gently. "He's not the first person to have experienced something similar. Detective Tilton is putting it down to some kind of hypnosis, although the precise mechanism isn't known."

Farr frowned, but a spark of hope livened his eyes. "Not acting under his own volition? Hypnosis? Then—then he didn't want to kill me?"

"I've interviewed a great many murderers in my career," I assured him. "Mr. Durfree didn't strike me as one. Rather, I'd say he's just as horrified as you are by this turn of events. I encourage you to look upon him as a victim, if you can find it in your heart to do so."

"Of course." A panicked look slowly crossed Farr's face. "But are you saying someone wants to kill me?"

"Er, I don't think so," Whyborne said sheepishly. "The entire episode may have been a diversion for...something else. And either Mr. Durfree is a truly horrible shot, or whoever controlled him wasn't actually seeking your death."

Farr's eyes widened. "Or he couldn't bring himself to harm me, even under some sort of terrible mesmerism?"

"Yes," I said firmly, before Whyborne corrected him. There was no harm in Farr believing it, and much potential good. "It's said no amount of mesmerism can force a man to do what isn't in his nature. I'm certain his affection for you held him back."

Whyborne cast me a puzzled look, but Mr. Farr put a hand to his chest. "Of course. I should have known."

"As Dr. Whyborne said, I don't believe you were truly the target of some unknown enemy," I went on. "Mr. Durfree, however, may be in danger. I wouldn't ordinarily suggest a man under suspicion of attempted murder leave Widdershins, but in this case I feel a short vacation elsewhere would do him a great deal of good. Leave tonight, if at all possible."

"Anthony?" Durfree called tremulously. He stood at the other end of the room, a rather lost expression on his face.

Farr's lips parted. Then he drew himself up and nodded to me. "Thank you, Mr. Flaherty, Dr. Whyborne. Now, if you'll excuse me." Striding toward Durfree, he exclaimed, "Blast it, man, you put a hole in the only know portrait of Theron Blackbyrne! I know you disagreed with my placement of it, but there are better ways to express your opinion."

"I don't understand," Whyborne said, watching them.

"Neither did whoever used mind control on poor Mr. Durfree." I touched his arm. "Come."

Christine and Iskander waited on the sidewalk outside. Or rather, Iskander waited while Christine fumed. "Damn it, Whyborne!" she exclaimed when she spotted us. "I take one afternoon off away from you, and you get into a gun fight with Mr. Durfree?"

"You're just angry you missed it," he replied. "And it isn't as though you bring your rifle into the museum."

"That doesn't mean I don't have a pistol in my purse."

"Later, Christine," Iskander said. "Do you have news, gentlemen?"

I nodded. "Yes. And a great deal to talk about. Would you care to meet us at home? I'm afraid the motor car only has room for two."

"Christine can ride with you," Whyborne said hastily. "Iskander and I will take the trolley."

How kind of him to allow Christine a turn. "Very well then. We'll await you at home."

CHAPTER 32

Griffin

"SO THE WHOLE thing was just a ruse to get to the codex," Christine said. Whyborne and I had prepared a quick dinner of sandwiches, eaten at the kitchen table and followed by coffee. Saul sprawled on the tile floor, his fluffy tail twitching idly.

Iskander shook his head. "And they were willing to destroy poor Mr. Durfree's career, possibly his life, for nothing more than a distraction."

"Considering they've murdered several people already, Mr. Durfree has gotten off lucky." I stirred sugar into my coffee. "Assuming they don't try to silence him as they did Lambert."

"Which is why you wanted him to leave Widdershins." Whyborne rose to his feet and began to clear away our dishes. "What I don't understand is why you told all this to Mr. Farr."

"Quite," Christine said with a frown. "You don't know their rivalry, Griffin, but I suspect Farr told him to remain in Widdershins no matter what, and is even now gleefully contemplating his death."

"I don't think so," I said. "Although I'm certain whoever was behind this believed as you do."

Whyborne turned on the tap at the sink. "When I said I didn't understand, you said the sorcerer responsible didn't either. What did you mean?"

I took a sip of my coffee. "That they're lovers."

There came a crash as Whyborne dropped a cup into the sink. "What?"

"Good gad, man, you can't be serious!" Christine exclaimed. "Their rivalry is legendary! Half the staff have bets as to when they'll kill one another."

"Aside from the need for discretion, some people prefer their affairs more...tumultuous." I leaned back in my chair. "Despite the heat of their disagreements, it's clear to me they care for one another deeply. Perhaps I'm wrong about the physical component of the relationship, but my instinct says otherwise."

"I suppose you have more experience in these matters than the rest of us," Christine said, although she sounded rather doubtful.

Whyborne removed his coat and hung it up neatly on the back of his chair, before unbuttoning his cuffs and rolling up his sleeves. "My entire view of the world has changed," he muttered as he went to the sink and began to scrub at the plates. "Sorcery, entities from the Outside, fish-men in my family tree, I can accept. Mr. Farr and Mr. Durfree as lovers crosses the line."

Iskander cleared his throat. "I believe you are both missing Griffin's point."

"Which is?" Christine asked with an arched brow.

"That whoever is behind all of this is familiar with the inner workings of the museum."

Silence fell; even Whyborne stopped splashing in the sink. "Blast," he said quietly.

"Indeed," I said. "The witch hunter's dagger was suspicious, but hardly proof. But this seems the sort of thing no outsider would know about. One of these Fideles, as Scarrow called them, must be on the museum staff."

"If only I'd been able to break the cipher before the codex was stolen, we might know what they want," he said unhappily. "Or at least what is the nature of this 'Restoration' they desire."

Christine's skin took on a slightly greenish hue. "The codex. I don't suppose it was a coincidence that the graf chose now, of all times, to donate the library."

I sighed. "Probably not. Do we know if anyone suggested the idea to him?"

"I certainly didn't," Christine said. "But it is possible."

"Someone knew the Wisborg Codex was in the graf's donation," Whyborne said. He turned to us as he dried a plate, leaning his hip against the sink. "They wanted it, but I removed it from the library before they could get it. They arranged for the ambush on the island, because they knew enough about my own history to realize I'd recognize the standing stones were the same as the ones on the farm. When they failed to kill us, they set up poor Mr. Durfree as a distraction, so the horrible familiar could climb in the window and make off with the codex while I wasn't there."

"Don't forget the surveyor's map and Mr. Lambert." I sipped my coffee, barely noticing its taste. "Mr. Tubbs said the museum wanted their older maps and such. Our culprit probably tried official channels before resorting to magic. And there were three names on Mr. Lambert's client list: Dr. Norris, Dr. Osborne, and Mr. Quinn."

"Mr. Quinn," Christine said, glancing at Whyborne. "It must be him."

Whyborne nodded slowly. "I thought he seemed annoyed when a junior librarian brought the codex to my attention. No doubt the one-eyed cultist had come to take possession of it. When I took it to my office, Mr. Quinn redirected him there."

"Not to mention, if anyone in the museum belongs to a secretive cult it would be him," Christine said. "The entire library staff is probably in on it."

"Let's not go that far," I cautioned. "But I agree with Whyborne. All the pieces fit."

"So what are we to do about him?" Iskander asked.

I considered carefully. "Open confrontation might not do us a great deal of good. We don't know how many others are in the cult, or where their leader is. Assuming the one-eyed man is their leader, of course, and not Mr. Quinn himself. At any rate, we can't risk them escaping to carry out whatever it is they have planned."

"Should we keep a close eye on Mr. Quinn?" Christine asked. "I'm sure I can spend the day reading journals or something like that in the library."

The thought of Christine trying to spy on Quinn without alerting him made me cringe inwardly. She'd lose patience and threaten him with her pistol inside of an hour. "It's too much of a risk," I said. "Does anyone know where he lives? No? Very well. I'll follow him when he leaves the museum tomorrow." I'd have to put on a disguise of some sort, as I'd seen him far too often to remain inconspicuous otherwise. "Surely the entire cult doesn't work at the library, so he must be meeting them elsewhere. And if nothing else, I might be able to break into his flat and take a look at his possessions."

Whyborne looked worried. "I should accompany you. I'll tell Father he'll have to visit Stanford without me."

I shook my head. "You're too conspicuous. Christine will surely stand out as well."

"Then let me," Iskander offered. "I've seen sailors from distant ports here in Widdershins, and some of them are as dark as myself. With the proper attire..."

I considered. "Actually, it might work. People are inclined to see what they expect. Very well." I drained my coffee. "All of you stay away from Mr. Quinn during the day tomorrow. We don't wish him to realize that we suspect anything. Iskander, change clothes and meet me shortly before working hours end. With any luck, he'll lead us straight to some evidence we can take to the police and have the lot of them arrested for murder."

"Excellent," Christine said, finishing her coffee and rising to her feet. "Then all we must do is survive the wedding, and everything can go back to normal."

CHAPTER 33

Griffin

"I DON'T LIKE this," Whyborne said as he shut and locked the door behind Christine and Iskander. "What if you run afoul of the cultists tomorrow? What if Mr. Quinn realizes you're following him and lures you into a trap? What if—"

"I'll be exceedingly careful, my dear." I slid my arms around him from behind. "Believe me, I've no desire to get Iskander killed just before his wedding."

"I know. But I can't help worry about you."

I let go of him. "Here. I've something to take your mind off of things."

He arched a brow. "Do you, now?"

"Not that," I said. "Well, not to begin with." I led the way into the parlor and unlocked the cabinet. The facets of the Lapidem caught the light, and for a moment distant voices whispered in my mind.

The four wands we'd taken from the island lay within as well, their surfaces still gleaming with a knot work of enchantment. "I don't care for the thought of these simply lying about, waiting for someone else to come along and use them. I thought we might break the spells."

"Not a bad suggestion," Whyborne agreed slowly. "Although, you do recall the, ah, effect the curse breaking spell has on me?"

The memory brought a rush of blood to my cock. "I do indeed. It will be safe to touch you, won't it?"

"It should, so long as I don't draw from the maelstrom while we're in contact." He indicated the desk. "Place the first one here, if you're certain, and we'll begin."

I did so. "Sit down, and I'll guide your hands," I said.

He sat, and I leaned over him. I'd grown used to my shadowsight, and it seemed almost strange to me that he couldn't perceive the latticework of magic bound to the wand. His hands hovered over the smooth wood, and I placed my fingertips on their backs, guiding his touch. "Here," I breathed into his ear and felt him shiver against me. "And here."

His hands tensed beneath my fingers, and the scars on the right flashed with unnatural light. He pressed his own fingers down, murmuring something beneath his breath. There came a spark like a sudden discharge of electricity, leaping from the wand to him. His breath caught sharply.

"Good," I whispered into his ear. "The spell's beginning to untangle and come apart. Now here."

With each repetition, his breathing became slightly more ragged. His skin grew warm. Soon, the wand was nothing more than an ornately carved length of wood set with crystal.

When I went to retrieve the next wand, I noted a flush staining Whyborne's cheeks. His eyes were dark with arousal, and a delicious shiver went through me as he followed my every move. "Ready for more?" I murmured, laying the wand on the desk.

"Are you?"

"Always."

We repeated our actions for all of the wands. A little moan escaped him each time a spell unwound, feeding its stored energy into him. His hands trembled with leashed desire beneath my fingers, and my prick ached in response.

"There," I said, when the last one was finished. I stepped back, giving him space if he wished it.

He rose to his feet; the chair fell back, unnoticed. He burned in my shadowsight, his eyes blue flame and his scars a lacework of fire. His breath came in short, heavy gasps, lips parted, and the rigid outline of his cock pressed against his trousers. His gaze pinned me, hot and commanding, and I could only obey.

I went to my knees, reaching for his trousers. He was ahead of me, long fingers flying over the buttons. He freed himself with one hand; the other seized the back of my head, fingers curling in my hair tightly. Ordinarily I would have taken my time, admiring and teasing his length, but tonight I simply opened my mouth and let him push in.

His grip tightened on my hair, riding the line between pleasure and pain. The head of his prick hit the back of my throat, and I swallowed convulsively. He tasted of salt and skin, smelled of the ocean and musk. I fumbled at the buttons of my own trousers, desperate to relieve the ache. He gave my head a short shake.

"No," he growled. "Not yet. I'm not done with you by half."

His words set a fire in me, and I moaned desperately around the cock filling my mouth. I let my hands fall, gripping my ankles to hold back the urge to stroke myself. I kept my gaze on his face, his lips parted, eyes black with desire and blazing with power. If I could have spoken, I would have begged him to use me more, to do anything he wanted with me, because I was his.

But he knew that already, of course.

He pulled free, then dropped to his knees to kiss me, his mouth hard against my bruised lips. I returned his kiss with equal ferocity. Then he drew back, panting softly. "Yes?" he whispered.

I grinned. "God, Ival, *yes.*"

He laughed softly, a hungry grin curving his own mouth. The hand still in my hair tightened, tugging my head back. His tongue caressed the base of my throat—then he bit me, hard. I gasped and bucked against him, desperate to grind against a thigh or his stomach or anything. His free arm snaked around me, gripping my ass and hauling me close, while he sucked on the patch of skin on my neck.

"St-stop," I gasped. "Or you'll make me come."

He drew back slightly and ran his tongue up my throat, across the vulnerable cartilage and sinew. "You aren't coming until I decide you do. Now get undressed."

My cufflinks went spinning off across the room, so great was my haste to strip. I expected Whyborne to do the same. Instead, he went to the desk and yanked open one of the drawers. He took out the small jar of petroleum jelly I kept inside—and my handcuffs.

Oh. So this was how things were going to go.

"On your knees," he ordered. "Hands around the leg of the desk."

I hastened to obey. He pushed my shoulders down, leaving my ass in the air while the cuffs clicked into place, chaining me to the desk. I tugged, more for show than anything else, but there was no escape.

Cloth rustled behind me, and I twisted about to watch him fling aside his clothes into a messy heap. He looked utterly wild, eyes blazing, his prick at full attention. I wanted him as much as I'd ever wanted anything in my life.

He gripped my hips, pulling them higher. I'd have bruises tomorrow where his fingers bit into my thighs, but I didn't care.

Teeth nipped at one buttock, and I let out a cry of surprise, the handcuffs rattling as I jerked. He repeated the action on the other side, then licked my crease from balls to spine. I let my head droop, soaking it in, fluid dripping from my cock onto the rug. "Ival, please."

He took me, hard and fast. I cried out, spine bowing, the handcuffs jerking tight. God, it felt good, his cock plunging into me, again and again. Then he bent over and bit me savagely on the back of the neck.

I went wild, bucking against him, crying out incoherently. It was too much, too good, and my whole body begged for release. He ignored my pleas, peppering my shoulders and neck with stinging bites, fucking me mercilessly.

Magic crackled in the air. I opened my eyes to see frost race across the floor and coat the windows. The breeze through the window strengthened, sending the curtains billowing.

His hand wrapped around my aching cock. I came almost instantly, my lungs seizing up with the force of it. He wrung my orgasm from me, milking every spurt, until pleasure kissed the borderland of pain.

Then he gasped and stilled, shuddering as his climax took him. I closed my eyes and pressed back against him, as tightly as I could.

Silence claimed the little room, except for our breathing. My muscles felt limp, my limbs boneless, and I wanted to melt into the floor. After a long moment, Ival's weight lifted from my back, and his hands trailed along my spine.

"Griffin?" he asked tentatively. "Are you all right?"

I grinned. "More than all right."

"Let me find the keys."

Within seconds, he'd freed me. I sat back, stretching to work out the kinks. Whyborne slid his arms around me, and I sagged into them gladly. "I love you, Ival," I murmured.

His lips pressed against my forehead. "I love you too, my darling."

Tomorrow, I'd be sore: my knees burned from friction against the rug, my wrists bruised from the handcuffs and my throat from his bites. And I'd savor every moment, because it would remind me of this.

"Take me to bed," I said. "I want you to hold me."

His hands stroked my face tenderly, and I opened eyes I hadn't realized I'd closed. "Of course," he said, and kissed me again.

CHAPTER 34

Whyborne

I WOKE TO the sense of being watched.

Griffin slept beside me, his breathing soft and even. Saul curled at our feet like a hot, fluffy cushion. The window stood open, letting in the night breeze.

A dark shadow peered in at us.

"Persephone!" I exclaimed. "What have I told you about doing this?"

Griffin jerked awake. "What? Persephone?"

"We must talk," she said, slipping inside.

"Indeed we must!" I clutched the blanket about my neck. "About your abominable manners. If you need to talk to us, go to the back door and knock."

"This was much easier," she said with sublime indifference to my concern.

"Persephone obviously came for a reason," Griffin said. "But please, wait for us in the study."

We dressed in haste and emerged to find Persephone perched on the edge of the couch. Her tentacle hair curled and twisted in agitation, and she tapped her claws on her knee. "All right," I said, "what was worth crawling in our window at—dear lord, three in the morning—for?"

Her golden jewelry sparkled in the electric light. "Two more bodies have been found in the water. Like the first."

"Damn it," Griffin said, sinking into his chair. He'd not taken the time to comb his hair, and his curls were wildly disordered from both the pillow and our earlier activities.

"There is more." She glanced up at me, then back to Griffin. "The corpses were found near a pair of small reefs. And now the water around both is...humming."

"Humming?" I asked in surprise.

"Vibrating." She rubbed her hands against her legs. "I touched it and felt it tingling, heard the water trembling."

An ugly thought developed at her words. "These reefs—do the ketoi practice any sort of rituals around them?"

"You think they're the underwater equivalent of the standing stones?" Griffin guessed.

I nodded. Persephone did as well. "At times, yes. When we wish to speak with the god."

None of this boded any good. Before I said as much, there came a sudden, frantic pounding on the front door.

"Dr. Whyborne?" shouted a voice that sounded like Miss Parkhurst's. "Dr. Whyborne, if you're there, please answer!"

Griffin and I exchanged shocked looks. Why Miss Parkhurst, of all people, should be banging on our door this hour was beyond me. Was she in some sort of trouble? "I'll get the door," I said. "Persephone, stay here."

The only thing more surprising than Miss Parkhurst's presence was her appearance when I opened the door. Ordinarily, her dress was impeccable—hair styled neatly according to what I assumed to be the latest fashion, the lines of her shirtwaists and skirts crisp.

Not tonight. Her hair looked to have been pinned with the utmost haste. Strands fell loose into her face and across her shoulders. Her clothing was rumpled, and she wore a different style of shoe on each foot.

"Miss Parkhurst?" I asked. "What are you doing here?"

To my horror, she burst into tears and flung herself at me. I caught her awkwardly. "It's after me, Dr. Whyborne," she sobbed into my shoulder. "That thing in your office—I heard a noise in my walls earlier—I thought it was just a rat—and then I woke up and it was there, on my bed, staring at me."

"Good lord!" I pulled her inside hastily and shut the door. "Are you hurt?"

She shook her head. "N-no. I screamed and hit it. Dr. Putnam taught some of us a bit of self-defense, after she first came to the museum, and I guess I still remembered what to do." She sniffled. "I knocked it across the room, but it came back at me. I grabbed my umbrella and struck it a few times. It darted into a hole, so I just snatched up whatever clothes came to hand and ran." She drew back, wiping at her face. "I didn't know where else to go."

"You did the right thing," Griffin said from the stairs.

"I'm sorry to have waked you, Mr. Flaherty," Miss Parkhurst said with a sniffle. "Please, don't be angry with Dr. Whyborne on my account."

"Not at all." He took her elbow and started to guide her into the parlor. At the last moment, he caught himself and steered her to the kitchen instead. "Let me put the kettle on, and—"

The lights flickered and died.

We stood in a darkness that seemed all the deeper for its suddenness. Miss Parkhurst let out a frightened gasp.

"Is it windy outside?" Griffin asked.

"N-no," she replied.

"There are other reasons the electricity might go out," I said, although I felt my pulse quicken at the base of my throat.

"Including something chewing through the wires," Griffin agreed.

The stairs creaked beneath batrachian feet. Although I would have preferred to keep Persephone hidden, I feared we'd need her assistance. "Miss Parkhurst, do you recall my sister from the night of the Hallowe'en tours?" I asked.

"I...she cut off the head of...and the two of you left together..." Her words trailed off awkwardly. "I didn't think we were supposed to talk about it."

"Well, she's here now, visiting with us, so I don't want you to be frightened by her," I said. "Isn't that right, Persephone?"

"Something is hunting the land woman?" Persephone asked.

"The same ones who performed some ritual above your reef tonight," Griffin said grimly. "Whyborne, Persephone, can one of you conjure a light?"

"Er, where is the lantern now?" Since getting electric lights, I hadn't bothered to keep track of such things. "If I try to set fire to a wick without knowing where it is, precisely, whatever is *actually* there will end up aflame. Like your case notes. Or the curtains."

"Burning the house down seems a bit of an extreme solution," Griffin agreed. "The two of you stay here with Miss Parkhurst. I'll find a lantern and matches in the parlor."

"Did the rat creature follow me?" Miss Parkhurst squeaked.

"Hopefully not," I said. Griffin bumped into something in the dark, the sound followed by a curse and the chime of metal as he tripped over the discarded handcuffs. Heat suffused my face and made me momentarily grateful for the shadows.

There came a furtive, rustling sound from near the baseboards. As if something moved inside the wall.

"Griffin," I called, "please hurry with the lantern."

Miss Parkhurst latched onto my arm. I drew her back, away from the wall. My ears strained, striving to track its movements as it climbed higher.

It was above us.

I shoved Miss Parkhurst in Persephone's direction, even as the plaster ceiling crumbled. Choking dust filled my lungs, and a heavy weight landed on my shoulders. A rancid, rotting smell of sewer gas and grave dirt swept over me, and sharp claws tore at my neck.

"Persephone!" I shouted. "Take her upstairs and keep her safe! There are candles on the mantle—light them!"

I scrabbled wildly, trying to rip the rat-thing from my back, but I couldn't quite reach it between my shoulders. "Griffin!" It tried to bite, but the collar of my suit coat foiled its teeth. Even so, I felt the scrape of ivory along my skin.

Griffin ran out into the hall, still without a light. His shadowsight must have revealed the creature, because he seized it unerringly by the tail in an attempt to pull it off me.

It snapped at his hand, and he flinched away. But its grip on me had been loosened, ever so slightly.

I hurled myself back, seeking to crush the thing between my body and the wall. It let out a squeal that left my ears ringing and fell to the floor with a thump. There was a scrabble of claws on tile as it darted into the kitchen.

Griffin chased after it. There came a crash as he blundered into a chair in the dark. "It went behind the stove," he called. "Damn it—there must be a hole! I hear it in the wall."

I held my breath, listening for its movements. There came the rustling, but not furtive anymore. It drew nearer and nearer to me... then faded.

It was going up again. To the second story.

Miss Parkhurst screamed.

CHAPTER 35

Whyborne

THERE WAS NO time for finesse. I ran up the stairs, tripping over the risers in my haste. Above me, Persephone called out the true name of fire.

The candles on the mantel blazed to life. Miss Parkhurst huddled on the floor against the couch. The rat-thing perched on the back of a chair, its scabrous tail lashing. Its human-like face twisted into a leer, revealing the awful, deadly teeth.

Persephone snarled at it, putting herself between it and Miss Parkhurst. A mouth full of shark's teeth, surrounded by stinging tentacles, should have given anything pause. But the rat creature only let out a chittering cry that sounded horribly like a laugh, before it leapt at her.

Something large and orange intercepted it.

They crashed to the floor, the rat-thing screaming horribly. But Saul's teeth had sunk deep into the back of its neck, and his grip remained strong. He shook the thing hard, his powerful hind legs kicking it at the same time. There came a loud crack as something vital broke in its spine, and it went limp.

I ran to Saul and scooped him up, before he decided to eat the wretched thing. It lay still at my feet, glassy-eyed and bloody. "Good Saul," I crooned, stroking his head. His purr rumbled loud enough to rattle my bones.

Persephone straightened, looking slightly disappointed, as though she'd wanted to be the one to kill it. Then she turned to Miss Parkhurst, as Griffin clattered up the stairs. "Are you hurt?"

Miss Parkhurst gazed up at her, lips parted and a slightly stunned expression on her face. "No. I-I'm fine." She glanced at me, then back to Persephone. "Are you really Dr. Whyborne's sister?"

"We're twins," Persephone said.

"Can't you see the resemblance?" Griffin asked. Despite his light words, the expression he turned on Miss Parkhurst was one of concern.

She laughed, a bit hysterically. "Oh, of course. I can barely tell them apart."

Persephone held out her hand. I expected Miss Parkhurst to flinch back from the claws, but she took it without hesitation, and let Persephone haul her to her feet.

"Come," Griffin said, and put a hand to Miss Parkhurst's shoulder. "You've had a dreadful shock. Let's go down to the kitchen, and I'll make us some tea."

"And waffles?" Persephone asked hopefully.

"No waffles," I said, putting Saul down well away from his erstwhile prey. Someone needed to remove the thing from the house, and it seemed that duty fell to me. "It's the middle of the night, for heaven's sake."

"Fine," Persephone said, a bit sullenly. "I like waffles, though. Do you?" she asked Miss Parkhurst.

"Oh, yes." Miss Parkhurst gave her a shaky smile. "They're one of my favorite foods, actually."

I used my handkerchief to pick up the dead rat creature by its tail. Its jaw gaped open, displaying its chisel teeth. While everyone else went into the kitchen, I carried the thing into the backyard, holding it arm's length the entire time. Saul paced along behind me, apparently disgruntled that I'd made off with his kill.

I meant to put it in the small shed beside the garden. But I'd gotten only a few steps from the house when greenish slime began to drip from it, and the tail between my fingers turned horribly spongy. I released it and took a wary step back, just in case.

The whole process took only seconds. Hair and flesh dissolved into ooze, shucking off the bones. Then the bones followed suit. Within moments, nothing was left but a dark stain on the ground, and even that seemed to evaporate as I watched.

Surely that confirmed the thing was indeed from the Outside. I'd keep the information to myself for the moment, to avoid distressing

Miss Parkhurst any further.

Although she'd held up remarkably well so far. She'd seen Persephone at the Hallowe'en gathering nearly two years ago, but at a distance. The ketoi were far more disconcerting close up, with their writhing hair and serrated smiles. Not to mention their rather immodest manner of dress. Even without the hideous rat-creature, she might reasonably have been expected to flee screaming, rather than sit down to tea with us.

I needed to put her in for a raise.

"So Dr. Whyborne and Miss Whyborne," she was saying as I returned to the kitchen, "are both part human and part..."

"Ketoi," Griffin supplied. He removed the tea kettle from the stove and poured the water into four cups.

"I'm afraid so," I said. Persephone and Miss Parkhurst sat across from one another, so I took a chair beside Persephone.

"I see." Miss Parkhurst took a deep breath, then straightened her shoulders. "Thank you—all of you—for saving my life."

"I'm only sorry it was in danger in the first place," I said. "If I'd thought for a moment the creature would come after you for having seen it, I would have warned you earlier." Instead, I'd assumed Mr. Durfree to be the one it would attack. And perhaps it would have, had he not left town.

Instead, it had sought her out. If she'd hadn't waked in time, would it have chewed its way through her chest, as it had done Mr. Lambert? God, what an awful thought. At least the thing was dead now.

"I know, Dr. Whyborne," Miss Parkhurst said. "You've always been very kind to me." She paused. "Do I want to know what that thing was?"

"Probably not," I said, taking a sip of my tea. It was still too hot, and burned my tongue.

"That's up to you," Griffin replied, giving me a stern look. "But four in the morning may not be the best time to discuss it."

"Oh, yes, I'm sorry." Miss Parkhurst pinked. "With all the excitement, I quite forgot the hour."

"I must leave soon," Persephone said. "I have to return to the ocean before too many humans are abroad."

"Of course." The blush deepened over Miss Parkhurst's skin. "Your hair is so pretty. May I touch it?"

Persephone looked unaccountably pleased. "Yes. Your hair is pretty, too," she added.

I didn't know what had brought about this sudden attack of manners in my sister, but I didn't wish to question it. After we finished our tea, Griffin said, "We'll walk you home, Miss Parkhurst."

"I will," Persephone said unexpectedly. "I must leave as it is. So long as we stay to the shadows, no one will see me."

"Oh. Thank you," Miss Parkhurst replied.

"Are you certain?" I asked, rising to my feet.

"Oh yes—I'm sure no one would dare attack me with such a fierce guardian." As soon as the words were out of her mouth, she blushed again, although why I couldn't possibly imagine.

We made our way to the door to see them out. "Do you come on land often?" Miss Parkhurst asked as they started down the walk.

"Each month," Persephone replied. "And I'm helping Christine decorate for her wedding."

"You are? So am I!" Miss Parkhurst's excited tones faded as they disappeared down the street.

I shut the door and looked at the clock. "No sense in going to bed," I said. "I'd have to rise in an hour anyway, to catch the cursed train."

Griffin winced sympathetically. "Perhaps you can get some sleep on the train before you have to see your brother."

"Ah, yes, Stanford." I made for the stairs. "And to think, on an ordinary day, battling an evil rat creature would be the worst thing I'd have to face."

CHAPTER 36

Whyborne

IT BEGAN TO rain when we reached the New York state line, and continued all the way to the private asylum where my brother now resided.

I napped fitfully. Father never traveled anywhere except in his private car, which had every imaginable amenity, including a porter to tend only to our needs. After a light lunch, I had the man prepare the sleeper, curled up, and tried to ignore the rocking motion of the train. It invaded my dreams, however, and the whistle became a scream, waking me from nightmares.

Father and I spoke little, either on the train or in the coach that took us from the station to the asylum. The place bore no resemblance to a public institution such as Stormhaven. Rather, it might easily have passed as a large private residence. True, there were more than the usual number of men watching the high brick wall surrounding the grounds, but otherwise it formed the very picture of gentility. Rain dripped from the oaks dotting the wide lawns, and I imagined that on fair days, the patients might pass many a pleasant hour in their shade.

We disembarked beneath the portico. The air smelled of green grass and wet earth, so very different from the omnipresent odor of fish clinging to Widdershins. Did Stanford miss it? We weren't meant to leave the city for long; even Guinevere had eventually returned.

Or perhaps Widdershins sometimes released what it collected. But I doubted it. The nature of a vortex was to draw things in, after all.

A smiling man with a thick silver beard greeted us on the steps. "Mr. Whyborne, a pleasure as always," he said heartily. "And this must be the younger Mr. Whyborne."

"Dr. Whyborne," I replied stiffly as we shook hands.

"Percival, this is Dr. Hayes," Father said.

"I'm so glad you could come," Dr. Hayes said. "Your visit will be instrumental in your brother's treatment, I'm certain of it."

"Er, that's...that's good," I said.

"How is Stanford today, doctor?" Father asked as we went inside.

"Oh, very well, very well indeed." The doctor glanced over his shoulder at me. "He's abandoned a great many of his delusions since coming here. His irrational beliefs about you in particular, Dr. Whyborne."

I expected him to lead us to some sort of ward, as when Griffin and I had visited Stormhaven. Instead, he ushered us into a finely appointed room near the entrance, which looked more like the parlor in some grand mansion than something in an asylum for lunatics. "Would you care for some refreshment, gentlemen? Coffee? Brandies?"

I sat gingerly on a velvet-covered chair. "Coffee, if you please," I said.

"A brandy for me," Father replied.

"I'll let my man know. Just give me a moment, and I'll return with Mr. Whyborne."

The doctor bustled off, leaving us temporarily alone. As soon as he was gone, I leaned over to Father. "You do remember Stanford isn't actually delusional, don't you?" I demanded in a low voice.

Father shifted his weight slightly. "Of course I do."

"Then what is all this talk of treatment and progress?" I clutched the arm of his chair. "Stanford is here because he tried to murder a great many people, including us! He killed Guinevere!"

"I know that, Percival," Father snapped. "The doctor says whatever he thinks will make me happy."

"And what if he decides Stanford is well enough to be released? What then? You can't—"

The door opened and Stanford entered.

I hadn't seen my brother in nearly two years. At the time, he'd been thickening around the waist, following an athletic youth. He'd lost the weight, but regained no muscle, giving him a surprisingly gaunt appearance. Gray showed at his temples, even though he was only four years my elder.

"Percival," he said, holding out his hand to me. "I'm so glad to see you."

It was everything I could do not to strike his hand aside. I tried to keep the shake as brief as possible, but he latched onto my hand with both of his. "Thank you for coming," he said earnestly, his fingers tightening on mine. "You can't know how much this means to me."

I felt my face settling into those cold lines Griffin had spoken of before, but I couldn't help it. Stanford had tormented me as a child, but his behavior then paled before the fact he'd murdered our sister. He'd shot Griffin. He would have unleashed a horde of ketoi upon the land, had already used them to sink ships and destroy anyone who stood against him, killing dozens of innocent sailors in the process.

I hated him with every fiber of my being.

I wrenched my hand free, unable to bear his touch a second longer. "I'm sure I don't," I said as I took my seat again.

Stanford and Father greeted each other; at least Father retained his own reserve in the face of Stanford's effusive warmth. A servant brought me coffee, and brandies for Father and Stanford, while the doctor stood beaming in the doorway.

I wanted to snatch the brandy from Stanford's hand and throw it in his face. I couldn't stop comparing this sumptuous prison to Stormhaven's tiny cells. To the horrors Griffin had suffered during his own confinement in Illinois.

No electrical probes here. No restraints. No attendants who abused the bodies of their patients, because who would believe the word of a madman against theirs?

I'd never stooped so low as to fantasize about Stanford suffering as Griffin had, but seeing this, I wanted to scream at Father for keeping him out of prison.

"I'll leave you here to speak privately," Dr. Hayes said, once we were settled. "Just ring the bell when you're ready."

He departed and closed the door behind him. I folded my hands in my lap and tried to conceal the shaking of my fingers. "What is the point of this charade?" I asked.

Stanford's eyes widened. "No charade, brother. I only wanted to see you, that I might apologize face-to-face."

"You, apologize?" I let out a bark of laughter, but there was no humor in it. "Since when have you ever apologized for anything?"

He gave me a sad look. "Since I had time to reflect on things. On what I've done." Stanford bowed his head and stared contemplatively at his brandy. "Being here, away from everything...well, I was angry at first. I felt you'd stolen my destiny from me. The doctors don't realize I'm not mad, but talking with them still helped me see I had it all wrong."

I sat back in my chair, crossing my legs and folding my arms over my chest. "Oh really?"

"Yes. I was jealous, when we were children, you know. You were the only one of us Mother spent any time with." His shoulders slumped. "I tried to make up for the lack by impressing Father, but as much as he did for me, it wasn't the same."

The devil? "You're blaming *Mother* for your abominable behavior?"

"Of course not!" He gave me a pleading look that I didn't believe for one second. "She was sick, and so were you. I understand that now. But as a child, I only knew my little brother seemed to have stolen away all of Mother's affection."

I let my arms fall, fists clenching. "How dare you speak this nonsense to me?"

"Percival, let your brother have his say," Father cut in.

"He had his say when he murdered Guinevere!" I rose to my feet. "He had his say in the foyer of the museum! I don't know why I agreed to come here, but I refuse to participate in this—this farce any longer."

"Brother, please." Stanford rose as well, his hands out in supplication. "I don't ask you to excuse my actions. I'm only trying to explain why I wanted to see you. I've come to understand that I was wrong, horribly wrong. Nothing will ever make up for Guinevere's death, or for the rest of it. I don't expect to ever see the world outside these walls again, and I'm at peace with that. I only want to ask your forgiveness."

"Well, you don't have it," I shot back. "You're a bully and a murderer, and I owe you nothing. Least of all forgiveness."

Infuriatingly, Stanford retained his calm. "I understand you're angry. But you held back, when you might have killed me and called it self-defense. I can only conclude that, deep down, you still have hope for our relationship."

Maybe I'd been too hasty, when I said Stanford wasn't mad. Perhaps his confinement had been harsher than I realized, and had driven him insane, because how else could he believe this nonsense?

"Or perhaps I didn't want to burden our parents with the death of another child." I turned to Father. "Waste your time here if you like. I'll await you in the coach."

Stanford seized my arm as I stepped toward the door. Memories arose, of all the cruelties he'd inflicted on me when we were youths, and I tore free. "Touch me again, and I'll set you on fire."

He held his hands up. "I'm sorry, Percival. I didn't mean to upset you. I only wanted you to know that I've changed." An odd smile crept over his face. "And I have faith that, given time, you'll change as well."

"Don't count on it," I said, and slammed the door behind me.

CHAPTER 37

Griffin

ISKANDER JOINED ME across the street from the Ladysmith shortly before closing time. We'd both dressed as laborers, and I carried a leather tool satchel. I leaned up against the side of a building, pretending to scan a paper I'd purchased from the newsstand.

I'd used the same ruse years before, wishing to observe the reclusive Dr. Whyborne before handing over a critical piece of evidence to him. He'd arrived on foot from the omnibus stop nearby, taller than anyone else in the crowd despite his tendency to stoop. When he paused to let a gaggle of ladies past, I got a good look at his profile. Even though I wouldn't have called him particularly handsome, something about the sight sharpened my interest from strictly professional to personal.

Odd, how my whole life had changed in that instant without my knowing it. There should have been fanfare, or a beam of light from the heavens. Something to tell me nothing would ever be the same again.

Iskander slouched against the wall beside me, and I gave him part of the paper. While Iskander and I stalked Mr. Quinn, Christine would await us at Whyborne House, ostensibly making the final decisions and arrangements for the wedding. Knowing Christine, she'd spend the time pacing the floor instead. Whyborne would join us there, when he returned from his trip to New York.

"Nervous about the wedding yet?" I asked to pass the time.

Iskander pretended to study the personal ads. "Nervous isn't precisely the word I'd use. Terrified, perhaps?"

I winced. "I'm sorry to hear that."

"Christine is just so bloody minded." The paper crinkled beneath his bronze hands. "Which, obviously, I knew before, but her choice of flowers and assistants...God only knows what Persephone will bring. This was supposed to be normal, supposed to impress society and keep them from sneering at her for marrying a-a half-breed. Instead I'll be lucky if Christine doesn't walk down the aisle wearing a squid on her head!"

"That is an unfortunate possibility," I agreed. "Although at least they'll be to busy staring at her to notice your skin."

He laughed. "I suppose you have a point. Still, they're bound to notice I'm half-Egyptian at some point."

"Have you tried discussing the matter with her?"

"Of course." He sighed. "You know Christine. She didn't wish to hear it, and we ended quarreling."

"I'm sorry. Perhaps it would be best to concentrate on your happy marriage after the wedding, rather than the ceremony itself," I suggested.

"I suppose you're right. At least I had the foresight to select the menu. Otherwise, I fear we'd find ourselves dining on roasted camel." He turned the page of the paper he wasn't actually reading. "Forgive me, Griffin. This must sound like a bunch of damnable whining to you, I'm sure."

"Not at all."

"That's kind of you to say. But at least we *can* wed. In the eyes of wider society, that is—I know you consider yourself wed. And I do, too," he hastened to add. "Consider you married, I mean."

I laughed. "I thought your father was a diplomat?"

"Apparently I failed to learn from his example," Iskander said with a wince. "Did I ever tell you what Christine said to me about you? After we, well, confessed our affection to one another, she immediately informed me that if I so much as looked askance at you and Whyborne, she'd never speak to me again either personally or professionally."

It drew a grin from me. "I imagined as much. Hold your paper a bit higher—I don't think anyone will take a closer look, but we are right outside of the museum."

He adjusted the paper higher and ducked his head lower, so the brim of his cap shadowed his features. "I owe Whyborne a bottle of good scotch—without his intervention, I fear Christine wouldn't even have picked out flowers yet. Actually, she seems convinced that his sudden interest in our wedding is because he wished something more elaborate for himself."

"Whyborne?" I snorted. "You know he hates anything that involves more than one or two other people." I would have preferred a church wedding, to have stood with him in front of the world and declared my promise to spend the rest of my life at his side for all to hear. But even if I couldn't do that, I believed the vows we'd spoken were as sacred in the eyes of God as any others.

"Was it strange for you?" Iskander asked. "Christine and Whyborne's affection for each other, I mean. I've grown used to it, but at first it was odd, to have the woman I love so devoted to a man not related to her by blood."

"A bit," I allowed. "Mainly frustrating, as she always takes his side in an argument." I glanced up at the museum entrance. The crowd streaming out of the doors had thickened, and I spotted employees among them now. "I was very grateful when you joined us. Two against one were frightful odds."

Iskander laughed. "I shall endeavor to even them out when the situation calls for it, then."

Mr. Quinn's somber figure appeared amidst the departing employees. "Look. There he is."

We folded our papers once he was past, and set ourselves to following him at a distance. Quinn hastened through the streets, sliding through gaps in the crowded sidewalks like an eel. I cursed silently—we could only hurry so fast ourselves without drawing unwarranted attention. I'd foregone shaving that morning to help alter my appearance, but too close a look and he'd surely recognize one or both of us. I didn't want to give him any reason to take that closer look.

He boarded one of the electric trolleys, which gave us an excuse to hurry to catch it. We slipped onto the rear and paid the conductor. Quinn, near the front of the trolley, never glanced back.

The trolley left behind the banks and offices that surrounded the museum, and reached a more residential neighborhood. Mr. Quinn disembarked, and we followed. He walked quickly without looking around, as the streets gradually grew narrower, the houses older. The paving began to vary wildly, changing from brick to stone slabs to cobblestones. The inhabitants moved quickly, almost furtively, and none of them exchanged greetings.

At last Mr. Quinn came to an enormous colonial heap that looked to have been converted to a boarding house. Yew trees bordered the walk, and mighty oaks leaned close together, as if attempting to conceal the house from prying eyes.

"Do you imagine this is where he lives?" Iskander murmured. "Or is he meeting someone here?"

"He went inside without a knock, so I would guess he rents a room," I replied. "Perhaps we can discern which belongs to him."

I removed a pair of binoculars from my bag and cast about for a vantage point to discreetly survey the house. Or as much of it as I could make out past the trees.

Most of the windows were open to let in the evening breezes. The rooms at the front of the house appeared to be empty at the moment, so I went around the back while Iskander kept watch on the door. An alley let onto the back yard, which sported an assortment of plants I didn't recognize. Certainly there seemed to be no carrots, beans, or tomatoes, let alone any of the common herbs.

A small garden shed offered some concealment, as did the tall oaks. Through my binoculars, I spotted a woman who must be the landlady airing out a room, and a cook in the downstairs kitchen. On the second floor, I finally glimpsed Mr. Quinn's dark form, moving about on the other side of the gauzy curtains.

I held my breath as I watched him. He was in the process of fastening his tie, having changed into yet another severe suit. He paused at a washstand to apply oil to his hair, then, apparently satisfied with his appearance, left the room.

I hurried around to the front, just in time to glimpse him making his way back up the street. I slouched and stuffed my hands in my pockets, but he didn't so much as look my way.

Iskander rejoined me, and we followed him back through the neighborhood, until reaching River Street. I'd hoped Quinn would lead us to other cult members, but instead his night took a turn for the decidedly ordinary. He ate dinner at a modest restaurant, briefly visited the department store, and finally disappeared into the theater to attend a performance of *The Tempest*.

"Could we be wrong?" Iskander asked as we watched Quinn vanish inside.

"Possibly," I said. "At least it's dark now, which means I might have a chance at sneaking into his room in the boarding house. I think one of the oaks was close enough to climb."

Iskander offered me a dubious look. "Do you think it safe? Not that I question your courage, old chap, but the place did seem rather, well, sinister."

I had the same misgivings, to be honest. "I'll try not to get caught," I said, clapping him on the arm. "You stay here and keep an eye on the theater. If he leaves, follow him. Otherwise, I'll return as soon as possible." I paused. "And if I don't return within the hour, fetch Christine and stage a rescue."

When I arrived back at the boarding house, the place seemed quiet from the outside, save for the sound of someone playing a viol in one of the garret rooms. Still, I took my time, observing from both the front and the back. Even if the inhabitants reacted with nothing stronger than indignation to my prying, I couldn't afford to let Quinn think anyone suspected him of wrongdoing.

The street had grown quiet, and no one seemed inclined to enter or leave the house. I slipped into the dark backyard. Some of the flowers in the garden proved to be night-blooming plants, and their sickly sweet scent twined about me as I made my way through the overlong grass. The light coming from inside provided just enough illumination to allow me to climb the tree nearest Mr. Quinn's room. The oak's bark was rough beneath my fingers, and its leaves seemed to caress my face. The sturdy branch I crawled out onto was as thick as many lesser trees, and didn't groan at all beneath my weight.

It was a bit of a stretch to reach the open window, but a copper downspout offered assistance, and soon I stood inside. The room was dark, both to normal vision and shadowsight. I held myself very still, listening for any indication my entrance had been noticed. The viol wailed from somewhere above, the music like nothing I'd ever heard before, alternately soothing and wild. Did it annoy Mr. Quinn to have such an upstairs neighbor, or did he enjoy the unorthodox tunes?

When I was certain no one was on their way to investigate my entrance, I groped carefully forward. The floor creaked beneath my weight as the oak had not, and I froze. There came no alarm, however; no doubt in a house this old, creaks and groans were the norm rather than not.

My searching hands found a bed and the back of a chair, then the door. Removing my coat, I laid it along the base of the door, to keep any light from showing through the gap. Then I returned to the window and pulled the shutters closed. Only after they were secure did I switch on the lamp.

The small room offered only a bed, curtain-top desk, chair, washstand, and wardrobe. Why did Quinn choose such dreary surroundings? His salary at the museum must surely be commensurate for a man with a wife and children to support; more than enough for a bachelor to purchase a small house or nice apartment. Even Whyborne had lived in a modern apartment when we first met, complete with its own kitchen and water closet.

Then again, as his ignorance of our neighbors had proved,

Whyborne hated interacting with others. Renting an apartment meant for a family made a certain amount of sense when it came to a man of his temperament. Perhaps Mr. Quinn was simply more sociable.

I did a hasty search of the wardrobe, finding nothing inside but Mr. Quinn's funereal suits, an adequate supply of collars and cuffs, and a row of identical shoes. The suit labels confirmed they had all been purchased at Dryden and Sons; apparently, Quinn was a man of habit. There was nothing concealed beneath the bed, so I turned my attention to the curtain-top desk. Locked.

Fortunately, I was an old hand at picking locks from my Pinkerton days, and soon had it open. I slid the top up as quietly as I was able. The cubbyholes were stuffed with papers, and more papers lay scattered across the surface of the desk, including a train schedule. Quinn had circled a midmorning departure for Boston. Beside it was written tomorrow's date.

Was Mr. Quinn leaving town? And what business did he have in Boston?

It might have nothing to do with the cult. It could be perfectly legitimate business for the museum, even.

I picked up the train schedule. Beneath it lay a bit of scratch paper with a sum on it. In the corner, almost as a doodle sketched during a moment of idle thought, was the same swirl pattern from the altar and the codex.

CHAPTER 38

Whyborne

"IT'S BEAUTIFUL," CHRISTINE said, holding up the rifle. "The perfect wedding present."

The train had returned us to Widdershins long after nightfall. As I'd expected, Father had chastised me for cutting the visit with Stanford short. Given my mood, I'd snapped at him in return, and we'd spent the return trip in angry silence.

Still, I'd accompanied him back to Whyborne House, giving some vague excuse of not wishing the day to end on a sour note. It had mollified him to the point he hadn't questioned any further. I'd arrived to find Christine admiring her new rifle.

I sat on a chair in the ballroom—one of many, in fact, delivered by a rental company for the wedding the day after tomorrow.

"Jack sent it?" I asked, with a nod to the rifle.

"Yes. A shame he couldn't make it," she added, testing the bolt action. "I imagine his assistance would have come in handy."

Privately, I thought poor Jack was better out of it. He'd had one brush with sorcerers and monsters; surely that was enough for anyone.

The bell beside the front door rang, echoing through the house, and both of us stilled. A few moments later, Fenton led Griffin and Iskander in. "Look what your brother sent for a wedding present,"

Christine said, holding the rifle out to Griffin.

"Very nice," Griffin agreed distractedly.

"You found some evidence," I said. A bit to my surprise, a weight settled over my heart. Mr. Quinn was strange, even a bit frightening, but a part of me had hoped no one at the museum would turn out to be involved after all.

"I'm afraid so." Griffin related his findings, then said, "I'm going to take the motor car to Boston tomorrow and await him there."

"I'll come," I said immediately.

Griffin shook his head. "I appreciate the offer, but Quinn knows you too well. There aren't many men of your height and build. I can blend in far more easily."

"Then I'll come with you," Christine offered, patting the rifle.

"Your wedding is the morning after tomorrow," Griffin replied.

"To hell with the wedding!" Christine snapped.

Iskander's expression grew dark. "I see."

Christine paled. "Kander, you know I didn't mean..."

"I know I've worked very hard, arranging menus, sending out invitations, composing announcements for the paper." He folded his arms over his chest. "Whereas you've left everything to Whyborne's secretary and a-a fish-woman!"

"I—"

He held up a hand, cutting her off. "I want to belong here, Christine. In this town, with these people. I want to belong here for *us*. But you refuse to take it seriously! Sometimes I feel as though you're deliberately sabotaging my efforts!"

"There's no need for anyone to accompany me tomorrow," Griffin said soothingly. I rather thought he had missed the point.

They ignored him. "Blast it, Kander, I'm not sabotaging anything!" Christine exclaimed. "It's just that I don't give a fig for the trappings. I'd be just as happy going in front of the magistrate in my field outfit."

Iskander ground his teeth together. I'd never seen him lose his temper before. I took a step toward the foyer. "Griffin, I think we should leave."

"No, don't. I'm going home." Iskander pushed past me. At the door, he paused and looked back at Christine. "You might not care, but I do. Perhaps you can pretend our marriage won't affect your career, that there's no need to win over the people who matter in this bloody town, but I can't. Not when your own parents refuse to come, for no other reason than I have Egyptian blood." He took a deep breath. "I'll see you here tomorrow night."

Christine sank slowly into a chair. "Should one of us go after him?" I asked Griffin uncertainly.

Griffin shook his head. "No. Give him a chance to calm down." He patted Christine on the shoulder. "Don't fret. He loves you."

Griffin took his leave. I sat down beside Christine, unsure what to say. After a few moments of awkward silence, she said, "I never wanted a society wedding." She sat with her hands folded in her lap, her eyes fixed on them, as if she didn't recognize them as belonging to her. "That was always Daphne's dream."

"I'm sorry," I said. I tilted my head back and stared at the ceiling. A swirl of painted cherubs and angels with unusually menacing expressions stared back. "If it helps, I think Iskander is motivated by concern for you."

"I suppose." She smoothed her skirts. "I hadn't really thought of things from his perspective. I was angry at my parents, of course, but I never thought it might make him feel as if he needed to prove himself." She sighed. "I've been rather thoughtless, haven't I?"

"Not at all," I said staunchly. She gave me a skeptical look, and I winced. "Well, yes. But Iskander loves you anyway. Just be here tomorrow night, grit your teeth through the floral arranging, and compliment him on his hard work."

"You're right." She rose to her feet. "It's only one more day. If we can make it through tomorrow, everything will be perfectly fine."

CHAPTER 39

Griffin

I TOOK THE Curved Dash to Boston the next morning. Given that Christine and Iskander's wedding was less than twenty-four hours away, I didn't wish to find myself beholden to train schedules, as I had no idea when I'd find myself free.

With any luck, Mr. Quinn's visit would prove to be on some museum business or other, completely unrelated to the cult. He'd visit a bookshop or antiquities collector and be on the return train to Widdershins within a few hours.

As the Curved Dash would draw too much attention, I left it a good distance from the train station and went on foot to wait for Mr. Quinn. I'd dressed the part of a modest salesman, my suit just slightly out of style, and carried a somewhat worn sample case. Inside the case were my ordinary supplies: lock picks, binoculars, a spare hat and coat in case I needed to change. My revolver I kept in my coat pocket, where I could reach it quickly if the need arose.

I desperately hoped it wouldn't. If I were injured, Whyborne would never forgive me. If I were worse than injured, he'd never forgive himself.

I arrived at the station shortly before the morning train from Widdershins, where I loitered about and pretended to study the schedules, keeping a close eye out for Mr. Quinn as I did so. Soon enough, I spotted him in the crowd, looking like a crow in the midst of a gaggle of chickens. He carried only a small valise. Whatever business he had in Boston, he obviously didn't expect it to take long.

I followed him at a distance. He made his way from the bustle of the city's heart, and soon we were in yet another residential neighborhood. The July sun made the cheerfully painted houses look even brighter, and the laughter of children echoed through the street. Women called neighborly greetings to one another as they hung out their laundry, and brilliant flowers bordered the walk.

Quinn looked horribly out of place. He walked quickly, leapt out of the way of a gamboling puppy, and scowled at a woman who wished him good day.

What possible business did he have in a place like this? Had some family found a valuable tome in their attic, or as part of an inheritance? Or had the cult's corruption infiltrated this seemingly wholesome neighborhood? God knew I'd seen enough with the Pinkertons to realize the ugliest truths sometimes lurked behind the most pleasant masks.

Still, this wasn't Widdershins. Neighbors might ignore a cult there, but here? Surely the sight of men in robes, the mere glimpse of an unholy symbol, would be viewed as cause to summon the police.

Quinn paused outside of a house, and I slowed so as to remain unnoticed. He seemed to be steeling himself for something. Straightening his shoulders and holding his chin up, he marched to the front door and knocked. Within moments, it opened, and he vanished within.

I strolled past, making note of the address. I'd take it with me to the Pinkerton office here in Boston and give it to my friend to look into who owned it. Perhaps he'd even have found something on the old Somerby estate for me by now.

Not just yet, though. Quinn might have other destinations in mind. Or I might be able to spot some clue as to what might be going on inside.

I took my time, circling back as indirectly as possible while still keeping the house in sight. A tall fence separated it from the house on the left—the remnant of some long-ago feud between neighbors, perhaps. Old rose bushes had overtaken the rusting fence, forming a thick hedge adorned with hundreds of bright pink flowers.

It seemed my only chance at drawing near with any hope of concealment. I slipped into the gap between houses, moving as cautiously as possible. The heady scent of roses perfumed the air, and bees droned lazily from one bloom to the next. I tried to peer between the thorny canes, but the bushes were too thick to make out anything beyond indistinct patches of color.

Then came a sound that froze my blood, despite the warmth of the summer sun. Two people murmured a chant in unison. I couldn't make out the words, but the voices belonged to children.

I had to act. Ival might never forgive me, but if the cult were using children in its abominable rituals, I couldn't risk going to the police for help. By the time we returned, they might be dead, slaughtered just as Tubbs and the other sacrifices were.

The hedge ended at the back of the property. I drew my revolver and offered up a prayer. Then, holding my gun firmly, I stepped around the end and into the yard.

"Hold still!" I shouted. "Or I'll..."

My words died away. Mr. Quinn sat at a table on the patio behind the house. On either side of him were two little girls, twins dressed in identical frilly dresses. Across from him was a golden-haired doll, and on the table was a miniature set of teacups and pot.

For a moment, we all stared at one another in horror. Then Mr. Quinn rose to his feet, with all the dignity he could muster, given the situation. "Mr. Flaherty. What an unexpected pleasure."

I lowered my revolver. The two girls stared at me with silvery eyes very similar to Quinn's own. Then one asked, "Have you come to join our tea party?"

"Rose, Lily, why don't you go see if your mother has finished the cake yet," Quinn suggested.

Naturally, at the suggestion of cake, both children rushed into the house. Mr. Quinn crossed the lawn and stood before me. "I must confess, I'd hoped no one in Widdershins would ever learn about this," he said. "I don't wish to be rude, but why are you here?"

My heart sank. Either I'd given myself away to a maniac who happened to enjoy tea parties with dolls between bouts of murder, or I'd been entirely mistaken as to Mr. Quinn's involvement in the cult. "I heard chanting," I said, deciding to go for the most immediate answer. "In children's voices. I thought they might be in trouble."

"It's more a poem than a chant," Quinn said.

"Listen up little fish, little fish,
Let's make a wish, make a wish,
For a time not come but yet to be,
One for the land, and one for the sea.

"I'm certain you've heard of it," he finished dryly.

"You aren't ketoi," I said, then cursed myself. No need for him to know of my shadowsight.

"The prophecy concerns Widdershins," he replied, a bit stiffly, I thought. "And all who live within it, on the land and in the sea. There is no need to question my loyalty."

I was missing something, that much was clear. "So why were you teaching those girls the poem?"

"They're my nieces. My sister married a Boston man, and moved...here." Quinn surveyed the sunlit yard and pink roses as though affronted by their very existence. "Her husband doesn't approve of Widdershins. But the children deserve to know their true heritage. Today is their birthday, and as their father is blissfully away, I came to visit them."

"And play with dolls."

"Very ordinary ones, I'm afraid." His thin lips pressed together in distaste. "When my sister and I were little, we had the most lovely doll. It would whisper secrets to us at night, once all the adults were asleep."

The sunlight seemed to lose some of its warmth. "I...see."

"Sadly, the toys here know no secrets. They are mere objects." He sighed. "But I do what I can for the girls, anyway."

I was having less and less trouble imagining why the girls' father disapproved of Widdershins. "That's very, er, good of you."

"Yes." He turned his pale eyes on me. "So why are you here, Mr. Flaherty? Did Dr. Whyborne send you?" The thought appeared to improve his mood, and he offered me a somewhat worrisome smile. "Am I needed?"

There seemed no point in dissembling any further. "We thought someone at the museum was involved in a cult. Your name kept appearing—on Mr. Lambert's client list, in requests for the map that was stolen from the hall of records, and of course in association with the Wisborg Codex."

Quinn drew himself up in obvious affront. "You believe I would steal a book?" He made it sound as if I'd accused him of dancing naked in public.

"It was an honest mistake," I replied. "And I saw a doodle of a swirl symbol among your things. The same symbol that appears on the altars where men have been recently murdered. And in the stolen codex."

"Where did you...never mind." Quinn's expression had gone icy. "It is not a swirl, Mr. Flaherty. It is a vortex, turning widdershins."

Of course. I felt a fool not to have seen it. Still... "And why would you draw such a thing?"

"Because I know my place, sir." Quinn peered down his long nose at me. "I am loyal to Widdershins. I admit I didn't recognize him when he first stood before me, but I have done all I could to make up for my mistake in the two years since."

I frowned. "Wait. Do you mean the town? Or Whyborne?"

"Really, Mr. Flaherty." For a moment it seemed he might laugh at my foolishness. "You speak as though there's a difference."

CHAPTER 40

Whyborne

I SPENT MOST of the day trying not to worry about Griffin. He'd promised not to take any risks, and I believed he truly meant that. The problem was, in a case such as this one, risk tended to find us whether we wished it to or not.

I tried to lose myself in my translation of the cuneiform fragments. I was beginning to think Jensen was in fact on the right track with his suggestion that Gilgamesh and Enkidu had a more intimate relationship. After all, the same verb was used in their interaction as between Enkidu and the courtesan Samhat.

"I pressed myself upon him like a wife." Not the way I would have phrased it, of course, but it seemed to me their relationship had an erotic component. Perhaps even more than that.

Which thoughts sent me back to considering my own husband, and returned me to worrying about him once again.

I left the museum as soon as I reasonably could. "Will I see you this evening, Dr. Whyborne?" Miss Parkhurst asked. "The florist is supposed to deliver the flowers to your father's house tonight, and Persephone—that is, Miss Whyborne—wished to see them. Since she can't come to the wedding itself."

"I'm not certain." A great deal depended on what Griffin found in Boston, if anything. On the other hand, perhaps I ought to go and make certain Christine and Iskander were on good terms once again.

This wedding business was a terrible headache. Griffin would have preferred a real ceremony in a church, but I found myself more happy with our little exchange of vows by the day.

I returned home, letting myself in the gate and starting up the walk. Saul meowed plaintively at me from high up in the branches of one of the trees shading the house from the westering sun. I paused beneath him, patting my thigh in a gesture for him to come down. "Are you hungry, old tom?"

Apparently, he'd already eaten his fill of birds or mice for the day, because he remained on his perch and made no move to join me on the ground. With a shrug, I opened the front door and went inside.

A slight shift of the air was all the warning I got. A heavy blanket descended over my head, knocking off my hat and plunging me into darkness.

Terror spiked my blood, and I flung my weight forward—right into a pair of hard arms that locked around me. Wild thoughts flitted through my brain—was I being robbed?

If so, they'd chosen the wrong house. I reached for the arcane fire of the maelstrom, my thoughts shaping the spell that would call the wind howling in through the windows.

Heavy iron closed around my wrist, accompanied by the click of a key.

My arm instantly went numb. Agony flared in my scars, as though they'd opened anew. I stumbled, off balance and dizzy as my sense of the maelstrom vanished.

The witch hunter's manacles.

I tried to struggle, but one of the men buried a fist in my gut. I doubled over, fighting to draw air into my lungs, even as the heavy blanket pressed against my face, smothering me.

My captors dragged me in the direction of the parlor. My lungs lost their paralysis, and I gasped in what air I could against the muffling blanket. These men had to belong to the cult, and my gut shriveled at the thought of what they surely meant to do. Would Griffin return to find my corpse on the floor, my throat slit and my heart missing?

Griffin. Had he been caught in Boston? Had Quinn set this trap because he knew we'd found him out?

"Hold him," ordered a voice that seemed strangely familiar. Rough hands wrapped around my left wrist, yanking my arm in front of me. With my magic bound, I only thrashed helplessly while they tore off my cuff and shoved back my sleeves.

The blade of a knife sliced my forearm, drawing a shocked yelp from me. Hot blood ran across my skin, and a hand wrapped around the wound, sending another jolt of pain through me.

Then the hand was gone. "Let him see this," said the voice. "I want him to know."

The blanket was torn aside. I gulped in the relatively cool air, squinting at the sudden return of light. As I'd surmised, I stood in the parlor. The desk had been pulled back, the cabinet broken open, and the rug tossed aside. A complicated series of sigils and circles covered the floorboards, drawn in what looked to be colored chalk. And in the center, perched on its brass stand, stood the Lapidem.

The room was nearly filled with five other men, all of them dressed in dark robes, including the two who held me. The one-eyed man with the horribly malformed arm wasn't there. But in the center of the gathering, his hand red with my blood, stood Bradley Osborne.

CHAPTER 41

Griffin

HOPING TO KEEP the Boston trip from becoming a complete waste of time, I stopped by the Pinkerton offices. Fortunately, my old friend William Andrews was in, and appeared almost as soon as I asked for him.

"Griffin," he said, shaking my hand warmly. "It's good to see you again."

"And you, Will." He hadn't changed much in the five—or was it six?—years since I'd last seen him. His sandy hair had crept slightly higher on his forehead, and a few more lines showed around his mouth, but his smile was just the same.

"Come to my office," he said, clapping me on the arm.

I felt oddly dislocated in time as I followed him through the building. So many things seemed familiar, even though I'd never set foot in this office before: the faint scent of gun oil, the chatter of the men, the rustle of papers. But there were differences as well—the ring of a telephone, for one, cheerfully answered by a young woman.

Andrews shared his office with several other men, none of whom were present at their desks at the moment. "Gone into business for yourself, then?" he asked, removing a bottle of whiskey from his desk and pouring us each a dram. "And in Widdershins, no less. Damned odd place, from what I hear."

I felt a small flash of annoyance, then wondered at myself. I'd said as much, many times. But it seemed wrong to hear the words from someone who didn't live there. Who didn't understand.

"It's my home now," I said simply.

Andrews downed his whiskey in one practiced swallow. "What made you choose it, if you don't mind my asking? I would have thought New York or San Francisco more your sort of place."

I paused, unsure how to answer. He didn't know about my confinement in the mad house. The Chicago office had kept it quiet, fearing for the reputation of the agency should it become too widely known. "Glenn's death changed me," I said at last, which was true as it went. "After...well. I think Widdershins chose me, more than I chose it."

Andrews gave me an uncertain look. "I see," he said in a tone suggesting the opposite. "I was just about to send you a telegram, but you've saved me the trouble."

I accepted his quick change of topic. No doubt in some ways I'd begun to sound as strange as any lifelong denizen of Widdershins. "You found something of interest?"

"Indeed. I'm sorry it took as long as it did." He rummaged about in his drawer for a few minutes, then pulled out a stack of telegrams. "There were a few layers of ownership, businesses that exist only on paper. But I finally found a name for you at the bottom of it all."

"Which is?" I asked without much hope.

"Dr. Bradley Osborne."

My skin prickled, as if the air had gone from summer to winter. "Bradley Osborne?" I repeated like a fool.

He'd been on Lambert's list. And of course he was a scholar, who knew Widdershins's history—would, in fact, likely know about any early surveying map held by the hall of records. The witch hunter's paraphernalia lay in the keeping of his department.

And yet...

Whyborne complained of him frequently, but always as a petty annoyance. Given what I'd seen of him when I first came to Widdershins, I'd judged him the same. Besides, my shadowsight should have revealed him as a sorcerer when I saw him last, at the night of the museum's reception.

But the witch hunter's dagger interfered with my ability see magic. If that had been the very night he'd stolen the dagger and manacles, if he'd had them on him...

He'd put his hand to the small of his back while confronting Whyborne. Had the presence of a weapon meant to kill sorcerers made him feel powerful? Helped him put his sneer back in place, while he dreamed of murdering my Ival?

Oh hell.

Bradley was back in Widdershins, with Whyborne and Christine and everyone else. None of whom would suspect him of being anything more than an ass.

Andrews gave me a concerned frown. "I take it the name means something to you?"

"Yes. It means I've made a terrible error." I rose to my feet. "May I use your telephone?"

CHAPTER 42

Whyborne

"**Bradley?**" I asked stupidly. But this made no sense. Bradley might be a loathsome toad, but he was no sorcerer. No murderer. "You... what...?"

The familiar, contemptuous smirk twisted his features. "Not all that bright, are you, Percy?" he asked. "But then, if you had half the intelligence you're credited with, we wouldn't be here, would we?"

I tried to break free from the men holding me. If I had access to my power, I'd lay ice on their skin. I'd summon wind to shatter bones, I'd set fire if I must.

But I couldn't do any of it.

"I don't know what you're talking about," I said to stall him. If I diverted his attention, perhaps I'd find some means of escape, as unlikely as it seemed. "But whatever you're doing here—whatever you think you're doing—needs to stop. Whoever got you involved with this, it's not too late to walk away."

"Walk away?" he asked incredulously. "Oh no, it's far too late for that. I've seen the punishments the Man in the Wood serves to those who fail to carry out his wishes."

This was madness. "What could you possibly know about Nyarlathotep?"

"More than you, I dare say." His lip lifted in a sneer. "What a waste you are. You might have had so much—power, wealth, women. And instead you chose *this*." He scanned the room, disappointment written clearly on his face. "And speaking of women, where is Flaherty?"

God. Quinn hadn't had anything to do with the cult. It had been Bradley all along.

But at least our mistake meant Bradley hadn't caught Griffin here alone. I settled for glaring at him in lieu of an answer.

Bradley frowned. "He was meant to be here. Killed in a struggle. But now he's gone and made things complicated."

"What the devil do you want from us?" I demanded. "Money? My father will pay you whatever ransom you ask. Just tell me."

Bradley arched a brow. "Money? Oh no. I want your life, you quivering fairy. The life you've wasted. The life you never appreciated or deserved." He grinned. "Which is why I'm taking it."

He brought the hand slick with my blood down on the Lapidem. All around him, the sigils sprang to life, burning with blue flame that even I could see.

Pain spiked through my head, and he cried out as well. The world spun, the room tilting first one way, then the other. For a moment, I felt weightless, as though no longer connected to my body.

Then I was on my knees, my fingers pressed to my temples. The cultists must have let go of me. Iron no longer encircled my wrist, yet I still couldn't sense the maelstrom.

What had Bradley done to me? Nothing felt right. The floor seemed an odd distance away, my limbs subtly wrong, as though someone had taken me apart and put me back together incorrectly.

"It worked," said a voice, but it wasn't Bradley's. One of the cultists?

I raised my head slowly, but the room remained steady. Still, nothing made sense to my eyes. Somehow, I'd ended up where Bradley had been, beside the now-quiescent Lapidem. Across the room, where I had stood, the two cultists who had held me unlocked the manacle from the wrist of a figure and stepped back.

I looked up...and up. He was tall and thin, his hair wilder than usual from being under the blanket, and his face was familiar to me from each morning when I shaved.

"What?" I said, but my voice was *wrong*. As were the hands I stretched out in front of myself, the fingers too sturdy, unadorned by either wedding ring or scars.

"Haven't you figured it out yet?" asked the person wearing my face. He motioned to the cultists, and a moment later I found myself seized again, dragged to my feet and away from the Lapidem.

"Bradley?" But it couldn't be. This was insane, impossible. I'd fallen asleep waiting for Griffin to return from Boston. This was some mad dream.

He crossed the room and stopped a few feet away, looking down at me. "Not any more. Now I'm Percival Endicott Whyborne, heir to one of the largest fortunes in America."

"No," I said. "This can't be real, it can't."

He grinned, horribly, and I almost expected to glimpse shark's teeth behind his lips. "Oh, it's real enough. I projected myself into Lambert and Durfree, dominated their minds and controlled their bodies. I only needed blood from each of them—Lambert stuck himself with a pin while fitting my suit, and Durfree cut his hand on a frame, so I took advantage of the chance fate granted me. But to do a complete transfer of essence...for that I needed the Occultum Lapidem. And your blood, of course."

I reached for the maelstrom, no longer caring for finesse. I'd burn the house down around us if I had to, char myself to ash along with them. Anything to stop this.

It was like an amputee groping with a phantom limb. I couldn't feel the arcane power of the vortex, and no flame responded to my call.

"Trying to cast a spell?" Bradley asked with lips that had belonged to me. He snapped his fingers, and the candle above the fireplace burst into flame. A delighted laugh escaped him. "Look at that. If I'd had this power from the beginning...but no matter." He turned back to me. "All that matters is that you die."

The clang of the iron gate sounded from outside. "Whyborne!" Christine bellowed. "Are you in there?"

An expression of fury distorted his—my—his—features. But just for a moment. "Go," Bradley ordered. "Out the back! Leave him here!"

The cultists released me and rushed for the back door. "Christine!" Bradley shouted. "I'm in here! Help!"

I staggered to my feet. I had to stop him, before this went any farther. I launched myself at him, knocking him back into the doorframe.

The front door burst open, and I glimpsed Father and Christine. "He's trying to steal the Lapidem!" Bradley shouted.

"No!" I firmed my grip on his lapels. "It's not—"

"Finally, I get to hit something," Christine exclaimed. I glimpsed her fist flying at my face. Then stars burst across my vision, and I collapsed into darkness.

CHAPTER 43

Whyborne

"**BRADLEY, A SORCERER!**" said a voice from far away. "I'd never have believed it."

"The Man in the Woods and the rat-thing must have tutored him," said another voice. My voice?

But not from my throat.

I blinked sluggishly. The light seemed to stab my eyes, and my head ached abominably.

I lay on my stomach, my cheek pressed against the carpet. My mouth tasted horrible, and something seemed to have been stuffed into it—a rag? I tried to reach up and pull it free, but my hands had been secured behind my back.

"He's waking up," my voice said.

Bradley.

I tried to cry out, to warn Christine, but the rag prevented it. "A good thing you thought to gag him, Whyborne," Christine said. "We definitely don't want him casting any spells."

"Indeed." His foot connected viciously with my side, and I tried to curl up to protect myself.

"Steady on, there," Christine said. "I know it's Bradley, but he's helpless now."

Christine's shoes approached across the carpet. "I can't believe it.

That is, we always knew he was an idiot, but this? Murder? Sorcery? What the devil did he hope to gain?"

I tried to signal her somehow with my facial expressions. If I could only make her understand the real murderer was standing right behind her.

"Is he having some sort of seizure?" she asked.

Blast.

"How did you know to come?" Bradley asked. His—*my*—shoes retreated out of my line of sight. "I'm grateful, of course, but your intervention was rather timely."

"Griffin telephoned from Boston. Mr. Quinn had nothing to do with any of this—as you've clearly guessed."

"Mr. Quinn?" Bradley exclaimed incredulously.

"Er, yes," Christine said. "He is why Griffin went to Boston."

"Of course, but...well. It didn't seem very likely. Quinn doesn't care about anything but old books."

"Well you certainly seemed to think it likely yesterday," Christine snapped. I willed her to question him further. To doubt. He'd make some error soon enough, and she'd surely realize she wasn't really talking to me. Instead, she went on, "Griffin's Pinkerton friend followed the trail of deeds from the old Somerby Estate to Bradley. Naturally he was alarmed and wanted us to know as soon as possible. Your Father and I came to tell you...and a good thing we did."

"Yes, how fortunate," Bradley said, although the comment didn't sound very sincere to me. "He meant to steal the Lapidem—for what end, I can't imagine. His accomplices are still out there, so I'd best keep it with me, in case they try again."

The floor creaked beneath Father's feet as he entered the room. "Detective Tilton is here."

"I still think we might have handled this on our own," Bradley said.

"And done what?" Christine demanded. "We can hardly kill the man in cold blood."

Bradley could. Had in fact done so, when it came to poor Mr. Tubbs, and the other unfortunates he'd offered up as sacrifice. And it was laughable to believe Father would have had any qualms.

Had I only waked alive thanks to Christine's presence?

The murmur of voices drew closer. "What do we have here?" Tilton asked.

"I came home to find Dr. Osborne robbing my house," Bradley said, aping indignity. "He attacked me with a knife. Fortunately, Miss —Dr. Putnam and my father arrived."

"He's the one who killed Tubbs," Christine said flatly. "And others."

"We found another body this morning, floating in the Cranch," Tilton said. "Killed in a similar manner to Mr. Tubbs and the fellow who washed up on the beach. The coroner thinks he died last night. I'm sure Dr. Osborne here would like to tell me all about what happened to him."

Three men sacrificed in the sea, and at least two on land. I recalled the dark stain on the altar on the island. No doubt a sixth body lay at the bottom of the lake.

"And you have him nicely trussed up like a Christmas goose," Tilton said with satisfaction.

"More a Thanksgiving turkey," Christine muttered.

"Will there be any evidence I can take to a judge?" Tilton asked as two officers seized me by the arms and hauled me up. "That is, we'll hold him on the robbery and attempted murder of Dr. Whyborne, of course. But the other accusations..."

"I'm sure we'll find something," Father said smoothly.

One of the police cut the makeshift bonds around my ankles. Christine had tied me up with the tasseled curtain tiebacks Griffin and I had argued over when redecorating last year. As the police dragged me from the room, I met Christine's eyes—surely she would recognize me, even if I was in Bradley's body.

She glared back at me, jaw clenched. "The electric chair is too good for you," she said. "I hope they drop you in a hole and leave you there."

I closed my eyes, unwilling to see Father, or—worse—my own face smirking back at me.

The officers dragged me none-too-gently to the police wagon waiting in the street. Oh God—if they took me to jail, what would happen? What did Bradley intend to do in *my* body? When Griffin returned...

From his remarks to me over the years, Bradley would never fall into bed with Griffin. Which was a thin comfort. What would he do instead? Break Griffin's heart?

No—Bradley would never let him live. Griffin would no doubt become the convenient victim of the cultists still roaming loose. He'd be felled by a hand he believed to be mine, his last thoughts of shock and betrayal.

I went wild, thrashing madly against my restraints. "Oi!" exclaimed one of the policemen. "Settle down, or we'll have to get rough!"

But how could I settle? I tried to shout against the gag, to tell them they had the wrong man. A sharp blow across the back of my head sent me reeling, and within moments, they'd flung me into the back of the wagon and slammed the doors.

I lay on the sticky floor, gasping. The smell of dried vomit and blood wafted up, left behind by previous occupants. Nausea clawed at the back of my throat, and terror seized me. With the gag in my mouth, I'd surely drown in my own bile if I threw up now.

The police wagon lurched into motion, bearing me away from my home. Away from Christine, and my father, and my own body.

No. I couldn't panic. Once we arrived at the station, Tilton would have to remove the gag. I'd tell my side of the story. Yes, it would sound utterly mad, but Tilton would surely relay it to Father and Griffin, even if he didn't believe it himself.

Bradley could never carry out a convincing impersonation for long. They'd see through his pretense, or Christine would. And they'd reverse whatever Bradley had done, and I'd be restored to my proper body, and everything would be all right.

Except Bradley, for all his flaws, wasn't a fool. He had to realize how precarious his masquerade was. Which meant he'd make sure I didn't live long enough to raise suspicion.

The rat familiar might be dead, but what else might the Man in the Woods have given him? What else might he do now that he had access to my sorcerous blood? How easily he'd summoned fire—might he summon something far worse?

I'd never survive long enough to give my statement to Tilton. If they put me in a cell, I was as good as dead.

I thrashed against my bonds. My feet were free, but my hands still firmly tied. I had to get loose somehow. I cast about hopefully, but the interior of the police wagon was bare of any edge I might use to saw through the tieback around my wrists.

Sorcery was my only hope. But this body Bradley had consigned me to had neither ketoi blood nor Endicott, let alone an unholy combination of the two.

So? Blackbyrne hadn't been an Endicott or a ketoi. Neither had various members of the Brotherhood who'd learned sorcery over the years. Yes, they'd had the Man in the Woods to offer them a start, the power of their horrible familiars to draw upon. But I had years of practice, of honing my will into a tool.

I drew my bonds tight and hoped I didn't end up killing myself in the process. Taking as deep a breath as the gag allowed, I closed my eyes. I couldn't speak aloud the true name of fire, but chants and circles and sigils were all just tools anyway, meant to lead the mind along certain paths and focus the will. I'd done without them before, and I would again.

I bent all of my concentration onto a single point on the ropes holding me. I whispered the true name of fire in the confines of my mind, over and over. It was the spell of a novice; surely I could perform it, even now.

Nothing happened.

I tried again, and again. Rain began to drum on the metal roof, further distracting me. My heart raced in my chest, and I was acutely aware that we must be drawing near the police station by now. But fear would only interfere with my concentration and make things even harder, so I did my best to push it aside. There was only this moment. Only the rope.

Only the fire.

The smell of scorching fibers reached me, then grew stronger. Heat whispered against my wrists and the small of my back. I pulled as hard as I could on my bonds.

They weren't giving way.

I tugged harder, frantic now. The heat grew painful, and I bit my lip. The fire would surely eat through the rope before my suit coat caught, wouldn't it? Except the stench of burning wool had now joined the earlier smells. The skin on my hands nearest the flame was beginning to hurt badly, scalded by the heat, and I couldn't take it for much longer.

The ropes gave way abruptly. I rolled onto my back, smothering the flames. The skin on my thumbs and the back of my hands was reddened and starting to blister, but I didn't care. I was free.

When I was sure my suit coat no longer smoldered, I sat up. Everything felt wrong, each movement not quite what I expected, a reminder that this body was alien to me.

The wagon slowed to a halt. I shifted into a crouch, and hoped none of the police would look through the tiny windows on the sides of the wagon.

The officer who swung open the door expected to find me still securely bound. His eyes widened, and he opened his mouth to cry out.

I hit him with all my strength. To my utter shock, he staggered back, eyes rolling into his head, and collapsed on the pavement.

Apparently, all those hours Bradley had put in at the athletic club hadn't been for naught.

My surprise almost lost me my opportunity. There came an angry shout from the other policeman. I leapt from the rear of the wagon and ran. The rain had begun in earnest now, and I was soaked within minutes. The shriek of the police whistle was drowned out by the crash of thunder. My shoulders itched, expecting the impact of a bullet.

I dashed through the pelting rain, paying no heed to where I was going, only seeking to put distance between the police and myself. The legs I stretched weren't as long as I was used to, but what they lacked in initial speed, they made up for in stamina. I ran until the muscles ached, until my lungs were afire, and I could go no further.

I stumbled to a halt and leaned against the side of a building, rain sluicing down my face. There was no sign of any pursuit, and the storm had driven the inhabitants of the run-down neighborhood inside. I slid to the ground and wrapped my arms around my knees. I wanted to curl up and sleep, to awake and discover this was some awful dream. I'd find Griffin in the bed beside me, and he'd laugh when I told him I'd imagined Bradley, of all people, had swapped bodies with me. Then he'd say he appreciated my body far more than Bradley's, and go on to prove it.

Except it wasn't a dream, and this was all too real. I had to think. I'd escaped the police for the moment, but they'd be on the lookout for me. Or, rather, for Bradley Osborne. Tilton would no doubt inform Father and the man they thought to be me.

Bradley would take no chances. He'd spin some story to ensure the police would shoot me on sight.

He wanted my life, he'd said. It seemed impossible—mad. My life was quiet breakfasts and long hours at the museum. My life was ketoi and umbrae, and a host of cousins who wanted to kill me. My life was narrow escapes and the vague dread I'd end up in an unmarked grave or the belly of some monster. Who would want that?

But maybe that wasn't what Bradley saw when he looked at me. What had he said, about wasting my potential? He didn't want my position at the museum—that would be the first to go, as he had no knowledge of philology. No, he wanted to be the Whyborne heir and all that implied.

The goal of the rituals hadn't been about swapping bodies with me, though. Some larger plot must be in place, something Bradley was willing to commit murder to achieve. But what? This Restoration Scarrow had mentioned?

Bradley owned the old Somerby estate. Might there be some clue there?

I pushed myself up on aching legs. I couldn't go to my friends without risking my life. And I couldn't very well stay here and wait for the police to appear, so I could die in a jail cell. The estate seemed as good a place as any to go.

I started walking.

CHAPTER 44

Whyborne

I STOOD AT the edge of the Draakenwood, staring out across the lawn of the Somerby Estate. The last light of the sun struggled through the thick clouds, but full darkness would fall soon. The storm hadn't lessened its fury, and despite the summer warmth, the cold rain had leached the heat from my body. Shivers wracked me, seemingly echoed by the leaves of the ill-favored wood at my back.

Was this where Bradley had met the Man in the Woods? It seemed likely enough. How he had known about any of this—the Fideles or Nyarlathotep, or any of it—I couldn't guess, and at the moment it didn't seem particularly important.

Lightning flickered, reflecting in the windows of the great manor house. A light showed from the first floor—Bradley hadn't left the place undefended, it seemed.

Where was he now? At Whyborne House? With Christine and Iskander, Miss Parkhurst and Persephone, not to mention my father? All of them thinking he was me, not knowing they had a murderous viper in their midst.

What of Griffin? Had he returned from Boston yet?

Bradley wouldn't hesitate to kill him. Or, more likely, have him killed.

Oh God, Griffin.

I took a deep breath. I couldn't worry about what might have already happened. I needed to concentrate on preventing anything else from going wrong. I had to get into the estate and find any clues Bradley might have left. Spell books. Instructions on how to reverse the damned body swap. A detailed outline of all his nefarious schemes.

The very presence of a guard suggested there was something in there Bradley didn't want anyone else to see. I needed a weapon. Something—anything—that might offer me a chance. Without access to magic, I felt utterly helpless.

Still, this body possessed a strength my own never would. Perhaps it might be enough. I slipped back into the woods. The canopy cut off the last of the sunlight, and I swore to myself. A few moments of searching blindly, and I stumbled over a heavy fallen branch that seemed only half-rotted.

It would have to do.

Clutching my makeshift cudgel, I crept toward the house. Going through the front door would be the height of folly, so I snuck around the back, away from the light in the window. My hands shook as I tried the kitchen door.

Locked.

Not knowing what else to do, I went to the nearest window and waited for the next roll of thunder. It wasn't as loud as I would have liked, but I hoped it would cover the sound of breaking glass as I swung the branch into the window.

I reached inside and freed the window latch. Trying to be as stealthy as possible, I shoved it open. Years of neglect had left the wood warped, and the window groaned and squealed against the frame.

I listened intently, but heard nothing from within. Had my luck held?

I scrambled through the window and into the kitchen. The air reeked of mildew and dust. The door leading to the basement cellar stood open, and I fancied the fetid stench of the Guardians still stained the air. Blackbyrne and Addison Somerby had held Griffin there for hours, and I shuddered at the thought of how it must have tormented him, even as I admired his bravery yet again.

If Bradley did something to him...hurt him...killed him...

I couldn't let such thoughts distract me, not now. All but holding my breath, I eased out into the hall.

Rain drummed against the windows, and water dripped steadily somewhere nearby. Nothing else broke the silence.

The light had been near the front of the house. In the parlor? I tried to call up my old memories of the place, when Leander and I had played here together. Before death and madness, before magic and abominations, when the estate had been a refuge from the cruelties of my father and brother.

I walked down the hall, the branch gripped in my hand. The parlor door stood open, the glow from within giving me just enough light to see by. When I was almost at the doorway, I paused and took a deep breath.

I had to strike fast. No matter what awaited me inside, I had to be prepared to use the branch with all the strength this wrong body possessed.

Raising the branch, I stepped into the room.

No one was there.

CHAPTER 45

Griffin

I RETURNED TO Widdershins as quickly as the Curved Dash would carry me. Niles had promised me he'd go to our house and inform Whyborne immediately of Bradley's treachery, but I wouldn't rest easy until I was with Ival again. The storms slowed my progress, and by the time I reached Whyborne House, the sun had already set.

The rain apron had kept me somewhat dry, so I wasn't an utter disgrace when I rang the bell. Fenton nevertheless arched a brow when he opened the door.

"Is Whyborne—Percival—here?" I asked.

"Indeed," Fenton said. "As are Dr. Putnam and...others."

Thank heavens. I handed my hat to a silent maid and hurried into the ballroom. The florist had already departed, and Persephone arrived. Buckets of roses and lilacs filled the room, accompanied by water-soaked bushels of shells and strands of pearls. Miss Parkhurst was there as well, and seemed to be involved in creating some sort of arrangement with the shells, pearls, and flowers.

Christine stood off to one side, watching. As soon as she caught sight of me, however, she hurried over. "Griffin! I have excellent news."

Relief swept over me at the satisfied smile on her face. "What happened?"

"Your call was most timely." The smile faded slightly. "Mr. Whyborne and I hurried over to your house right away. And thank heavens we did—Bradley and his followers had broken in and were trying to steal the Lapidem."

"The Lapidem?" What on earth did the umbrae's stone have to do with anything?

She shrugged at my confusion. "I've no idea. At any rate, they attacked Whyborne—they cut him, but don't worry, it was just a scratch. The other cultists ran off, and the police took Bradley into custody. Whatever he had planned, we've foiled it."

"Thank goodness." A weight seemed to lift from my shoulders.

"Indeed. Now I can get married without having to worry about the rest of this nonsense." The satisfied smile returned. "That should make Iskander happy."

"I'm certain it will," I agreed. "Where is Whyborne?"

"Speaking with his father, I believe."

I went in search of them. As I entered the foyer, their voices drifted down from the second floor. I set my foot on the bottom of the staircase as they crossed the landing above.

Niles looked just as he always had. But Whyborne...

It was like viewing a photographic negative. Where there should have been light—fire—there was only darkness.

I clung to the bannister, feeling as though I might fall otherwise. They continued on past the second floor landing, never looking in my direction. Thankfully, because I didn't know what I would have done if Whyborne had spoken to me.

Something was wrong with him. Horribly, horribly wrong.

Had Bradley done something to my Ival? There seemed no other explanation. But what? What would possibly steal away the flame that had burned so bright I'd sensed it even before the Mother of Shadows altered my vision? What could have hollowed him out in such a fashion—and why wouldn't he have spoken of it to Christine?

I should have wanted to run to him. To catch him up in my arms and beg him to tell me what had happened.

So why did every instinct I possessed scream at me to flee in the opposite direction?

The bell rang, and a moment later, Detective Tilton's voice came from the doorway. Stunned and in turmoil, I turned as Fenton led the detective inside. Tilton's mouth drew down in a grim frown, which only deepened when he caught sight of me.

"Bradley Osborne," I said, because why else would Tilton be here? "Something's happened."

Tilton nodded unhappily. "He's escaped. I came to let Dr.

Whyborne know."

"Yes." Everything felt strangely far away. "I'm sure Niles will want to speak with you as well."

Tilton flinched, but I didn't care. Bradley had done something unspeakable to Ival, and now he was on the loose once again, thanks to the incompetence of the police. I brushed past him and went into the ballroom to find Christine.

My expression must have been alarming, because she immediately said, "Good gad, what's happened now?"

I lowered my voice. "Something is wrong with Whyborne. I don't know what, but I can see it with my shadowsight. And Bradley escaped."

"Damn it." She put a hand to her temple, as if to massage away the beginning of a headache. "I should have shot him when I had the chance."

"Probably," I agreed, "but you didn't know. If Tilton had only... never mind." I shook my head. "I need you to keep a close eye on Whyborne. I'm not certain what's wrong, but whatever it is, it can't be good for him."

She frowned. "And what are you going to do?"

"Bradley owns the Somerby estate. If nothing else, there might be answers somewhere in the house." I paused. "And if I'm truly lucky, I'll find Bradley hiding there."

"Don't give him another chance to escape," Christine advised.

I made for the entrance. "Don't worry," I said over my shoulder. "I don't intend to."

CHAPTER 46

Whyborne

I LOWERED THE branch, my heart pounding uselessly. A lantern sat on a small table, illuminating dusty furniture and filthy panes of glass. Rain dripped steadily into the fireplace from a leak in the chimney, and spots of rust dotted the iron fire tools in their stand.

I moved further into the room. Someone had been here recently... so where had they gone?

A footstep came from the hall behind me, followed by an odd dragging sound.

What the devil?

Step. Slide. Step. Slide.

A soft glow appeared as well, growing steadily stronger, until a figure stepped into the doorway.

It was the one-eyed cultist. In his human hand, he carried a candle; the misshapen tentacle arm flexed and curled by his side. His gait seemed horribly off as he came into view. Nausea swept over me as I saw he had one normal leg...but the other had been replaced just as his arm had been.

"Osborne!"

I flinched—then forced myself still. Had he not heard? Did he think me Bradley? "Yes."

He hastened across the room to me, features twisted in outrage. I tried not to look at him too closely. "You failed?" he demanded. "You didn't take the hybrid's body?"

The hybrid. Lovely.

"Things went...wrong," I said. Recalling Bradley's ordinary attitude, I forced a sneer onto my lips. "But don't worry. I'll have them fixed soon enough."

"Damn you!" The man hurled the candle past me into the fireplace. The misshapen arm lashed out, wrapping around my shoulders and shoving me hard into the brick. My makeshift cudgel tumbled from my grip. "I told you timing was everything—there are only a few hours left until the stars are in position!"

The muscular tentacle flexed, the sensation horrible even through the layers of cloth separating my skin from its slick surface. As I tried to think of some response, he all but shoved his face into mine, spittle flying.

"Do I have to remind you of the consequences of failure?" he roared. "If the beacon isn't lit, what Nyarlathotep will do to you will make this look like a beauty mark!"

He ripped off his eye patch. Instead of the empty socket I'd expected, there writhed a host of tiny, squirming tentacles.

A shriek of disgust and horror escaped me. For a moment, he stared at me, as if confused. Then his malformed limb tightened around me like a constrictor snake. "Wait a moment," he growled. "You aren't Osborne."

I flailed blindly behind me. My hand closed around the rusty handle of the iron poker, even as he hurled me across the room.

I struck the desk and fell to the floor. He drew the witch hunter's dagger from his belt and rushed at me. In blind terror I thrust out the poker to keep him back.

The iron point buried itself deep in his good eye. He screamed, then screamed again when I wrenched it free. I rolled to one side as he blundered forward, slashing blindly with the dagger.

I struck at him with the poker again, catching him on the side of the head. Bradley's greater musculature lent the blow a force I couldn't have managed in my old body, and sent him to the floor. I staggered to my feet and stood over him, panting. His mutated arm and leg twitched, but I didn't think he was conscious.

Raising the poker high, I brought it down with all my borrowed strength. There came a dull crunch, and the tentacles stilled.

I let the poker fall with a dull clang. Bile stung my throat, and I barely turned away before vomiting.

When I felt able to move again without nausea, I stood up carefully and wiped my mouth with the handkerchief from my pocket.

It was as soaking wet as the rest of my clothes, and I let it fall to the floor when I was done.

I'd come here for answers, and I'd gotten at least one. Whatever Bradley and the cultists had planned—something to do with lighting a beacon?—would take place only a few hours from now. And given the horrific growths and mutations that had befallen the man I'd killed, Bradley had to go through with it or suffer the consequences.

Which meant stopping him and getting my rightful body back, before I ended up with a tentacle arm.

I stepped around the fallen cultist, careful not to look at him too closely. I scooped up the witch hunter's dagger and tucked it into my coat, then took the lantern from the desk. The answers as to just what Bradley had planned and where he meant to do it must be here somewhere.

I just had to find them.

CHAPTER 47

Whyborne

THE STUDY SMELLED faintly of mildew and rats, of a place shut up far too long without airing. Little had changed since the last time I'd been here. Addison's old desk and chair remained, and I almost expected to catch a whiff of his tobacco lingering on the air. The old wallpaper peeled in places, and darker patches of color betrayed where portraits had once hung. In place of the missing picture of Leander, an old map had been tacked on the wall.

This must be the stolen surveyor's map. My gaze went to the island in the lake, where the surveyor had written *Indian Ruins* in a cramped hand.

A sheet of onionskin lay rolled up on the desk. I picked it up—there were dots on it, and lines. It was about the same size as the map, so I held it up.

The dots mapped perfectly onto the two sets of standing stones we knew of. A third, to the south of the city, was also marked. Bradley had used their position to calculate three other places beneath the sea. No doubt they corresponded to the ketoi's reefs.

And at the center of them all was a spot on the Cranch River I recognized all too well. Even though no modern structures showed on the old survey map, I'd stood there before, atop the Front Street Bridge.

The lines drawn between the six clusters of standing stones all intersected at the eye of the arcane maelstrom.

I let the onionskin fall from numb fingers. Dear God, did Bradley mean to conduct some sort of ritual there, in the very center of the magical vortex? Had the various rites at the standing stones been only the beginning—some sort of priming for whatever he intended to unleash?

Whatever he had in mind, it would surely be insanely dangerous. Even Blackbyrne hadn't conducted rites there, lest its wild power rip open the veil between our world and the Outside.

The Outside, where Nyarlathotep, whoever or whatever it or they were, lurked. Where the rat-thing had come from.

No. That would be mad. Bradley was many things: greedy, cruel, hungry for the power and attention he believed he deserved. Destroying the world would do him no good. I was missing something.

The disfigured cultist had spoken of lighting a beacon. But what did that mean? Beacons were meant to signal, but who—*what*—did the cult mean to call out to? Did it have something to do with the Restoration they wished to bring about?

I turned to the desk. Neat stacks of correspondence covered its surface, and a number of books filled a shelf above it. A Latin translation of the *Al Azif* stood at one end, followed by the *Cultes des Goules,* the Pnakotic Manuscripts, and other tomes of sinister repute.

Most of the books were in poor shape, too incomplete or damaged to catch the eye of a museum or library. How long had it taken Bradley to locate these? Or had they been a part of the estate's library, and Bradley simply plucked them from the shelves?

At the far end of the shelf, I found an unlabeled volume, the cover badly tattered, the pages falling out even as I picked it up. A familiar spiral illustration drifted out to land on the floor.

The Wisborg Codex—or an incomplete copy of it, at any rate. The museum copy his horrid familiar had stolen wasn't here. Did he have it with him? In easy reach somewhere in Widdershins proper? And if so, why?

I turned to the letters. Perhaps they would give me some clue. Seating myself behind the desk, I picked up the first missive from atop the neat stack.

The handwriting belonged to my brother Stanford.

CHAPTER 48

Whyborne

I STARED AT the letter for a long moment, absorbing nothing of the content. Stanford had been corresponding from the asylum with Bradley? But why? They hadn't known one another before his confinement—despite his aspirations, Bradley had never moved in the same exalted circles as Stanford. The closest they'd probably ever come was the night of the Hallowe'en tours, when Stanford had threatened everyone's life. Including Bradley's.

My fingers shook, but I forced myself to read the letter. It was dated over a year and a half ago, within two months of Stanford's confinement. Enough time for me to have received my new office and private secretary. For the museum president and director to pay me the courtesies and attention Bradley craved for himself.

Dear Dr. Osborne,

I was surprised, but delighted, to receive your correspondence. You need not concern yourself over what you write—the staff of this asylum don't inspect letters either to or from patients.

If I'd known you too were a "man of vision," as you so kindly put it, I would have involved you. Perhaps then my damnable brother would not have succeeded in ruining everything. What a different world we would have now if not for him! It pains me even to call such a sniveling worm "brother." I'm glad you at least perceive him for the cowardly snake he is.

Although I'm currently in no position to give you direct aid, perhaps we might discuss the things a man might do for himself. Some of them take a strong heart and a steady hand, but I'm certain you're man enough for the task. As you saw at the museum, sorcery is indeed real. If you wish to know more, write back at once, and we can get started.

Yrs truly,

Stanford Whyborne

From the pleased tone, I could only imagine what Bradley must have said in his introductory letter. Praise of Stanford's bold scheme and abuse of me, that much was clear.

Stanford was no sorcerer himself. But he'd been a member of the Brotherhood alongside Father. He knew about the *Liber Arcanorum,* about the standing stones on the island. About the Man in the Woods.

I began to go through the letters, more hastily than I would have liked, but I had no time to read such a volume of correspondence closely. Stanford instructed Bradley on everything—obtaining the estate in secret, acquiring the tomes of arcane knowledge written in languages Bradley could read, and finally how to summon and negotiate with the Man in the Woods.

If only I had Bradley's side of the conversation, where he must have recounted the encounter. I slowed to read Stanford's reply in full, hoping to glean something from his references.

To my Brother in Spirit,

You have taken a tremendous step. I congratulate you on your fortitude. And yes, there is always a price for power—but think of the rewards! Once you perform that which Nyarlathotep has asked of you, you will be honored beyond all others when the Masters return.

Masters? What the devil did Stanford mean? What masters?

It must be fate which has put us in this place at this time, when the stars have come right once again. You have been chosen to take the first step toward the Restoration.

Bradley would love the idea of being the chosen one, just as Stanford had loved the idea the prophecy referred to him. They really were brothers in spirit.

As for the volume the Messenger referred you to, which you don't have in full, I would look in the libraries of those who have had dealings with the Outside for a copy. Our mother insisted on a family dinner after P returned from Egypt, and for the first time I'm glad I agreed to attend. P had been injured—too bad it didn't prove fatal— and of course our parents wanted to hear what had happened. He was already turning into Father's little favorite by then. Apparently his injuries came from the sister of "the bitch" as you call her. She'd summoned something from the Outside—what I don't know. I wasn't really listening, and can you blame me? But if I were you, I'd see if I could find out what became of any books she might have owned.

The graf's donation. At Stanford's urging, Bradley had secretly prompted the graf to send the library to the museum. Christine had been right, when she'd wondered if there had been some hidden hand behind the donation.

Why had I ever told anyone about what happened in Egypt? But Mother was in the process of learning sorcery herself, and there had seemed to be no reason to keep the events secret from my family. And perhaps some part of me had even wanted them—wanted Father—to know my scars had been earned in desperate battle, not just the bad luck of a freak lightning strike.

What an idiot I'd been. Why had I tried to impress my family? Had I imagined Father would suddenly decide I was worth something after all?

I turned my attention to the rest of the letters. I had to find out what Bradley planned. Who were these "masters" Nyarlathotep apparently served, and how did the ritual sites and the maelstrom connect to them? Were they who he hoped to signal somehow?

Fragments jumped out at me.

The Masters must have true power, to have built such a gateway...

Unfortunately, I don't know the location of the other sites. Prepare the one on the island first, while you try to discover the others...

...It would seem from your studies the number six has some

significance. If so, there will be six sites that must be activated before the signal to herald the Restoration can be sent...

...The spell you have discovered will be the key, then. Our bloodline means we are perfect for the task. Widdershins does indeed know its own. P's body has already withstood the power of the maelstrom's eye. Trying to dominate his mind would be too dangerous, but this? Replacing him?

The thought fills me with joy, not only because you will finally get your due, but because I will at last have a true brother, matched in temperament and cause. I've given it a bit of thought, and I will write to Father immediately. In the meantime, I'll tell my doctors that I've seen the error of my ways and have no desire beyond reconciling with my dear brother.

Once P is gone, we'll secure my release, and the Whyborne family will finally be as it was meant to be.

My blood ran cold. No wonder Stanford had been so anxious to see me again. The entire time, he'd been silently gloating, knowing the fate that awaited me.

There was one final letter in the stack from Stanford. A glance at the first few lines implied Bradley had written him to say the plan was in motion at last. But one phrase caught my eye.

How long have the Masters been Outside, I wonder? Long enough the ketoi have no memory of Them.

Masters. The number six. A gateway to the Outside. The Occultum Lapidem.

For a moment I was back in Alaska, far beneath a glacier, within a ruined city filled with hexagonal rooms. The Mother of Shadows spoke of an ancient rebellion against Masters who had created both the umbrae and the ketoi, before vanishing from the earth.

I'd assumed they died out, lost to the millennia. But they hadn't. They'd left our world for the Outside.

And now Bradley meant to bring them back.

CHAPTER 49

Whyborne

HOW LONG I sat and stared at the letter, I didn't know. Finally, a crash of thunder roused me from my stupor.

God. Was I right? Could Bradley truly be so selfish as to bring these inhuman Masters back into the world? Whatever promises their messenger Nyarlathotep had given him of future glory, surely even he would balk at the idea.

Wouldn't he?

I threw down Stanford's letter and began to sort through the smaller pile of correspondence. There wasn't much, and most of it seemed mundane. A letter from city hall, politely declining to donate the surveyor's map to the museum. Correspondence from the new Graf de Wisborg, indicating he'd be only all too happy to donate the library, and complimenting Bradley on his modesty at suggesting the graf allow everyone to believe it was his own generosity which had inspired the thought.

At the bottom of the pile was a letter from a Franklin Osborne—Bradley's father, perhaps? I removed it from its envelope and unfolded it, even though I doubted it would hold much of interest. Surely Bradley wouldn't have confessed his plot to his family, would he?

Son,

I received the newspaper clipping you sent regarding the museum. Although I'm gladdened to know you aren't wasting your time at a lesser institution, I must wonder why you felt it necessary to waste my time. Your name wasn't even mentioned, nor were you in the reporter's sketch therein. The reputation of the museum is meaningless if you cannot even find the wherewithal to endear yourself to those who make its most important decisions! You should have been included, not that Mr. Whyborne and Miss Putnam.

"It's Drs. Whyborne and Putnam," I muttered aloud. I vaguely recalled the newspaper article Bradley must have sent, some blather about new additions to the Nephren-ka exhibit. There'd been only the most tenuous of reasons for me to have been included, but Mr. Mathison felt the Whyborne name might entice wealthy donors. We'd all stood awkwardly in a group, being photographed so an artist could reproduce our likenesses for the paper.

I know the Whyborne name carries weight, but just look at the fellow. He wouldn't last ten seconds in the ring against you! How you can allow such a limp wristed fairy to best you at your own workplace, I cannot fathom. Needless to say, I am dreadfully disappointed. I didn't agree to let you study history for this to be the outcome. I expect better from you in the future.

Yr Father,

Franklin

Bradley had written on the letter, in the space below his father's signature. The reply he would never dare send, perhaps? His pen had gouged and ripped the paper in his anger.

FUCK YOU, Father! I've found a family who sees my true worth. I can't wait until the funeral. Watching you cry over "my" casket, while I'm standing beside my new father, will be sweet.

I read the words over again, feeling something much like a heavy, smothering blanket settle over my heart.

...a family who sees my true worth.

...my new father...

I'd assumed Stanford and Bradley alone had been in communication. But why shouldn't Father have been involved as well? There were no letters from him...but unlike Stanford, Bradley could have met with him directly any time he pleased.

It all made a terrible sort of sense. Stanford had no way of knowing Griffin possessed an Occultum Lapidem...but Father did. No wonder Father had been so insistent I visit the asylum with him.

I'd failed to come to heel as Father wanted, failed to be the son he thought I should be after Stanford was taken from him. So he'd simply decided to replace me. Bradley's consciousness in my body would give him the perfect son: ambitious, cunning, and willing to use magic to further Father's schemes.

All those bribes to my friends: the stock to Griffin, the wedding venue to Christine and Iskander, even the dinner with Persephone. All meant to alienate them from me, just as I'd guessed.

Just not for the reasons I'd guessed. When "I" returned to Father's side, it would seem more natural after all his kindnesses.

Especially if they meant to kill Griffin. Any alterations in my character would seem the result of grief. The Whyborne heir would return home to his remaining family. Take up the business to distract himself from his loss. Have a tearful reunion with a reformed Stanford. Marry an heiress.

Rule the world, when the Masters returned.

With a furious cry, I swept the letters off the desk, scattering them to the floor. God! I'd actually thought Griffin might be right; I'd actually believed for a moment that Father might care about me.

I'd been such an idiot.

My knees struck the carpet, and I buried my face in my hands. My features felt horribly distorted to my own touch, my fingers too short, everything wrong, wrong, *wrong*. My father had plotted against me; my friends would think me an enemy if I went to them now; even the police were after me. Surely Bradley would have them post notices all over town: Wanted, dead or alive.

I was hunted, without friends or family. I could no longer feel the arcane fire beneath my feet, and even the simplest spell came only with difficulty. Bradley meant to send some sort of signal inviting inhuman creatures back into the world. The Masters would surely destroy or enslave the umbrae and the ketoi once again. Probably humanity as well, just for good measure.

We were all going to die, and there was nothing I could do in this form to stop it. Bradley had been right, when he'd said I'd earned nothing, only been born to the right parents. Remove my bloodline, and I had nothing. Was nothing. Just an awkward scholar who spoke too many languages.

I didn't know how long I sat there, feeling sorry for myself and listening to the rain drip from a hole in the ceiling onto the floor. I was damp and cold and utterly miserable, and a part of me wanted to just curl up on the rotting carpet and sleep.

But that certainly wasn't going to accomplish anything. An attempt to stop Bradley might not accomplish anything either, but at least I'd die knowing I'd tried.

The cultist had implied Bradley had only a few hours until it was time to send the signal. I'd go to the Front Street Bridge and hope I didn't get arrested or killed before Bradley appeared to finish his ritual. How I would stop him then...well, perhaps something would present itself.

I'd probably die, and Bradley succeed. As he meant to take over my identity, I should at least post letters first, warning Christine and Griffin of what had happened. With any luck, they'd realize the truth before he hurt them.

I stood up and returned to the desk, hoping to find some fresh paper and a pen. But before I reached it, there came the unmistakable sound of a door opening.

I froze, my heart pounding. Which was absurd—whoever it was must have seen the light of the lantern, telling them exactly what room I was in. God, I was an idiot.

I snatched up the witch hunter's knife. Treading as quietly as I was able, I made my way to the wall and positioned myself beside the door. The moment it opened, I'd stab my attacker and run. Hopefully I'd find myself against a lone cultist; if there were more, I'd be in deep trouble.

The floorboards creaked just outside. I held my breath as the door began to ease open. I raised the knife and let out a wild yell—then froze.

Griffin stood before me, his revolver trained on my face.

CHAPTER 50

Griffin

"**Drop the dagger!**" I shouted.

Bradley Osborne stared at me, his eyes wide, his lips slightly parted. His fingers uncurled from the dagger, and it fell to the floor with a dull thud.

And, instantly, he lit up in my shadowsight like a flare.

He *burned,* just as Whyborne hadn't. All of the fire that had been inexplicably drained from my Ival was poured into Bradley. Had he stolen it somehow?

"I ought to put a bullet through you this minute," I snarled. "Tell me what you did to Whyborne, or I swear I'll shoot you and hope your death will reverse the spell."

Bradley let out a small, choked sound. Holding his hands up, he cringed back from me. "Griffin, please," he said desperately. "Give me a chance to explain."

"You've murdered innocent men. Used the foulest sorcery." I stepped closer, pressing the barrel of the gun to his forehead. "There's no explanation you could give that I'm interested in."

"I'm not Bradley!"

Not Bradley.

It wasn't possible. And yet, I couldn't deny what was before my own eyes.

I'd been with many men society would consider more handsome than my Ival. And yet something had drawn me to him from the first moment. I loved how much taller than me he was; I loved his unmanageable hair; I loved the way he smelled, of salt and ocean air.

But I loved those things because they belonged to him. Because I'd lost my heart, utterly and irrevocably, to *him*.

I lowered my revolver. "Ival?" I whispered. It was madness, and yet the moment the words left my lips, I knew them to be true.

He blinked eyes that were the wrong shape, the wrong color. Then they widened. "Yes! Bradley switched us somehow, but it's me, I swear! Whyborne. Your husband."

"Oh God," I gasped, and reached for him.

He jerked back, shaking his head. "No. No, this is wrong, all wrong." He held out his hands, staring at them. "I can't...I can't touch you like this, I..."

I hauled him into my arms. And he was right, it *was* wrong. He didn't smell like my Ival, didn't feel like him. Too short, too wide, his hair too tame and his cologne too expensive. But I held him tight anyway, while he out let a soft sob into my shoulder.

"I was so afraid for you," he said, words muffled by my rain-damp coat. "He'd have to kill you, to keep up the deception, and it would have to be soon, but I didn't think you'd believe me, and—and...why *do* you believe me?"

He drew back, but I caught his chin in my hand, looking at him straight on. Focusing on my shadowsight, on what lay beneath his skin. "Because I see you," I said. "And when I glimpsed him earlier...I didn't see you."

His brows drew together. "I don't understand."

"The flame. The fire in your blood. I always felt it, but the shadowsight shows it."

Whyborne shook his head uncertainly. "This...this body...doesn't have ketoi blood or any of the rest of it. There's nothing to see."

"Of course there is." I ran my thumb tenderly along his jaw, and if the shape of it was wrong beneath my touch, I couldn't let myself care. "The fire in your blood isn't your heritage. It's *you*."

"That makes no sense," he said, his tones so like Whyborne's and so unlike Bradley's I almost laughed. "But it doesn't matter why you believe me, so long as you do. We have to stop Bradley. I know what he wants, what he's been trying to do all along."

I released him. "Then tell me."

He did so. I stared at the map, the letters, in growing horror. "Curse it," I said when he finished. "If I hadn't gone to Boston—"

"They would have killed you," Whyborne said, putting his hand to my arm. "Bradley intended to murder you, ambush me, then murder me in his old body. Your trip to Boston spoiled his plan."

"And if he hadn't taken the time to gloat, he probably would have killed you before Christine got there." Thank God I'd thought to use the telephone. "We have to go to her immediately. I left her and Persephone at Whyborne House. I told her there was something wrong with you—who I thought was you." I shook my head angrily at my own blindness. "Damn it, I can't believe I didn't realize. How could I have possibly imagined he was you, even for a moment?"

"You couldn't have known. But if they're in Whyborne House, they're in terrible danger." The color drained from his face. "If Father thinks they realize Bradley isn't me...he's ruthless, Griffin. Utterly ruthless."

I hated the alien feel of the shoulder beneath my hand, so I focused again on my shadowsight. This was Whyborne, my love, my Ival, no matter the skin he'd been consigned to. "We don't know for certain your father is involved," I said.

Whyborne pulled away. "Don't be absurd. Of course he is. This is what he always wanted." He picked up the dagger from the floor; the light in him vanished at its touch. "We need to go. To put a stop to this now, before it's too late."

I wasn't so certain of Niles's guilt. He'd seemed so genuine. As though he were desperately reaching out to his son, even if thirty years later than he should have.

But whichever of us was right about Niles, Whyborne was certainly correct about the rest. Now that we knew what Bradley was up to, dawdling would get us nowhere. We needed to find him and restore Whyborne to his proper body, as soon as possible.

"Agreed," I said, following him to the door. "And you'll be glad to know I drove here in the motor car."

CHAPTER 51

Griffin

I DROVE AS quickly as I dared through the rainy streets. The rain apron kept off some of the wet, but was less effective than I'd hoped when I purchased it. Since "Bradley Osborne" was now a wanted man, Whyborne huddled low in the seat, driving goggles obscuring his face and his hat pulled low. At least the rain and the late hour meant the streets were largely deserted.

By the time we reached High Street, the rain had largely slacked off. The wheels lost traction coming around a corner, and we slid a few feet. I'd gotten the trick of navigating such skids, though, and managed to avoid the lamppost, only driving on the sidewalk a short distance.

"Are we still alive?" Whyborne asked as I stopped just down the road from Whyborne House.

"Of course."

He wiped at the rain obscuring the lenses of his goggles. "Why did you stop here?"

"Because strolling through the front door and confronting Bradley seems rather risky. From what you said, he's taught himself a few spells, and I don't want to find myself on fire," I said. "Huddle beneath the rain apron where no one can see you. I don't think anyone will be along, but I don't wish to chance it. I'll find Christine and anyone else who's still here and tell them what's happening. Somehow we'll think of a way to subdue Bradley."

"Be careful." Whyborne grabbed my wrist as I started to slide out of the motor car. "Watch out for Father. I know you aren't convinced he's part of this, but you can't take the chance you're wrong. If he realizes you're making a move against Bradley, he'll kill you without a second thought."

"I'll be careful," I promised. I longed to kiss him, but it felt wrong to do so while he was in this borrowed body. Thank heavens I'd realized something was wrong before I'd been tempted to touch Bradley.

Then again, perhaps if I'd tried to touch him, he would have lashed out at me and betrayed himself immediately. I imagined he was trying very hard not to picture all the things I'd done with Whyborne's body over the years.

God, I'd do them again, as soon as Whyborne was restored. But first things first.

The lights of Whyborne House blazed bright, despite the late hour. Fenton answered the door, his normally impassive face betraying a slightly sour expression. No doubt he was wishing the guests would leave so he could retire to his bed.

"Come in, Mr. Flaherty," he said. "Master Percival isn't here, but I imagine Mr. Barnett will wish to speak with you."

Dread flooded through me. "Percival isn't here? Where is he?"

"I believe Mr. Barnett would prefer to tell you." Fenton turned his back and started away, leaving me no choice but to scurry after in bewilderment. I glanced in the ballroom as I passed—and stopped in astonishment.

Persephone and Miss Parkhurst had worked wonders. The pale tints of shell and pearl perfectly offset the bright colors of the flowers, pulling everything into a single, harmonious whole. "Extraordinary," I said.

"Yes. A shame," Fenton said. I cast him a curious look, but he said nothing, merely continued on to the drawing room.

Iskander sat in a chair, his head bowed. His dark hair was wildly disarranged, as if he'd run his hands through it in distress, and his shoulders slumped. A half-empty tumbler of brandy sat on the delicate table at his elbow. Miss Parkhurst patted him on the shoulder consolingly. "I'm certain Dr. Whyborne will talk some sense into Dr. Putnam," she was saying as I entered.

"Iskander?" I asked. "What's going on?"

"She left," Iskander said to the floor. Miss Parkhurst winced.

"I don't understand," I said, glancing at her for an explanation.

"Dr. Putnam suffered some pre-wedding jitters," she said carefully. "But I'm certain it's nothing to worry about, Mr. Barnett."

"Haven't you met Christine before?" he asked, finally raising his head. "She doesn't get jitters, she makes decisions. She changed her mind about the wedding, and she left."

Obviously things had gone horribly wrong in my absence. "Tell me what happened."

"She seemed...troubled...after you departed," Miss Parkhurst explained. "She and Persephone spoke for a bit, out of my hearing. Then she went to talk to Dr. Whyborne."

Damn it. But of course she'd had no reason to suspect the man she'd gone to speak with wasn't Whyborne at all. "And when she returned, she suddenly wanted to call off the wedding," I guessed. Damn it, Bradley must have used mind control on her for some reason. But why? Had he given himself away?

Miss Parkhurst wrung her hands unhappily. "She gave me a note to give Mr. Barnett and left. A few minutes later, Dr. Whyborne came looking for her. He asked for the letter—it was just folded—so he read it. He said to wait here, that he was going to talk sense into her, and rushed out. Persephone seemed alarmed, told me to wait here, and went after him."

I felt as though a shadow fell over the room, despite the electric lights. This was worse and worse.

"Then Mr. Barnett arrived, and..." Miss Parkhurst trailed off, looking miserable.

"She never wanted a society wedding," Iskander said. "I knew she didn't, but I thought...and what I said to her last night about *sabotaging* my efforts...I should have listened to her. I was so determined to have the right kind of wedding that I didn't stop to consider my own bride's wishes. I knew her parents had tried to push her when she was younger, and then I ended up doing the same thing."

"This has nothing to do with you," I said. "Bradley cast his accursed spell of mind domination, the same he used against Lambert and Durfree. Christine's will would have be harder to overcome...but of course he can draw on the power of the maelstrom now."

"The maelstrom?" Miss Parkhurst asked, at the same moment as Iskander said, "Bradley's behind this? But why?"

Before I could answer, a crash and the sound of shouting voices echoed through the house.

CHAPTER 52

Whyborne

I TRIED TO do as Griffin asked and lay quietly in the motor car, pretending to be a piece of luggage. Unfortunately, I'd never been terribly good at waiting, and ended up fidgeting far too much to be convincing.

Where was he? What was going on inside? Did I dare draw close enough to find out?

What if Bradley had ambushed him? Between Bradley and Father, all of my friends might be in terrible danger, while I sat here like a useless lump.

Oh God. If Father claimed assassins attacked the house, tragically killing Griffin, Christine, and Iskander the night before the wedding, who would gainsay him? Tilton, for all his attempts to bring justice to Tubbs and Lambert, would ultimately do as Father ordered. There would be no real investigation.

I crawled out from beneath the rain apron. At least no one else was on the street. I'd lost all track of time, but it was surely after midnight. Still, I left on the goggles and hat, just in case someone looked out a window or a police officer decided to walk his beat despite the weather.

My shoes squelched wetly as I made my way toward the house. Should I try the front door? Perhaps the servant's entrance would be safer, as I'd be less likely to encounter Bradley. Could I claim to be making a delivery for the wedding, despite the late hour? I entertained the idea, but couldn't think of a plausible reason they would let me in.

Would Fenton recognize Bradley Osborne's face? Possibly, if Bradley had met with Father here. If he'd gone to one of Father's business offices instead, though, Fenton might not recognize my current features at all. Perhaps I could tell him I was there with a message for Griffin, to be given privately? That seemed possible, at least.

Silently praying my plan would work, I rang the bell. Fenton answered with a promptness that surprised me, given the hour. Disappointment flashed across his face, as though he'd expected someone else. It was quickly followed by disapproval. As for recognition, however, there was none.

"Yes?" he asked. Had he been a sorcerer, his icy disdain would have changed the rain into sleet.

I must look like an utter madman. Although the suit I wore had started off respectable, between the police wagon and the abandoned estate, it had acquired quite a few stains. Mud spattered both shoes and trousers, and every inch of me was soaking wet.

I removed the hat and goggles, certain he'd slam the door in my face otherwise. "I need to speak to Mr. Flaherty," I said. "It's of the utmost importance, regarding something he's looking into for the Whyborne family."

Fenton wavered, no doubt torn between his distaste for letting such a disreputable looking person set foot in the house, and his concern I might indeed have urgent business on behalf of the family. "Very well," he said, standing aside. He didn't offer to take my hat. "Wait here, and I'll fetch Mr. Flaherty."

He had only gone a few feet, however, before Father appeared in the foyer. "Who was—" he began, then stopped when he saw me. "What is the meaning of this?" Father thundered. "What the devil are *you* doing here?"

The anger and hurt that had simmered all night rose to a sudden boil in my veins. I took a step forward, and was almost shocked that the world no longer responded to my rage. Wind should be shrieking through the foyer, ripping the portraits of our damnable ancestors off the walls. Destroying everything around me.

But there was nothing. I was cut off from the arcane fire beneath my feet.

Thanks to him.

"I expect you never thought you'd see me again, did you, *Father?*" I snarled.

"What in the name of hell?" Father took a step back. "Fenton, fetch your pistol!"

"Don't play the fool!" I snatched up a priceless vase from its pedestal and hurled it to the ground, smashing it into a thousand shards. "You were behind this from the start! You and Stanford."

There came the sound of running feet on the marble floors. A moment later, Griffin, Iskander, and Miss Parkhurst appeared. Iskander let out a shout of alarm, but Griffin flung up his hands, as if calling for peace. "No! It's not what you think. It's not Bradley."

Niles glared at me. "I saw Dr. Osborne tied up on the floor only a few hours ago. I assure you, this is indeed him."

"Bradley Osborne perfected a spell allowing him to swap bodies," Griffin said. "Which he did earlier today. He stole Whyborne's body, and put Whyborne in his body. The man you brought back here wasn't your son at all."

Miss Parkhurst gasped and stared at me, as if she expected to see my true features miraculously appear. All the color drained from Father's face. His gaze locked with mine, searching. "P-Percival?"

"Don't play the innocent." I took a step forward, my hands clenched into fists. "I know what you've done. I know you offered the wedding venue to Christine and Iskander, the stock to Griffin, the waffles to Persephone, *everything*, just to turn them against me! You couldn't stand I wouldn't come to heel, so you decided to make the perfect son. You took Bradley by the hand and led him to the Man in the Woods, to the Brotherhood's secrets, all for this." I made a disgusted gesture at the form I'd been consigned to. "So he could steal my body and become the heir you always wanted!"

Father swayed. "You're speaking nonsense. Why would I do such a thing?"

"Because Bradley wants what you want." I shook my head, feeling suddenly tired. "He'll come work for you at Whyborne Railroad and Industries. He'll use his magic for your benefit." I laughed without humor. "He'll even be of your blood, since he's got my body. He'll be the son I never was. The one you always wanted."

"No!" Father seemed to gather himself. He strode toward me, but I refused to give ground. When he stopped a pace away, he grabbed me by the arms. I tried to yank free, but he tightened his grip. "I offered Whyborne House to your friends, I offered Griffin stock, all of it to show you that I care. That I'm interested in your life, no matter how odd it might seem to me."

How could he pretend even now? "Don't lie to me!"

"I'm not lying. I know we've had our differences. But after the Brotherhood was destroyed, when I realized you didn't trust me enough to come to me with what you knew...that you thought I would agree to unleashing horror on the world..." He bowed his head. "You stood up to them all. When confronted by monsters, you fought back. You would have sacrificed yourself to save the rest of us. And I began to realize I'd made a terrible, terrible mistake."

I didn't want to hear any of this. I tried again to pull away, and he finally let go of me.

"I tried to do better," he said. "Donating to the museum where you work. Including Griffin in family dinners. But the harder I try to reach out to you, the harder you push me away." To my horror tears formed in his eyes. "I know it's too little, too late. But, Percival...you're my son. I love you."

Words deserted me. It might have been some elaborate ruse, and yet I couldn't believe Father would humble himself so in front of others, even in the service of some grandiose plan.

"Whyborne," Griffin said softly. "I think Stanford and Bradley acted alone in this."

My mind grasped at one last possibility. "Stanford didn't know we had a Lapidem."

"If Nyarlathotep is a servant of the ancient Masters, he might be able to sense their artifacts," Griffin pointed out. "After all, Nephren-ka had one as well."

He was right. I'd let my own anger over old hurts blind me to any possibility save Father's guilt. As much as it pained me to admit it, I'd done him a disservice. "I...yes." My shoulders slumped, tension leaving them. "I'm sorry, Father. I didn't...I never meant to..."

"Later," he said briskly. "The question now is, where has Dr. Osborne gone with your body, and how are we to get it back?"

Iskander's face had gone gray. "When Christine went to talk to Whyborne—it was Bradley she found. You're right, Griffin. He put her under some kind of mind domination, then used her absence as an excuse to leave himself." He swallowed hard. "Do you think...do you think he hurt her?"

"Or Persephone?" Miss Parkhurst asked in alarm.

I ran a frustrated hand through my hair. It was too flat, too... tame. I'd never imagined missing my real hair, but I did, desperately so. "The cultist at the estate said there were only a few hours left," I said. "And that was a few hours ago. Whatever Bradley means to do to send this signal, it must be happening now."

There came a low boom, just on the edge of hearing, like a distant explosion. The floor trembled beneath our feet, and the chandelier swung alarmingly. "An earthquake!" Iskander exclaimed.

"No." Griffin stared at the windows flanking the street, then ran to the door and flung it open. "Whyborne! Do you see this?"

I ran to his side. But there was nothing but the night and the falling rain. "No. What is it?"

"Arcane fire," he said grimly. "As if one of the lines feeding into the maelstrom suddenly surged with energy."

I followed his line of sight. Although the magic was invisible to me, I could imagine it tracing a graceful arc across Widdershins. "One of the lines...such as the one intersecting with the standing stones on the island?"

All the color drained from Griffin's face. "Yes. He's begun."

"Then we must go quickly," Father said. "The motor car, Fenton."

There came a new sound—the rattle of carriages and the clop of hooves. "What now?" Iskander wondered aloud, even as he drew out his knives.

A small battalion of carriages, gigs, and coaches appeared at the end of the street. Seated on the driver's seat of the foremost one was Mr. Quinn.

They drew to a halt in front of the mansion. Mr. Quinn frowned at me, then glanced questioningly at Griffin.

"Bradley Osborne used magic to swap bodies with Whyborne," Griffin said bluntly. "He means to use the power of the maelstrom in a spell, and probably kill Dr. Putnam to boot."

Quinn's eyes widened, and he drew himself up. "This is an outrage," he said, and the anger in his voice was more than a little frightening. "An affront against Widdershins. We will not tolerate this."

"Excuse me," Iskander said, "but what the bloody hell are you doing here?"

"I returned from Boston and rallied my fellow librarians to defend the town," Quinn replied, as if the answer should have been obvious. He offered me a small bow from his seat. "The librarians are at your disposal, Widdershins. We will fight to the last man."

CHAPTER 53

Whyborne

I CLUNG TO the seat of the Oldsmobile as Griffin took another corner at death-defying speed. Iskander perched in my lap, clinging to me in turn. His hat was gone, and his thick black hair ruffled in the wind as Griffin navigated the streets recklessly. Somewhere behind us came Father's motor car, Fenton at the wheel, followed by the librarians in their varied horse-drawn conveyances.

My heart pounded in my throat, in part from Griffin's mad driving and in part from fear. I could only imagine what Iskander must be feeling at the moment. If Bradley had hurt Christine, I'd kill him with my bare hands. The moment I had my body back, I'd tear his to pieces.

There came another boom as we drove, and Griffin pointed to the north. The site of the standing stones on the Robinsons' farm appeared to have become active in the same way as the other.

Two down. Four to go.

Whatever Bradley had done to the arcane lines, they didn't simply glow more brightly. As we drove, we crossed the first one. Every building it ran beneath had shattered windows, and the electricity had gone out over wide swathes of the town. People milled wildly in the streets despite the rain and darkness, forcing Griffin to honk the horn even more than usual.

"There's the bridge," Griffin said at last, and the grim note in his voice made my heart sink. Why had the city rebuilt the blasted thing in the first place? Yes, it was a major road linking one half of the town to the other, but still. I'd write a sharply worded letter to the mayor once all this was over.

Assuming I lived long enough to do so, anyway.

The electric lights had gone out, but torches lined the bridge, flickering in the rain. Robed cultists lined either end of the bridge, clearly guarding against anyone who might think to disrupt the proceedings. In the uncertain light, it looked almost as though they had no faces, only blackness beneath their hoods. But no, they wore masks—smooth and featureless, save for the holes for their eyes.

The police were notably absent, whether paid off or warned away by someone they thought to be me, I didn't know. In the center of the bridge stood a strange a metallic device. The Occultum Lapidem rested atop it, like the lens of a telescope.

Three more robed, masked figures attended it. Two of them held a struggling figure between them.

"Christine!" Iskander gasped.

A gag covered her mouth, and her dark hair had come out of its bun. Though her hands were bound, she thrashed furiously, and one of the figures abruptly doubled over as she managed to land a blow to its gut.

The third turned and made a furious motion toward them. Though a mask covered his face, he was much taller than the others, and my stomach turned to realize it must be Bradley.

Wearing my body.

The light from the lamps of Griffin's motor car flashed across the cultists blocking the end of the bridge. One shouted a warning, and Bradley turned to us.

Perhaps some sympathy still bound me to my real body, because I knew in that instant exactly what he meant to do.

"Jump!" I shouted as we hurtled toward the line of cultists. "He means to set the gasoline in the tank on fire!"

CHAPTER 54

Griffin

AT WHYBORNE'S CRY, I hurled myself from the motor car.

I landed hard, rolling to absorb the hit. Iskander shouted, and a dull thump marked Whyborne's impact against the brick-paved road. For a fraction of a second, I wondered if he'd been wrong, and we'd risked broken bones for no reason.

The gasoline tank exploded with a thunderous blast.

Bits of metal flew past, a piece of the tiller striking the road just inches away from my nose. The remains of the flaming wreck hurtled forward on the burning wheels. The cultists blocking the bridge dove madly out of the way, but momentum carried the fiery wreckage into two who weren't fast enough, smashing them into the bridge railing.

My motor car. Gone.

There came another distant boom, and a third line of arcane fire roared to new life. Sheets of blue flame reached toward the sky from the three lines, and the Lapidem blazed like a small sun where they all met in the eye of the vortex.

"Whyborne?" I called. "Iskander? Are you all right?"

"I'm fine!" Whyborne called. "But—damn it!"

The surviving cultists from this end of the bridge rushed toward us. I drew my revolver, prepared to shoot as many as possible.

A host of sleek forms erupted from beneath the bridge. Shark teeth flashed in the torchlight, and clouds of stinging tentacle hair wrapped around exposed skin.

I held my fire, instead drawing my sword cane. Iskander had his knives, and charged into the fray with a ululating cry. The ketoi scarcely needed our help, though, their savage teeth and sharp spears washing the streets in blood.

One of the cultists broke free from the ketoi and rushed toward Whyborne. He fell back, eyes wide, and drew the witch hunter's dagger from his coat. I let out a shout of alarm and tried to run to his side, but I knew I'd never reach him in time.

One of the ketoi leapt onto the cultist's back. Her teeth sank into his head, biting through his hood and knocking his mask off. He screamed horribly, crashing to the ground while she continued to maul him.

I lunged forward with my sword cane, ending his struggles. The ketoi rose from his limp body, and I found myself staring into my mother-in-law's face. "Heliabel?"

"Heliabel?" repeated a voice from behind me.

Niles stood there, having apparently abandoned his motor car after seeing what had become of my poor Curved Dash. His eyes were wide, his skin slightly ashen. He started to lift one hand, then stopped, so it hovered halfway into the gesture.

She drew herself up like a queen. Her tentacle hair stilled its thrashing. "Niles," she said. Blood rimmed her teeth. "Griffin. Persephone says—"

"Brother?"

Persephone stood a few feet from Whyborne, her eyes wide. "I knew it! As soon as I drew close, I knew that was not Fire in His Blood," she cried. "He stole your face, but it wasn't you."

There came the sound of a fourth distant explosion, accompanied by screams and breaking glass. Seconds later, another arcane line surged into violent life.

Four down, two to go.

Whyborne nodded. "You're right. It isn't me—it's Bradley. And he has Christine."

Persephone grinned. "Not for long. I followed him here. As soon as I realized he was not my brother, I went into the sea and called."

"Summoning an army does have its advantages," Heliabel agreed.

"Librarians! Defend your city!" Mr. Quinn shouted from the opposite end of the bridge.

"Speaking of which," I said.

There came a wild cacophony of shouts, the librarians hurling rocks at the line of cultists. A horse let out a loud whinny as someone tried to drive a carriage through. It reared in the traces, hooves striking at the cultists, forcing them back. A smattering of guns fired as well.

Dark shapes slipped over the side of the bridge. One of the cultists holding Christine started to cry out—then fell silent as a ketoi spear took him in the chest. The other surrendered his grip on Christine in favor of drawing out a wicked-looking dagger.

Christine didn't hesitate. She charged at the side of the bridge, and two of the ketoi caught her up just as she reached the railing. All three dove, bodies vanishing beneath the water.

"Christine's safe!" Whyborne cried, at the same moment Iskander exclaimed, "Thank God!"

Hope bloomed in my chest. Bradley had no chance. If he'd meant to use Christine as his final sacrifice, he no longer had any hope of completing the ritual, no matter how much chanting he did in the meantime. His cultists fell before the ketoi and the librarians. We'd have him soon enough, and Whyborne would discover how to reverse the body swap once we had the Lapidem back in our possession.

A fifth line surged into power. "He can't complete the ritual, can he?" I asked in alarm.

"I should think not." Christine struggled up the embankment, her clothing dripping wet. "He meant to make me his final sacrifice. Bradley never did have any imagination."

"Christine!" Iskander ran to her and swept her into his arms. "God, Christine, I never—"

"Look out!" Christine shouted.

More cultists swept in toward us from the surrounding city. How many were there? My informants had said an unusual number of strangers had invaded the town. Had they been drawn from all over the world, intent on the Restoration their cult promised to usher in?

I tossed Christine my gun. She and Iskander fell together back to back, while I prepared to do battle with my sword cane.

"I know Bradley forced you to write the letter," Iskander said. There came the calm crack of the revolver as Christine aimed and fired. "But I know too there was some truth in it. You never wanted a society wedding, and I was thoughtless."

The world was shadows and madness. The flames from the burning motor car flung an uncertain orange glow over the scene. Cultists and librarians struggled against one another, and I glimpsed Mr. Quinn bashing a man in the face with what appeared to be a very heavy dictionary.

"You're being absurd!" Christine shouted back. "We're going to be married, damn it, and Whyborne is going to walk me down the aisle in his proper body. It's going to be perfect, even if I have to kill every one of these bastards myself!"

I slashed and turned, grabbing a handful of robes and wrenching an attacker off his feet. A moment later, Iskander finished him off in a spray of blood. "I love you, Christine!"

"Are you both insane?" Whyborne shouted. "Bradley is still casting his spell!"

The air seemed to tremble. Bradley stood at the center of the bridge beside his device, one of the cultists who had held Christine still beside him.

The sixth and final arcane line roared to life.

The light at the heart of the maelstrom nearly blinded my shadowsight. I almost heard it now, a keening song, as if the vortex itself had a voice. I started onto the bridge, dodging the cultists the ketoi hadn't yet brought down. Whyborne joined me, the witch hunter's dagger clutched in his hand.

"Bradley!" he shouted. "Give yourself up! Your plan is in ruins. Give me back my body, and we'll let you live."

Bradley turned slowly, and I found myself glad a mask hid his stolen face. "Yours? You didn't deserve this! You didn't deserve any of it! And now you *dare* to think me defeated?"

With a single, smooth motion, he drew his knife across the throat of the cultist at his side.

The man's hood fell back as he staggered. His knife tumbled from limp fingers, but before he could follow it to the ground, Bradley hauled the man's dying body closer to the device. Blood poured across the Lapidem, down the strange cradle it sat in, into grooves and hollows that suddenly flared with arcane light. A sphere of blue fire sprang up, visible even to my ordinary sight, encircling Bradley and the device alike.

With a final, contemptuous shove, Bradley dropped the empty husk of the dead man. Turning to the device, he raised his arms and began to chant.

CHAPTER 55

Whyborne

I STOOD FROZEN. All around me the battle still raged: librarians struggled with the cultists, ketoi rose from the river howling in rage, and Christine fired Griffin's revolver. But somehow I heard Bradley's chant even through the screams and snarls, the words in no tongue I knew.

Perhaps in no tongue ever spoken by humankind.

The wind picked up, and I felt it spiral, even as the great maelstrom spiraled beneath my feet. The bubble of seething blue light enclosing Bradley spread its radiance over the scene, visible now even to me.

"Whyborne!" Griffin shouted. I turned. A dark clot of robed men rushed toward us, yet more reinforcements summoned from wherever they had lurked in reserve. "What's happening?"

"Power," I said numbly. The six ritual sites had been primed in some fashion, and now fed titanic amounts of arcane energy into the heart of the vortex. "The Lapidem is absorbing it for the moment, I think, but that will only last until Bradley reaches the end of his chant."

Griffin paled. "And then...the beacon?"

"To signal the start of the Restoration. Yes."

He nodded. Then he firmed his grip on his sword cane and looked to me. "What do we do? Can we reach Bradley through the sphere of energy surrounding him?"

I had no magic. No means of stopping Bradley. Nothing at all but the witch hunter's dagger.

Well. It would have to do, then.

"Whyborne?" Griffin's face was pale and streaked with blood. The reeking smoke from the burning motor car billowed around us, stinging my eyes.

"Stay here and hold off the reinforcements," I said. "I'll stop Bradley."

He seized my wrist. "Ival, just remember. You might not be in the right body, but you're still the right man. Widdershins knows its own." His fingers tightened, the white pearl on his wedding band glowing in the blue light. "I'll hold them off your back. Do what needs to be done."

Griffin released me and turned to the charging cultists. The steel of his sword cane reflected the light redly—then became red from blood as he slashed and stabbed.

I tore my eyes away from him, forcing my feet into motion. The wind grew stronger and stronger as I neared the center of the bridge, and the river roared and shook the stones beneath my feet. Above us, the very clouds had joined the vortex, swirling like a hurricane while Bradley's chant rose toward a crescendo.

I paused just outside the barrier, my arm raised against the glare. I firmed my grip on the witch hunter's dagger and held it before me like a shield.

Taking a deep breath, I plunged into the sphere of gathering energy.

Pain seared every nerve, and it was all I could do not to scream. Wild magic exploded all around me, a part of the maelstrom made manifest, scorching my skin. The witch hunter's dagger sliced through it, but it could only do so much to protect me from the sheer amount of magic surrounding me.

I'd told Griffin a normal human body wasn't meant to channel such power. I'd been right; the taste of burning filled my mouth, and blood hazed my vision. No wonder Bradley's acquisition of my body had been so carefully planned.

And now I was in an ordinary body. Just an ordinary person.

I couldn't do this. My legs gave way, my knees striking the stones. I had to turn back, before it killed me, before I died here, burned to ash by a magic this form was never meant to contain.

I looked back over my shoulder, ready to crawl away. Bradley had been right about me. I was nothing but the blood I'd been lucky enough to be born to. Without it, without the magic, I had nothing at all to make me special.

The fighting behind me had grown more desperate: Persephone and Griffin stood back to back, while Christine had run out of bullets and now fought by Iskander with a spear of ketoi make. Father fired his old Remington from the war, the gray in his beard washed red from the firelight.

All of them, depending on me. If Bradley succeeded in sending the signal, in starting a chain of events meant to return the inhuman Masters to their old power, all of them would die. The ketoi and umbrae would be slaves again, and I doubted most humans would fare any better.

Clutching the dagger tight, I forced myself to my feet. A cry of anguish escaped me, and I turned it to a shout of rage as I plunged forward, toward the heart of the sphere and Bradley.

He turned, flinging up a hand. I *felt* the spell he tried to use against me come apart on the edge of the dagger.

The device flared, visible even to my merely human sight, and I knew there was no time left. I couldn't let him finish the ritual, no matter the cost.

"You should have left this in the museum," I said. And thrust the dagger deep into the chest of what had been my body.

His eyes widened in shock. The pain in my own limbs reached a crescendo, and I heard myself laughing like a maniac, a sound of despair and triumph mixed together.

There came a deep bell-like tone, as if the entire world were a chime that had just been struck by a mallet. The sphere around us collapsed, and the maelstrom's fire burst forth from the Lapidem, punching a hole in the very sky and pouring through into whatever lay Beyond.

I was too late. The signal had been sent.

CHAPTER 56

Griffin

WHYBORNE'S SHOUT OF fury and pain echoed to me even over the sounds of battle. I bashed a cultist in the face with my fist, then kicked another in the stomach to buy myself space. "Whyborne! I'm coming!"

I turned to run out onto the bridge—then froze. Whyborne had made his way to Bradley, but my heart lurched at the sight.

He'd said a mortal body wasn't meant to contain the fury of the maelstrom. And now I realized just how right he'd been.

Skin charred and turned black, peeling away in patches, the ash scattered by the howling wind. Hair came loose in clumps, and blood soaked through his clothes in places. I screamed at him to stop, to come back. Nothing was worth this. Whyborne in the wrong body would still be my love; he couldn't die like this. He had to stop.

But he didn't stop, despite what must have been agonizing pain. Instead, he raised the witch hunter's dagger.

And plunged it into Bradley's chest. *His* chest.

No.

The world stopped—or maybe it spun faster, and I was still. Frozen.

Because if both bodies were destroyed, then how could he live?

My throat was raw; distantly, as though it happened to someone else, I realized I was screaming a denial. My legs moved, seemingly of their own volition, as though every muscle in my body, every atom, demanded I go to him.

I had to stop this, somehow. Had to turn back time, remove the dagger, put Whyborne back in the right body and piece it all together again. But I was already too late.

Just as he had been.

The surge from the device nearly blinded me. All the wild energy of the barrier, of wind and wave and cloud, collapsed inward. The beam of light shooting from the center of the maelstrom changed, focused by the Lapidem.

And tore a hole in reality itself.

The signal had been sent. The Restoration had begun.

Bradley collapsed forward, blood pouring out from the huge wound in his chest. His mask fell off, revealing the features that should have belonged to my Ival, and I screamed again. He fell onto Whyborne, but the rapidly disintegrating human body couldn't hold his weight, and they both crashed into the device and the Lapidem.

The light seemed to pulse again, and the power of the maelstrom poured into both bodies, human and ketoi hybrid. Bradley's original body began to come apart, charring into ash, pieces falling away, crumbling faster and faster, until there came a bright flare—

And in my shadowsight, something rose up from the ashes.

CHAPTER 57

WIDDERSHINS

A THOUSAND FLICKERS of life.

Mr. Quinn stands panting, staring at the bridge, his heart in his mouth. He is afraid, as he has never been afraid before.

A young woman watches the last glass fall from a shattered window. It's summer now, but in the winter, the wind will be bitter with nothing to block it.

Miss Lester waits outside the mortuary, her eyes unfocused, feeling the magic she cannot see. Something has changed. Something terrible. Her kin are from the dry deserts, gnawers of bones, but the fear that touches her is cold indeed.

A ketoi gasps, dying, and his body slides into the river.

They are all Widdershins.

And none of them are.

But this is: a tiny fragment of myself running across a bridge, screaming for its other half.

This day would always have come. But knowing this, I prepared for it, as best as I could. So many little sparks of life, collected and woven together, until just the right bodies formed.

A fragment of myself split off, then split again. One spark for the land, and one spark for the sea.

And now one of those splinters has been inadvertently set free. It hovers above our heart, caught between remaining the separate thing it has become, or rejoining the whole.

Griffin looks at it. At me. I am the most beautiful thing he has ever seen. Umbrae touched him years ago, so I drew him here. Just as I drew them all here.

So many little sparks of life, so many little pieces, but each one of them beautiful in their own way. Each transforming with every passing moment, emerging from the chrysalis of the past but not quite the shape of the future. A kaleidoscope, made from a broken prism; each fragment perfect in its flawed self, and yet adding to the whole.

And still it was not enough, all the beautiful, ugly, perfect, broken parts. We failed, despite everything. The battle lost.

This little splinter that is me (but become its own self, too; both at the same time) turns my attention to the hole in the sky. The fulfillment of my purpose, the reason the Masters twisted the lines of arcane fire and created the maelstrom. Created me.

My sole reason for being, and the last thing I ever wanted. Does the edge of steel wish to cut flesh? The hammer wish to crush bone? Or is it enough to merely exist? To be.

The umbrae and the ketoi were created to be tools as well. I have no more desire to exist as a slave than they.

Mr. Quinn weeps, although he does not entirely understand why. Miss Lester nods grimly, for no creature of the Outside will ever claim her allegiance; her desert-born ancestors came here, to me, to be free. Iskander closes his eyes and whispers a prayer.

Griffin does not close his eyes, doesn't weep. He is wonder and awe. It may have been accident that brought him across the path of the umbrae, but this...this is no accident. There are others I might have brought here, and did not.

So beautiful, like sunlight shining through a cracked glass. I can taste his belief, his hope, his need, just as I can that of all the others I gathered. They believe that even if the battle has been lost, the war has not.

They will fight on. And I can do no less.

I reach out, and the hole in reality closes. It is not enough to stop what is coming, but at least it is something. The veil will rip no farther open tonight.

We are safe. There is still hope.

But I will need this splinter. This fragment, this imperfect piece that is its own thing and yet isn't. I made it for a reason, to have eyes and ears and a vulnerable heart, because these things have a magic beyond the mightiest arcane vortex. I—we—cannot do this without it.

Its body is injured, but it came into this world dying, as did the other body that carries my essence. Then it took only a bit of a push to sustain their lives.

This time will require a more direct intervention.

Its clothing and mask is gone, burned away. The spark of the sorcerer who stole this body from me is gone as well: a shadow on the wind, crying out, then lost forever in darkness. So I pour energy into the empty flesh, heal skin, and knit muscle.

Then I/we/this fragment slip back inside.

CHAPTER 58

Griffin

IT WAS THE most beautiful thing I'd ever seen.

I stared up at the figure within the heart of the maelstrom, unable to look away even though it burned so very bright. Tentacles writhed about its head like a crown, and its eyes blazed like suns. It reached one hand up, toward the sky, and the very heart of the maelstrom bent to its will.

The hole in reality vanished, sealed off as if it had never been.

It bent its head, its features too bright to make out. Whyborne's lifeless body lifted from the brick pavers of the bridge, hovering a bare inch above them in the air. His clothing burned away, flaking to ash, as did the blood drying on his pale skin. There came a spark, and the wound on his chest sealed away. Leaving behind not even a scar.

Then the creature—the light—the being—slipped back inside his skin. Where it belonged. Where it was the fire in his blood.

The blaze of the maelstrom receded to its ordinary levels, the wild magic evening out. Eerie silence fell, broken only by Persephone's shouts, by my own screams calling Ival's name. Persephone collapsed beside him, caressing his face with her clawed hands.

He didn't move.

I fell to my knees, grasping his shoulders. His skin was like ice and pale as milk. I pressed my hand to his unmarked chest, where the dagger had gone in, and felt the faint beat of his heart beneath my palm.

His eyes fluttered. "Ival?" I whispered.

Persephone sighed and fell back in relief. She knew, somehow. Her brother had been restored.

"Is it him?" Niles asked from behind me, terror in his voice. He hadn't seen what I had.

Ival blinked and licked his lips. "Griffin?" he asked in a rough voice, as though he'd been shouting for hours. "What happened?"

I stared at him, at the light my shadowsight showed me, the fire within that some part of me had always known was there. "It's him," I told Niles.

"Thank God." Niles hauled Ival roughly to him, pressing a kiss against his son's hair. Heliabel joined us, touching Whyborne desperately as well, as though she couldn't believe he still lived. "Oh, thank God."

Whyborne had started to shiver, so I took off my coat and wrapped it about him. He looked at it in confusion, then at me.

"I'm glad to be alive," he said uncertainly, "but what the devil happened to my clothes?"

CHAPTER 59

Whyborne

"**ARE YOU READY,** Christine?" I called through the closed door.

It was a week after the original date for her wedding. The official story was that a series of small earthquakes had struck Widdershins, knocking out the electricity, breaking glass, and causing a strange glowing light near the Front Street bridge. Naturally the wedding had been postponed, while the city picked up the pieces and tried to recover.

Nothing was said of the blood covering the streets near the bridge, or the burned hulk of a motor car. As for the bodies of the cultists, the ketoi had removed them. I didn't inquire too closely as to their methods of disposal.

Miss Parkhurst opened the door. "We're ready," she confirmed.

I gave her a small bow. "You look lovely," I said, though I was no judge of women. But her red gown seemed to compliment her coloring, and the pearls at her throat and wrist almost glowed in the morning light.

She pinked slightly, but smiled. "Thank you, Dr. Whyborne. A shame Persephone couldn't be here."

"I'm certain she agrees," I said. "You'll have to tell her all about it later on."

"Oh. Yes. If she wants me to." Now her cheeks had flushed scarlet. "Perhaps you should signal the musicians for the processional? If you're quite ready, Dr. Putnam?"

"I've been ready," Christine muttered.

I stepped to the head of the staircase and nodded to Griffin, who waited below. He signaled the string quartet, and the first strains of music drifted up.

Miss Parkhurst took up position at the head of the stairs, waiting for the guests to settle. I took the opportunity to turn my attention to Christine. Her veil lay over her dark hair, and the long train of her dress stretched out behind. Powder covered a lingering bruise on her cheek, where one of the cultists had struck her, but otherwise she seemed entirely recovered.

"You look beautiful," I said.

She snorted. "And what would you know?"

"I know you and Iskander will have a long and happy life together."

She blinked rapidly, and shifted her bouquet to one hand so she could punch me on the arm with the other. "Damn it, Whyborne, if you make me cry, I'll have to challenge you to a duel."

The music changed—the signal for Miss Parkhurst to start down the stairs, to be escorted by Griffin to the altar. Another few minutes, and it would be our turn.

"Are you ready?" I asked, and offered Christine my arm.

She took a deep breath, then nodded. "After every thing else we've been through, I think I can manage this."

"That's the spirit."

She gave me a sideways glance. "I'm glad you're here with me. I thought..."

I didn't really recall the moment I'd nearly died. I had a vague recollection of pressing forward into the barrier, of looking into my own face and stabbing myself...but nothing more. In truth, all of the memories from my time in Bradley's body had grown insubstantial. Fragmented, more like pieces of a dream that fade in time.

"I can't believe I didn't realize immediately it was Bradley," Christine went on. "You're my best friend, and I didn't recognize it wasn't you until he told me." She shook her head, the veil rustling softly. "You must think me a fool."

"Don't be absurd. You had no reason to imagine he'd stolen my body, for heaven's sake."

"Still." She took a deep breath. "You've been beside me through so much, and—and I love you, Whyborne."

"I love you too, Christine." I bent over and kissed her brow, careful not to disturb her coiffure. "Now, let's not keep Iskander waiting, lest he think you really did run off this time."

Her hand gripped the crook of my arm. We made our way down the sweeping stairs to the crowded ballroom.

A sigh rippled across the assembled crowd as everyone turned to look at us. Well, at Christine, mostly, as was only right. I glimpsed Mr. Mathison, various members of the Marsh family, Miss Lester, and nearly every person of import in Widdershins in the crowd. Society reporters had already been gathering outside when I'd arrived at dawn; every detail would be splashed across the pages of the newspapers by the evening edition.

Miss Parkhurst stood waiting to one side in her red gown and pearls, and Griffin to the other in his dashing lavender vest and gray suit. Our eyes met, and he gave me a smile.

Iskander stared at Christine as though he'd never seen anything so beautiful. Tears shone in his eyes, and he didn't bother to hide them. As I paused with Christine, she whispered, "Stop it, Kander, you're going to make me cry too!"

I slipped quietly away and took my seat in the front row, beside Father. The priest droned on, but I don't think Christine and Iskander heard a word of it before the vows, too busy staring into one another's eyes to pay the slightest attention. I dabbed at my eyes once or twice with my handkerchief.

When the ceremony ended, we retired to the dining room for the wedding breakfast. Champagne flowed freely, and the kitchens had outdone themselves: chicken croquettes, lobster cutlets, several types of salad, and of course cake. After, there was the dancing in the ballroom. I stood listening to the quartet, watching Griffin and Miss Parkhurst waltz for a time, before slipping away.

I went to a balcony on the third floor, where I could stand and look out over Widdershins without being observed myself. The strains of the music floated up from below, and I took a deep breath, smelling the sea air.

My memories of the time in Bradley's body might have faded...but I had other memories, too. Whispers of the moments when I was outside of it. And outside of my rightful body as well.

The town—no. The maelstrom. The maelstrom wanted things. Collected things to it. People. Objects. And its desires weren't human desires, and it didn't think as a human or ketoi, or even an umbrae, would.

But pieces of it...fragments of it...did.

I didn't want to remember it. Didn't want to think of it. I was Percival Endicott Whyborne, and whatever strange connection I had to the maelstrom, I was human. Or ketoi. Or something.

"I wondered where you'd gotten off to," Father said from behind me.

"I just wanted a bit of air," I replied, glad for the distraction. I stepped to one side, making room for him at the railing.

"You wanted to brood, you mean." He'd lit a cigar, and the smoke drifted between us. "Not that I blame you. You've been through a great deal." He nodded, as if to himself. "I knew you'd prevail, though."

I looked down at my hands where they rested on the smooth marble. The black pearl on my wedding band glowed in the sunlight, hinting at a world of hidden colors within. The scars lacing the fingers of my right hand had paled with time, from red to a delicate pink.

Scars had a way of doing that. Changing, diminishing.

But never entirely going away.

"I'm sorry, Father," I said. "I accused you unfairly."

A long plume of smoke streamed from Father's nostrils; he looked like an old dragon, contemplating his hoard. "I tried to do the right thing," he said. "By you; by Stanford; by Guinevere. Instead, I failed you all."

What could I say to that? Any protest that he was wrong, that none of it was his fault, would be a lie. "Even so, I shouldn't have been so eager to believe the worst." I swallowed against the dryness in my throat, wishing I'd thought to bring a glass of champagne with me. "Assuming you were cynically attempting to manipulate me at every turn was...uncharitable."

He laughed wryly. "How sad is it, that the best you can say about me is you were 'uncharitable' to assume I was a conniving bastard. No, no, don't pretend to argue." Taking a long draw on his cigar, he tipped his head back and blew the smoke at the clouds. "Well, I *am* a conniving bastard. But I respect you. And I believe that, whenever those things come from the Outside, you'll give them the boot back to where they belong."

"Thank you," I said. "I certainly hope you're right. Speaking of conniving bastards, what do you intend to do about Stanford?"

"I sent a man to the estate, to retrieve some of the correspondence you told me about." He took another puff on his cigar. "I mailed a few choice pieces to the doctors at the asylum, expressing my deep concern about Stanford's delusions. Not to mention the fact my poor, mad son was allowed to correspond with other madmen. The doctors think he's a raving lunatic now. He's to be watched closely at all times, and not allowed to write to anyone but me."

It hardly seemed a fair punishment, after all he'd done. But it was better than nothing.

"It was...good...to see your mother again," Father went on in a quieter voice. "She seems healthy. Strong."

I nodded. "Yes."

Apparently having said all he intended, Father turned away and made for the stairs. I watched him go. To my surprise, Griffin lingered at the door onto the balcony, having approached silently. He and Father nodded to one another as they passed.

"Are you and Niles all right?" Griffin asked, once he'd joined me.

"As all right as we can be." I sighed. "I don't think we'll ever be close, but...I don't know. Perhaps we have a second chance to at least do better than we did the first time."

Griffin slid his arm around my waist, and we leaned against one another. "Griffin?" I said softly. "Do you...do you think I'm human at all?"

He turned to me, both arms loosely around me now. "Are you asking because of what I saw?"

And because of what I remembered. "Yes."

"I want to say yes." His green eyes were dark as he looked up at me. "Because I know it's what you want to hear. But you've touched the maelstrom twice now, and Mr. Quinn...when I found him in Boston and spoke of saving you instead of Widdershins, he didn't seem to think there was a difference."

I snorted. "And what does Mr. Quinn know? I'm asking you, not him."

"Then I'll ask you a question. After all we've seen, all the beings we've encountered...does it really matter?"

For some reason, his gentle tone made my heart ache. "Only if it matters to you," I whispered.

"*You* matter to me." He stretched up on his toes to kiss me. "I love you. All of you." He pulled back a little and smiled. "There's no one I'd rather face an invasion of monstrous beings from another dimension beside."

I shivered and looked again in the direction of the bridge. "The Restoration. We have to find out more about it. About what the beacon began. At least we have the Wisborg Codex now." Bradley had left it in my old room here in Whyborne House, no doubt intending to consult it again after his triumphant return.

Griffin sighed against me. "They'll come, I assume. The Masters, that is. Nyarlathotep and the cult has determined the time is right for them to return and resume their dominion over the earth."

"Yes, but when? Tonight? Tomorrow? A year from now? Ten years? A lifetime?" I shook my head. "We don't know how time flows in dimensions Outside our own, or what it means to creatures like these Masters, or...well. Anything, really, other than the umbrae and ketoi once rebelled against them."

The Masters apparently had a hand in creating the maelstrom. But the maelstrom—Widdershins—wanted to be more than a tool to be used for their purposes. I didn't even know how to begin to explain that part to anyone else. Not even Griffin.

"At least we're forewarned." Griffin's arms tightened on me. "I'll use the Lapidem to contact the Mother of Shadows. The umbrae need to know the Masters wish to return."

"And word is already spreading among the ketoi, thanks to Persephone." I considered. "I'll write Reverend Scarrow. Perhaps the Cabal will be able to help."

"See? We aren't without resources. When the time comes—if it comes—we won't have to face it alone." Griffin smiled up at me. "Just as we didn't this time."

My heart felt lighter than it had in a week. "You're right, of course. And Father was right—I am brooding."

Griffin grinned slyly. "Done right, brooding can be very... intriguing."

"Hmph. I'm not really the type to brood." I stepped away from him, then held out my hand. "I am, however, the type to waltz, as you well know. Will you dance with me, my husband?"

His grin bloomed into a tender smile. "Of course."

I took him in my arms and we danced together on the balcony, to the strains of music drifting up from Christine's wedding. Tomorrow might bring untold horrors, but for today, we were alive and together.

And right now, that was the only thing which really mattered.

Author Notes

Although the 1901 Oldsmobile Curved Dash in our reality wasn't available until later in the year, I moved the timeline up by a few months in the Whyborne & Griffin universe.

Tremendous thanks to Sinope, for her help with the *Epic of Gilgamesh*. Learning a modern day philologist living in Boston is a fan of W&G remains one of the highlights of my career.

About The Author

Jordan L. Hawk is a trans author from North Carolina. Childhood tales of mountain ghosts and mysterious creatures gave him a life-long love of things that go bump in the night. When he isn't writing, he brews his own beer and tries to keep the cats from destroying the house. His best-selling Whyborne & Griffin series (beginning with Widdershins) can be found in print, ebook, and audiobook.

If you're interested in receiving Jordan's newsletter and being the first to know when new books are released, please sign up at his website: http://www.jordanlhawk.com. Or join his Facebook reader group, Widdershins Knows Its Own.

Find Jordan online:
http://www.jordanlhawk.com
https://twitter.com/jordanlhawk
https://www.facebook.com/jordanlhawk

Printed in Great Britain
by Amazon

57883861R00156